NECROPOLIS

Other Books from Jordan L. Hawk:

Hainted

<u>Whyborne & Griffin:</u>
Widdershins
Threshold
Stormhaven
Necropolis

<u>SPECTR</u>
Hunter of Demons
Master of Ghouls
Reaper of Souls
Eater of Lives
Destroyer of Worlds
Summoner of Storms (July 2014)

<u>Short stories:</u>
Heart of the Dragon
After the Fall (in the *Allegories of the Tarot* anthology)
Eidolon (A Whyborne & Griffin short story)
Remnant, written with KJ Charles (A Whyborne & Griffin / Secret Casebook of Simon Feximal story)

NECROPOLIS

(Whyborne & Griffin No. 4)

JORDAN L. HAWK

Necropolis © 2014 Jordan L. Hawk
ISBN: 978-1499153521

All rights reserved.

Cover art © 2016 Lou Harper

This book is a work of fiction. Names, characters, places, and incidents are products of the author's imagination or are used fictitiously. Any resemblance to actual events or locales or persons, living or dead, is entirely coincidental.

Edited by Annetta Ribken

CHAPTER 1

I ELECTED TO have Christmas dinner in hell and took my lover with me.

Not a literal hell, of course. As a materialist, I didn't believe in such things. But if proved wrong and condemned by a deity cruel enough to fashion me to love men, then proceed to damn me for it, I rather imagined I'd find myself spending eternity here in my childhood home.

But at least this version of hell contained an angel. "Griffin, I'm glad you came," my mother exclaimed, kissing him on the cheek.

Griffin's smile removed some of the lines of care from his face. I always found him damnably handsome, with his overlong chestnut curls and bright green eyes, but his grin brought out all of his devilish charm.

"Thank you for the invitation, Heliabel," he said. "May I say how lovely your home looks? I don't think I've ever seen a Christmas tree quite so large."

I eyed the monstrosity in the foyer. Like everything in Whyborne House, it was absurdly ostentatious, as if Father refused to take the chance any visitor might forget just how rich and powerful a man lived here. The pinnacle of the towering evergreen brushed the ceiling twenty feet above, and its boughs hung low beneath the weight of ornaments, ribbons, and softly glowing candles. Melting beeswax perfumed the air alongside the spice of conifer.

The sights and smells transported me involuntarily to the

holidays of my youth. Most of which featured my brother opening great mounds of presents, and myself making do with a few books from Mother and an orange from Miss Emily.

"Father gave me a child-sized pair of boxing gloves one Christmas." I hadn't thought of those in years.

Griffin arched a brow. "Did he? That seems...an unlikely gift."

A charitable way of saying I wasn't the most athletic of men. "He had unrealistic hopes," I muttered, glaring at the tree. I itched to speak the words which would set it on fire, but burning down the house seemed a bit much. Even on Christmas.

"Have you investigated any interesting cases lately, Griffin?" Mother asked, rescuing the conversation.

Griffin began to relate the details of a kidnapping he'd recently looked into—successfully, I should add, with the abducted tyke returned to his family unharmed. I stood back and watched them. Griffin looked quite fine, dressed in his best suit, wearing the emerald tie I'd given him for a Christmas present. With his broad shoulders and trim form, he presented the very image of vigorous manhood.

Mother stood in sharp contrast. The year hadn't been kind to her...but none ever were. Her health broke when she delivered my twin sister and me into the world. My sister never even took a breath, and I'd spent a good deal of my childhood sickly.

Mother hadn't left the house for years; I couldn't recall the last time she'd set foot across the threshold. But she had abandoned the refuge of her room and dressed for dinner, and if her skin held an unnatural pallor and her smile wore lines of pain around the edges, I couldn't help but feel even more grateful for her kindness to Griffin.

Had it merely been the three of us, I would have looked forward to the afternoon with great anticipation. Unfortunately, I possessed other family members.

"Percival," Father said crisply, striding into the foyer as if onto a battlefield such as he fought on under the command of General Grant. Although the years had grayed his hair and beard, his back remained unbent and his eyes still glittered like knives. His lips pressed into a thin line, but he nodded in Griffin's general direction. "Mr. Flaherty."

Mother folded her hands together. "Wasn't it kind of Griffin to join us for the holiday?" she asked pointedly.

Father had been involved in a cult which first unjustly confined Griffin to a madhouse, then tried to sacrifice him to an undead abomination. I rather thought it beyond kind for Griffin to respond to the invitation at all, instead of just flinging it into the fire.

Society, however, would more likely overlook Father's crimes than the one Griffin and I committed by virtue of falling in love.

"Yes," Father grated out, glowering as he did so. "Most kind."

"Thank you for the invitation," Griffin said, not warmly, but with more graciousness than I could have summoned.

The gong rang to announce dinner. Even though this was, in theory, an intimate family gathering, all the formalities must be observed. Seeming relieved, Father hurried to the dining room, while servants swung back the ponderous doors to allow us entry. Griffin offered Mother his arm, which she accepted.

Compared to the last time we'd dined here, the atmosphere was a bit more cheerful, thanks to the evergreen boughs above the hearth and the bows tied around the pikes held by the suits of armor. Not to suggest our family descended from European aristocracy—the Whyborne lineage consisted of thieves and whores who fled to the colonies to escape the hangman. But the money, which fueled our ascension in society, encouraged certain lapses in memory when it came to our sullied past.

Five settings lay at one end of the immense dining table, and I resigned myself to the presence of my elder brother. As we took our places, with Father at the head of the table, Mother to his right, and Griffin and I to his left, Stanford wandered in. From the flush on his face and his unsteady gait, it seemed he'd begun the festivities early.

Griffin's eyes narrowed at the sight of my brother. I hadn't the slightest idea if he'd been exposed to Stanford when the Brotherhood kidnapped him. If so, did it count as some sort of formal introduction?

Fortunately, Mother took matters in hand. "Stanford, I don't believe you've met our guest. Mr. Griffin Flaherty, this is my eldest son, Stanford Preston Whyborne."

Stanford grunted in Griffin's direction and didn't bother to extend his hand.

The servants poured wine and laid out the first course: oysters on the half shell. The conversation limped along: Father asked about my job at the Ladysmith, and I yet again explained my utter lack of interest in becoming the head of the Antiquities Department, let alone the director or—heaven forbid—president of the museum. Mother inquired as to whether I'd read anything by Mr. H.G. Wells. I hadn't, but Griffin admired adventure fiction, and the two of them animatedly discussed *The Time Machine* through the soup and custard courses.

Father glowered but didn't interrupt, no doubt consigning Griffin onto the pile of womanish frivolity alongside me. Stanford drank glass after glass of wine in silence, while the rest of us pretended not to notice.

For us, it was practically a scene of familial bliss.

Which of course meant it couldn't last. The servants set out the chestnut-stuffed turkey and presented another bottle of wine. As they worked, Stanford cast a small, piggish eye on Griffin.

"Why is *he* here?" my brother slurred.

Silence fell. The servants pretended not to hear, but I could only imagine they strained to catch every syllable. My face grew hot. I didn't know what, if anything, our parents had said to Stanford about Griffin, let alone why Griffin spent the day with us rather than visiting his family in Kansas.

Mother set her fork carefully down beside her plate. "Because everyone deserves to be with family on Christmas."

Stanford snorted into his wine glass. "Doesn't he have one of his own to go to?"

This silence was even tenser than the first. Griffin's expression slipped into a mask of polite indifference. But anger turned the food in my belly to acid. How dare Stanford? I'd spent my youth enduring his taunts and torments, but I'd be damned if I let him callously dig into Griffin's barely healed wounds.

I pasted a false smile on my lips. "And where are Darla and the boys?" I asked in the most pleasant tone I could manage. "I would have thought you'd want to spend the holiday with your wife and sons."

Stanford's face flushed brick red. "Shut up."

"I only asked a question, as innocent as your own."

"Innocent," Stanford spat. "You don't know the meaning of the word. How dare you expose our mother to your perversions—"

"You blasted—"

"Boys!" Mother slammed her hand down on the table. The wine leapt free of every single glass along the table, curling in the air for a moment before falling to stain the cloth.

For a long moment, no one spoke, as we all absorbed what we'd seen. Then a delighted laugh escaped me. "You've been practicing!"

Mother's cheeks flushed with pride. "Well, yes."

"Practicing?" Father's tone bordered on horror.

Mother's shoulders went back a touch. "I asked Percival to teach me some of his little spells."

"What?" exclaimed Griffin, at the same moment Father thundered, "There are no *little* spells!"

Drat. I'd not intended for Griffin to find out this way. Well, technically, I'd not intended for him to find out at all.

"Mother requested to be tutored in a few *small* spells," I said, aiming the words at Father. "The water spell came easiest to me, so I thought it might as well to her." My annoyance gave way to excitement. "And it did! You used it on wine—what a brilliant idea!"

She smiled fondly at me. "Well, wine is mostly composed of water, of course."

"No." Father gripped his fork in one hand as if he meant to stab someone, as soon as he decided which of us to target. "Sorcery is a dangerous matter, Heliabel. I forbid you to conduct it within these walls."

Her thin shoulders rose in a shrug. "Stop me."

Griffin cleared his throat in the ensuing shocked silence. "The papers reported on a body partially exhumed and eaten yesterday," he said. "I don't suppose anyone here knows anything about it?"

Father beckoned for more wine.

Two hours later, escape lay within reach. Father denied all connection with cannibalistic grave robbers and seemed offended Griffin even asked the question. This despite the fact his history with the Brotherhood of the Immortal Fire made it a reasonable inquiry. Griffin accepted his assurance, and we all had another round of wine. Or in Stanford's case, several.

Dinner ended, and Mother stated her intent to retire for the evening. Although she voiced no complaint, the lines around her eyes drew tight with pain. It seemed a good time to make our excuses to leave. While Father retreated to his study with Stanford, no doubt for brandy and cigars, Griffin and I walked Mother to the grand foyer to say our farewells beneath the great tree. How many Christmases did we have left with her?

"Percival," she said fondly, kissing my cheek. Turning to Griffin, she took his hands. "Griffin. Thank you for coming. It was very… generous of you." The corner of her mouth curled in a rueful smile.

"It was generous of you to invite me," he replied solemnly.

"I rather thought it the least we could do, considering…" she trailed off with a sigh. "At any rate, pay Stanford no mind. He's suffered some personal disappointments as of late. You're always welcome here."

Griffin eyes grew a touch bright. "Thank you, Heliabel. Truly."

She squeezed his hands, before turning slowly, painfully toward the stairs. One of the maids hastened to assist her, and within a few moments, she vanished upstairs.

"Your coat and hat, Master Percival," Fenton said at my elbow.

I started, not having heard the butler come up on us. His habitual icy sneer didn't alter in the slightest, but I imagined him silently condemning me for frailty of nerves.

"Thank you," I said, pretending I wasn't perfectly aware he wished to remove me from the premises as quickly as possible. God knew I didn't want to linger, now that Mother had retired.

As we donned our coats and scarves, a heavy tread approached from the direction of the study. "Fenton!" Stanford bellowed. "Bring the motorcar around. I want to go out."

Fenton stiffened, almost imperceptibly. He'd always worshipped the ground Stanford walked on, and I wondered at the change. Had Stanford's drinking alienated the staff, as it had his wife?

"Right away, Master Stanford," Fenton said. He departed, and I made for the front door. Unfortunately, Stanford blundered into the foyer and cut across the room to intercept me before Griffin and I could make our escape.

While I'd inherited Mother's willowy build, Stanford took after Father's stockier frame. Though Stanford had been athletic in our youth, he'd run to fat in recent years. His fashionable Fifth Avenue waistcoat strained around his paunch; it must have been some time since he'd visited the tailor. Because other things occupied his mind, or because he'd spent all his money on gambling debts?

I didn't care. Stanford could squander every cent of the family fortune on cards and women, as far as I was concerned. I'd given my inheritance up when I walked out at age eighteen, Father bellowing threats at my back.

"You," Stanford said, grabbing my arm.

I sensed Griffin stiffen behind me, poised to give assistance. But this wasn't his fight.

"Me," I agreed with a cold smile.

I'd been a thin, sickly boy, while Stanford grew up hearty and strong as any red-blooded American male might wish. Most of my memories consisted of him locking me in dark closets, or dangling me over the second-story railing, or striking me about the legs with a baseball bat. I'd grown up in terror of his whims.

No more. If he wished to make a scene in front of a guest, I'd oblige. "Darla's threatening divorce, isn't she?" I asked, my gaze boring into his eyes. "And taking the boys with her, I hear."

"I'll get her back. She's a woman. She can be bribed." His breath could have stripped paint. "But you. How dare you?"

Heat flared in my chest, like banked coals raked over, to expose the fire beneath the ashes. "How dare I what?"

His eyes narrowed belligerently. "That." He gestured vaguely in Griffin's direction. "How dare you bring *him* to a family dinner and flaunt your perversions in front of Mother?"

The heat grew, boiling my blood. How dare *I*? How dare Stanford. "The invitation was formal. Which means Father and Mother both agreed to it. If you have an issue with their selection of dinner guests, I suggest you take it up with them."

He shoved my chest, hard enough I staggered. Griffin started forward, but I flung out a hand, gesturing him to stay back. Stanford noticed, of course, and his expression shifted from anger to a contemptuous sneer.

"Finally found someone to fight your battles for you, Percival? I suppose it's easier than growing a spine of your own."

My heart thundered, but I forced an ugly smile onto my mouth. "At least I haven't come slinking back to Whyborne House like a whipped dog. Has Father called you to heel yet, or does he still delude himself into thinking you'll change your ways?"

Stanford stared at me, open-mouthed, as if he couldn't believe I'd spoken to him so. I could barely believe it myself. Our entire lives, I'd swallowed down my vitriol and choked on it. But I refused to stand here in front of Griffin and let my odious brother make him feel unwelcome.

"You rotten little fairy," Stanford sputtered, even though I stood almost half a foot taller than him. "You're the one who's delusional, thinking your nancy cares about anything other than getting his hands on the family money."

The Christmas tree shivered in a sudden breeze. My hands curled into fists, and I took a menacing step toward Stanford. A bit to my surprise, he shrank back, his eyes darting toward the tree.

"Not. Another. Word," I warned. The breeze grew stronger. The ornaments tinkled, and the flames on the candles guttered wildly.

"You dare threaten me?" he demanded, but the words lacked force. "I'll tell Father—"

I laughed. "Are you twelve? Father won't—"

He swung at me.

His blow would have landed, if Griffin hadn't grabbed the collar of my coat and yanked me back. Blind fury ignited in my blood. I wrenched loose and threw myself at my brother. My fist impacted with his jaw, even as a huge gust of wind brought the enormous tree crashing to the floor.

Chapter 2

"Ow," I said, as Griffin gently applied a warm washcloth to the blood on my knuckles.

We'd returned to our house...although first I'd suffered the humiliation of Father scolding Stanford and I for brawling in front of the servants like a pair of common hoodlums. Although brawling was rather a strong term for it. My blow to Stanford's jaw felt as if it had broken my hand, and resulted in the both of us standing there in utter shock: myself at the pain, and he at the fact I'd actually struck him. Meanwhile, the servants and Griffin rushed to make certain the candles in the toppled tree didn't burn down the house.

Father charged in from his study like an enraged bull, bellowing at us both and further compounding Stanford's surprise. Father always took his side during our childhood, ruffling Stanford's hair while telling me I needed to toughen up. When Griffin led me out the door a short time later, Stanford still stood in the foyer looking dazed, as if he couldn't quite comprehend what had just happened.

Now Griffin tenderly took my hand in his and felt the bones. "Nothing seems to be broken," he pronounced. "Just bruised and bloodied."

"I'm sorry," I said as he dipped the washcloth back into the basin. "My family is an utter horror. I shouldn't have dragged you there with me. I only thought..."

There existed no way to finish the sentence without bringing him pain. "I should have known better," I finished unhappily. "Nothing good ever came out of that house."

He put the washbasin aside and sat back on his heels, looking up at me. "Not so." He rested his hand on my knee, his fingers warm through the cloth of my trousers. "You came out of it, after all. Even if you are trying to turn your mother into a sorceress."

I didn't bother to suppress my sigh. I'd known he'd bring up the matter sooner or later. "No need to lecture me. I know how you feel about the *Liber Arcanorum* and the spells within, and about my use of them. You know as well as I do nothing bad has happened thus far."

"The wind which blew over the tree. Did you summon it deliberately?"

"It had nothing to do with me," I protested. "A fluke breeze."

He didn't seem convinced. "Quite the fluke."

"You know I have to draw a sigil to summon wind. Did you see me do so?"

"No," he admitted reluctantly. "But you didn't need a sigil at Stormhaven, either."

Not an incident I wished to recall. "The dweller possesses its own magic. Under its influence, I had use of its power. Which isn't the case now."

"I suppose." Griffin's look remained pensive. "Your mother…"

If the man couldn't make an argument one way, he'd find another. "Mother asked me to teach her. What was I to say?"

"Did it occur to you not to tell her in the first place?"

"Of course not!" For the second time that evening, anger roused in my chest, although far less sharp than what I'd felt toward Stanford. "Mother has spent the greater part of her life confined to the house thanks to her illness. If not for books, for knowledge, her world would be tiny indeed. Am I to make it even smaller by keeping from her the existence of the arcane? She's not a child, or a fool whose fragile mind must be protected from the truth."

"I suppose," he agreed reluctantly. "But to teach her to actually cast spells…"

"She is not a child," I repeated. "She can make her own decisions. She asked me to teach her, and I saw no harm in it. Nor do I now."

His green eyes darkened for a moment, but he didn't speak whatever thought troubled him. "You're right," he said eventually. "Heliabel is an adult, and a very capable one. But I won't pretend to like the idea of the *Arcanorum's* secrets spreading even this much."

"We will simply have to disagree on the matter," I said, a bit stiffly. Would the man never come around to my way of thinking?

He still knelt before me, his fingers on my knee. "Yes. Forgive me. I don't wish to argue tonight, of all nights." He shifted closer, hand sliding higher, onto my thigh. "Given no one made an attempt my life, I think we can call the visit to your family a success, don't you?"

His fingers traced little circles on my thigh, making it hard to think. "Up until the bit with Stanford, anyway."

"Hmm, yes. It occurs to me I haven't yet thanked you for your valiant defense of my honor." His eyes gleamed wickedly, and his hand moved yet higher, making it clear what sort of thanks he had in mind.

Desire tented the front of my trousers, and my breath quickened, responding to his touch. "No," I said, my voice rough with need, "you haven't."

He shifted between my knees, a wicked grin on his lips. The electric lights we'd had installed a few weeks ago brought out glints of gold amidst his chestnut curls. I still didn't know what I'd done to capture the attention of such a man, let alone his heart, but I was grateful beyond words to have done so.

He undid the buttons of my trousers slowly, teasing my rapidly hardening length by rubbing deliberately against it through the cloth.

"D-do you want to go upstairs?" I asked.

"No. Just stay where you are."

I wanted to protest we were in the *kitchen* for heaven's sake, but the firm grasp of his fingers as he drew my member free drove all such thoughts from my mind. I shifted slightly in the chair to give him better access, a soft sound escaping me as he fondled my sack. "Griffin…"

"Watch," he commanded. I obeyed, loving the hungry look in his eyes almost as much as the sensation of his tongue as he licked me slowly from base to head. The wet, red tip of his tongue flicked lightly at the slit, teased at the edges of the hood, and generally made me whimper and stiffen with the lust for more. And all the while, his gaze remained fixed on my face, every emotion and change of expression bare to him. A part of me wanted to close my eyes, to hide whatever vulnerability he might see, not because I didn't trust him, but out of old habit and nebulous fear.

Then his mouth closed around me, and I gasped, hands clenching on the arms of my chair. He slid down slowly, hot and wet, all the way to the base before repeating the action. I gripped the chair harder, holding back the urge to thrust into his mouth. When his eyes closed briefly, and he moaned around my cock, I knew he'd unfastened his trousers and put a hand to himself as well.

I gave myself over to it, letting pleasure wash over me, through me, all centered around the length of hard flesh in his mouth. He moaned, picking up the pace of his ministrations. God! It all felt incredible, and the sight of his swollen lips wrapped around me, his eyes dilated with pleasure as he stroked himself, undid me. I groaned his name as a warning, even as my sack tightened and my body clenched. He moaned encouragement around my cock, and I shuddered with ecstasy as I spent myself in his throat.

He swallowed eagerly, coaxing out everything I had to give him. When I relaxed back against the chair, still panting and shaking, he let my softening cock slip from his lips. Arching his back, he gave me a view of his erection, flushed deep red against the paleness of his hand as he worked himself. "Yes, Griffin," I said hoarsely, wanting to see.

His orgasm took him, and he cried out, spending himself on the tiled floor. He stroked his length a few times more, before slumping to rest his head against my thigh. I leaned forward and wrapped my arms around his shoulders, pressing my cheek against his hair.

"Was that adequate thanks?" he asked, when his breathing slowed enough to allow it.

I nuzzled his hair, delighting in the scent of sandalwood and musk. "Mmm, yes. I'd offer to play the knight errant more often, but I fear I really would succeed in breaking my hand."

He chuckled softly, then shifted position to kiss me. "Thank you for a wonderful Christmas, Ival."

I still thought him too generous. "You're welcome. But perhaps next year we'll keep to just the two of us."

He sat back with a smile. "I like hearing you talk about our future," he admitted. "It makes me feel…I don't know how to say it, exactly. Wanted. Permanent."

"I'm glad." I set about to getting my clothing back in order. "But for tonight, let's clean up here and go to bed."

I awoke late the next morning. The museum closed for the holiday, so we'd set no alarm. I reached blindly to Griffin's side of the bed, only to find the sheets empty and cold.

I sat up, hoping to find him at the washbasin. We'd spent the night in his room, which contained his shaving kit. We kept two bedchambers, for the sake of appearances, as a woman came in once a week to clean and take away the laundry. But we never slept apart, rather alternating nights in the two beds.

Before coming to Widdershins, Griffin worked for the Pinkerton Detective Agency, a career which ended in a double set of horrors: his partner dead in the clutches of some otherworldly abomination, and himself shut away in a madhouse. His experiences left him prone to nightmares and fits, which stole his sleep on a regular basis. But the fits had grown less frequent recently, and I hadn't waked alone in some time. A bit concerned, I rose and pulled on a dressing gown, before going in search of him.

I found him in the second-floor study, staring fixedly out the window at the barren hedges beyond. His face reflected in the window, drawn and pensive. I'd discovered him in such a mood several times over the last few months, ever since...

Well. Ever since his family turned their backs on him for daring to love me.

"Griffin?" I asked tentatively. "Is everything all right?"

He blinked back to the present and turned to me with a smile. "Of course, my dear. Breakfast?"

I wanted to say...something. He'd given up everything for me, and I...

I didn't know if I was enough. If I could ever *be* enough. And I was too much of a coward to ask and find out for certain.

"Breakfast sounds wonderful," I said. "Shall I cook?"

"You? Voluntarily offering to cook? It's a Christmas miracle."

"Hilarious," I muttered. "Keep it up, and you'll be wearing your eggs instead of eating them."

After a lazy breakfast, I retired to the study to relax with a new book on cryptography. Griffin remained in the downstairs parlor where he kept his office and attended to his account books.

There came a knock on the door sometime just before lunch. I ignored it; one of the many advantages to living with Griffin was his willingness to interact with postmen, delivery boys, and neighbors. Not to suggest I disliked any of them in specific, so much as I never felt comfortable with people in general. I didn't know what to say, and my attempts at small talk generally failed miserably and made social situations even more awkward. Griffin, on the other hand, enjoyed such interactions and excelled at them. I thought it best for all concerned if I left them up to him.

The faint murmur of voices floated up to me, followed by the sound of the door shutting. The stairs creaked beneath Griffin's weight, and I set my book aside as he joined me. "Who was at the door?" I inquired.

"The telegram boy."

"Word of your brothers?" I asked. After the falling out with his adoptive family, Griffin decided to attempt finding his two older brothers, whom the orphan train had separated from him.

"No, I'm afraid not." Disappointment muted his voice as he crossed the room and extended the telegram to me. "Actually, it's a message for you."

"For me?" I straightened in my chair and took it from him. Who on earth would feel the need to contact me in so urgent a fashion, let alone do it at home rather than at the museum?

The telegram read:

CAN'T EXPLAIN BUT NEED YOU IN EGYPT IMMEDIATELY STOP WIRE WHEN YOU HAVE DATE OF ARRIVAL SECURED STOP

DR. CHRISTINE PUTNAM

"This is an outrage, even by Christine's standards," I fumed. "What is she thinking? I'm not about to just drop everything and rush off to the other side of the world on a whim!"

We sat to either side of the kitchen table, our lunch of fish chowder in front of us and the offending telegram lying to one side. Our cat, Saul, circled the table in hopes we'd let him jump up during an unguarded moment. I considered crumpling the telegram and throwing it for him to chase about on the floor.

"Egypt isn't on the other side of the world, precisely." Griffin pointed out. "More of a third of the way round."

"Oh, well, I'll just nip right over," I muttered, clanking my spoon against my bowl a bit more forcefully than necessary.

"Given Christine is well aware of your aversion to travel, she must have some compelling reason to ask you to come."

"Ask? More like ordered." My appetite had vanished, so I set aside the spoon and sipped on my coffee. "And if she has a compelling reason, she should have told me what it is."

"Perhaps she didn't wish to commit it to writing, or wire, in this case," he suggested. "She's conducting further excavations near Nephren-ka's tomb, isn't she?"

As if she hadn't gone on about it for months before leaving. "Yes. Looking for evidence of a lost temple or some such. Nothing which would possibly require my expertise, at least not urgently. If she wants something translated, she can mail photographs or a sketch."

Griffin didn't look certain. "Some of the objects from his tomb held the secrets of dark sorcery, at least judging by the scroll the Brotherhood stole last year. What if she doesn't want your expertise as a philologist, but as a sorcerer?"

I gave Griffin an annoyed look. "I wish you wouldn't call me that. I'm a scholar, nothing more."

"Forgive me, my dear. But you're changing the subject."

I broke off a piece of bread and nibbled on it to give me an excuse not to respond immediately. West Virginia marked the farthest I'd ever strayed from Widdershins. I'd hated the heat and mosquitos, but at least we'd had a hotel and other civilized amenities. What if Christine expected me to sleep in a *tent*?

"I don't know," I said at last. "Christine is my friend and not given to flights of fancy, but...how am I to excuse taking several months away from the museum to the director?"

Griffin shrugged. "Show him the telegram. He knows Christine; I doubt he'll think anything of its abruptness. He'll assume she wants your skill at translation. If I'm not mistaken, the expedition is of great importance to the museum, especially after the revenue her previous discovery brought. Surely he'll be more than happy to send you to Egypt if he thinks it will secure similar results."

I put down my coffee and glared at him. "Are you on my side or not? You're supposed to be helping me find reasons not to go, not chipping away at the ones I have."

He hid a smile—unsuccessfully—behind his cup. "I'm sorry. I thought you wished my honesty."

"Hmph." Blast the man. He always knew what to say. "I'm not convinced. I'll write to Christine and ask for more information. I wish to help her, but she thinks of nothing of these long journeys. Possibly the matter can be handled via post."

"Possibly," Griffin agreed, although he didn't sound as if he believed it. For that matter, neither did I.

Chapter 3

    I WENT TO work the next morning, still angry with Christine. Griffin thought me unreasonable, but how could he understand? He'd traveled all over the country, almost into Mexico even, while working for the Pinkertons. When it came time to start his life over, he'd moved to Widdershins and set up shop despite never having set foot in Massachusetts before.

    I didn't have his courage, let alone Christine's. I'd been born in Widdershins and would probably die here—especially if I kept running into monsters and cultists. It was a fine town, and had everything I needed: a job I enjoyed, a man I loved, and a comfortable house. I liked knowing where everything was located, and going home to the same bed—well, beds—every night. Why should I have to go jaunting off across the ocean, staying in strange places and eating exotic food? If I wanted to see the world, I would have signed up for one of Mr. Cook's tours.

    I tried to put the matter from my mind and took out the *Arcanorum*. With Christine in the field, no one ever visited my little basement office, so I could at least be sure of no interruptions. I would have preferred to work on my arcane researches at home, but Griffin's absurd attitude toward both book and spells made such an arrangement impossible, or at least inconvenient. Learning new spells required concentration, which meant I had no hope of doing so with his dire warnings ringing in my ears.

    The harmless spell I currently attempted to master made such warnings seem even more ridiculous. Supposedly it would allow me to shatter stone or open a rent in the earth, neither of which had the slightest application I could think of. The exercise was purely an experiment, nothing more.

And, thus far, a failed experiment. After the ease of the water spell, I'd assumed this one would prove no more difficult. Instead, it completely eluded me.

But today would be different. I felt focused. Calm.

I took a small river rock from my drawer and put it in the center of the desk. With will and words, I would break it into two pieces. Putting aside all mental distractions, I concentrated on the stone.

Really, it was completely unfair of Christine to blithely ask me to join her in Egypt with no explanation whatsoever.

Drat, no, I needed to focus. Not think about Christine's ridiculous telegram. I took a deep breath and fixed my attention on the stone again.

After all, if I went to Egypt, it would mean leaving Griffin behind. True, Griffin occasionally went on short trips for his job, but never farther than Vermont or New York. I could bear to be parted from him for a few days. But Lord only knew how many months would pass before I returned home again. It would take the better part of a month just to reach Port Said, and the same amount of time to return. I didn't want to be away from him so long.

Oh, to hell with it. I'd never get the spell right in this state.

Hoping to clear my mind, I wrote Christine a stern letter, saying she must send an explanation if she meant to demand my presence in so distant a place. But once finished, I hesitated over giving it to Miss Parkhurst to post. Perhaps a telegram would be better, if it truly was an imperative matter. Then again, if she were in the field at the moment, would either have a hope of actually reaching her?

Christine kept a copy of her itinerary in her office while away, in the event of urgent news or correspondence. Surely it would indicate whether a message could be expected to reach her now, or whether it would sit at a hotel or embassy for weeks until her return. I obtained the key from the security office and let myself in.

Christine's office was quite a bit tidier than mine. One could actually see the floor, and both chairs were clear of everything but a layer of dust, the janitorial staff apparently having decided any cleaning could wait until immediately before her return. A rather large stack of accumulated mail teetered on one corner of her desk.

She kept the itinerary in the upper right hand drawer, if I recalled correctly. As I made my way around the desk, my elbow brushed against the tower of mail.

I grabbed wildly at it, but too late. Letters, fliers, and small parcels went everywhere, scattering across the floor in a drift of paper.

Drat. Going to my knees, I began to collect letters from where they'd slid beneath the desk. Most seemed to be ordinary correspondence, but one proved to be surprisingly heavy for a mere letter.

I paused, inspecting the envelope. Postmarks indicated it had made its way across the Atlantic from Berlin. The pressure of the mail stack had embossed the outline of what appeared to be a coin or token contained within on the envelope.

I bit back a sigh of annoyance. Clearly the sender had improperly addressed the letter to Christine, probably having seen her name in the papers and assuming her an expert on everything historical. As the Ancient Egyptians had no monetary system, the contents of the letter clearly needed to be passed on to someone else, probably one of the Classical scholars, since the public often misunderstood the rarity of Roman era coins.

Restacking the rest of the correspondence, I retrieved Christine's letter opener, a dagger purchased in the Cairo markets. Despite my expectations, the coin was no Roman denarius, but rather a token of clearly modern origin. On one side it bore an Egyptian cartouche, inscribed with the name *Nitocris*.

Why did that sound familiar?

On the other side was a symbol I recognized from the *Al Azif*, meant to offer protection against certain gods. Which meant the thing had true occult power, if only in a limited fashion.

Baffled as to why anyone would send such a thing to Christine, I withdrew the letter enclosed with it. Written in German with a tremulous hand, it said:

I write this in haste but with great sincerity. If you value your life, do not return to Egypt. Nitocris has risen from the dead and seeks the power hidden within the faceless god's temple. Her followers gnaw on corpses, as—God help me!—I have done.

I have enclosed the token they use to know one another, so you may recognize their sign. Do not go to Egypt and do not trust any who seek you out here. My life is forfeit; even now I hear their howls on the wind. Sending this is likely to be my final act.

What a bunch of rubbish. Either the entire thing was a hoax, or the writer was a madman.

Although the protective symbol gave me a bit of pause. That was genuine, at least. And Christine had apparently run into some sort of difficulty in Egypt…

I tucked the token into my vest pocket and left her office without consulting the itinerary.

Instead of the paper on the use of laryngeal theory in reconstructing the Proto-Indo-European language I needed to work on, I spent the afternoon searching for any references to Nitocris. Most likely the letter writer was an ordinary lunatic, but I wished to quell the sense of doubt itching in the back of my mind and disrupting my focus.

I soon recalled where I'd heard the name before. Herodotus had mentioned Nitocris as an early Egyptian queen who tricked her enemies to a feast, before drowning them all by diverting the Nile into the room where they dined. An unlikely tale, to say the least, even discounting the wilder claims she'd recovered their bodies and feasted on *them* instead.

Her name appeared again, centuries later, in *Cultes des Goules* the 18th century manuscript by Francois-Honore Balfour. He claimed Nitocris held court as Queen of the Ghūls, an eater of the dead and near-goddess to subjects more jackal than human.

The final reference occurred on one of the artifacts taken from the tomb of the necromantic pharaoh Nephren-ka, which Christine had so famously discovered. The back of a gilded throne depicted what seemed to be a domestic scene of the pharaoh and one of his wives. The cartouche beside her was the same as that on the token from the letter.

Nephren-ka had been a heretic and sorcerer of the worst kind. After his death, the priests had done their best to expunge his name from history along with the names of his wives and children. I took the coin from my pocket and turned it over and over in my fingers while I thought. Could there be any truth to the warning? Had Christine run afoul of something occult and so needed my help? Was that why she hadn't been more specific in her telegram, not wishing to be labeled a madwoman by anyone else who might read it?

Blast.

I glanced at the clock and started guiltily. My researches had taken longer than I'd realized, and it was now well after closing.

Gathering some papers to take home, I cursed my own inattention. Hopefully, Griffin wouldn't be upset at the delay in dinner, especially as it was my turn to cook. Of course, he'd lived with me for a year now, so he really ought to be used to my tendency to lose track of time.

Resolving once again to be a better housemate, I put on my coat and hat and started for the exit. The janitorial staff had largely extinguished the gaslights for the night, and I had to return to my office for a lantern. Although I'd never admit it to Griffin, the new electric lights in our house had proved rather more convenient than the old system of gas.

My footsteps echoed eerily as I made my way through the deserted galleries. There was a night watchman around somewhere—or, rather several of them, all on their separate rounds. But given the quiet and shadows, I felt as if no one remained in museum—perhaps the entire city—save for me.

I shivered at the fancy, before firmly telling myself to stop being foolish. Still, I quickened my pace, angling past the new Isley Wing toward the grand entryway. As I did so, I caught the rusty scent of blood.

I froze in my tracks, my heart rabbiting in my chest. Perhaps I was wrong…but no, I'd encountered far too much blood over the last year to mistake the odor for anything else. And it was strong, as if a great deal of it had spilled.

If there had been some earlier excitement, surely Miss Parkhurst would have come to inform me of it. Wouldn't she? Perhaps Mr. Farr and Mr. Durfee's feud finally got out of hand, leading to a duel over the proper display of post-Colonial paintings.

Which would have been horrible, but not the worst possibility I could think of, unfortunately.

I took a deep breath and shone my lantern about the great entry hall. I saw nothing, save for the fossilized bones of ancient beasts and shuttered ticket booths. And no sign of the night watchman who should have stood near the front doors.

Blast it.

I should go for one of the other guards without delay. But what if the man—what on earth was his name?—had become injured through some accident? If he lay bleeding to death and needed immediate aid to survive?

There really was nothing for it. I reluctantly turned my steps in the direction where the scent of blood seemed strongest. I wished my lantern were of the type the police—and Griffin—used, which cast a single strong beam. The silence of the sleeping building pressed against my ears, so every footstep echoed abominably loud.

There came a soft scrape from inside the Isley Wing. The portion of the museum, I couldn't help but note, where many of Nephren-ka's treasures were on display.

No light came from the exhibit hall. Perhaps the night watchman had fallen and his lantern went out. But why the smell of blood? Had he hit his head on one of the stone statues, perhaps?

The small pool of light around my feet fell across a dark shape lying almost in the arch leading to the first room. I found the watchman sprawled there, obviously dead. Sharp-edged cuts, as if from a knife, sliced open his clothing, and the flesh beneath...

No knife made those wounds. Something had fed on his body.

Horror washed through me, and I stumbled back. What had Griffin said at Christmas dinner, about a corpse exhumed and partially eaten a few days ago?

My lantern swung in my hand, casting its illumination deeper into the room. The light fell across the expressionless face of a colossal statue of the pharaoh, and made the carved animals on the side of an alabaster chest seem to ripple with life and movement. A pair of eyes reflected back the light, like a cat's.

Dear Lord, had some sort of wild beast slipped into the museum and killed the guard?

The owner of the eyes stepped into the light of my lantern. They belonged to a man after all. Blood covered his hands and face, and his sharp teeth showed red when he offered me a horrible, rictus grin.

I bolted in the other direction.

The lantern swung wildly in my hand, flinging crazy shadows on the walls, the floor, the great bones of dinosaurs. My shoes slipped on the polished marble as I darted around an exhibit. Footsteps pounded behind me. The sound of my racing heart in my ears nearly drowned out the strange dog-like bark of excitement.

The intruder had murdered the guard and eaten him, and no doubt intended to do the same to me.

But he didn't know the museum's labyrinthine floor plan as I did. If I could just keep ahead of him, I could surely find some place of concealment. Once he left, I'd locate one of the other watchmen, or run screaming through the streets for the police, whatever it took.

My long legs gave me some advantage, at least over the short distance. I ducked through a staff door, down a hallway, around a corner, and through a second door. The door let onto a large, open room where the desks of the general secretaries sat at ordered intervals.

I ducked behind the nearest desk and pressed myself against its solid wood frame. I quickly shuttered the lantern, and strove to suppress my need to breathe, lest my gasps give me away. Surely the intruder was no ordinary thief, but some kind of cannibalistic maniac.

A door creaked in the distance. God, let it be one of the watchmen coming. I'd warn him, and we'd sound the alarm.

Stealthy movements came from the hall outside, accompanied by a strange snuffling. Definitely not a watchman.

What could I possibly do to stop him? The water spell would be useless here, and I hadn't noticed anything particularly flammable on him. I might ward him off with a wind spell, but I needed to draw a sigil to act as a focus, and it took precious moments for the wind to gather.

The secretary had left an umbrella propped against her desk, no doubt forgotten when she left at the end of the day. I snatched it up and clutched it in both hands. Not as good as a knife or a gun, but at least I had some sort of weapon now. The only illumination came from the mixture of moonbeams and gaslight seeping through the tall windows at one end of the room.

The door creaked open. Cloth rustled, and a shoe scraped against wood, but I heard no footsteps. Barely daring to breathe, I peeked around the edge of the desk.

The intruder crawled on all fours, sniffing the floor like a dog following a scent. In the moonlight, his eyes glowed like a pair of corpse candles.

I gasped inadvertently at the sight. The man's head jerked up, and a grin split his face as he spotted me.

I leapt up from behind the desk, even as he surged to his feet and rushed me. I swung the umbrella as hard as I could. The wooden shaft let out a loud crack as it shattered against his skull.

The man growled savagely and dashed the broken umbrella from my hands. I stumbled away, nearly tripping over a chair. "St-stay back!" I warned him.

He rushed me a second time. I twisted away, around another desk, and sprinted for the open door.

A hand closed on my jacket, shoving me hard against the wall. I managed to turn to face him, just in time to see his other hand aim a knife at my throat.

I grabbed his wrist and clung to it, fighting to keep the blade away. "Help!" I bellowed at the top of my lungs. "Thief! Murder!"

My attacker let go of my jacket and closed his hand around my throat. My shouts ended in a strangled sound as his fingers squeezed mercilessly. It took all my willpower to cling to the hand holding the knife instead of clawing at the one cutting off my breath. My vision began to darken around the edges, and a strange rushing sound, like waves, pounded in my ears. A ruffle of wind touched my face, blowing from where I didn't know, but it was weak and dying.

Like me.

There came the thunderous report of a pistol. The grip on my throat slackened, and the wrist in my hands went limp. I collapsed against the wall, gasping and coughing. My assailant staggered two steps, blood frothing about his mouth, before slumping to the floor. His hands twitched one final time, as if seeking to grasp me, then stilled in death.

"Dr. Whyborne! Are you all right?"

The youngest watchman knelt in front of me, his earnest face worried. "Y-yes," I said, but my voice sounded as if I'd gargled with rusty razors. I coughed and tried again. "I think so. But the Isley Wing...he killed the watchman there."

The man went pale. "Will you be all right here alone, sir?"

"I-I think so."

He nodded and left, blowing his whistle loudly to summon help from the other guards. I huddled against the wall, my gaze drawn involuntarily to the intruder's face. Even in death, his lips drew back from his teeth in a rabid snarl. Although dressed in a plain sack suit, he had the coloring and features of an Arab.

Could this incident have some connection with the wild letter sent to Christine? The unknown writer claimed to have eaten the flesh of the dead while following Nitocris. And the guard's body...another shudder went through me at the memory.

I didn't want to go near anywhere near him. But the watchman would return soon. Crouching beside my assailant, I gingerly peeled the blood-soaked coat away from his chest, half-expecting him to surge back to life and grab my wrist as I did so. A quick pat of his vest pockets yielded a watch but nothing else.

Taking a deep breath and trying not to think too hard about what I was doing, I slid my hand into the right pocket of his trousers. His flesh was still warm, and my stomach turned.

My fingers brushed metal. Probably just a silver dollar.

I drew it out and held it in my palm. In the dim light filtering from the high windows, I could just make out the cartouche of Nitocris.

Chapter 4

"Are you certain you're all right, my dear?" Griffin asked some time later.

When I'd finally arrived home, having given my statement to the police, the head of the museum's security, and the museum director himself, Griffin greeted me with an annoyed expression. It had quickly cleared when he saw the bruises ringing my neck, and the bloody smears on my suit.

I'd let him dote on me a bit while I told him the gist of the story: ushering me onto the couch, removing my coat and vest, fetching a cup of tea to soothe my throat.

"I'm fine," I assured him. My voice scraped coming out, and he scowled.

"You should have summoned a guard at once instead of investigating," he said. "If the watchman who answered your cry for help had responded any slower, your corpse would lie beside your attacker's!"

I hesitated, but what could I say? "You're right. I didn't want to look foolish if I proved wrong, but it would have been the better alternative."

He relaxed fractionally, and when I set my empty teacup aside, reached for my hands. I was glad for the contact, twining my fingers through his. His thumb gently rubbed back and forth across my knuckles.

"Do you know what the man was looking for in the exhibit?" he asked.

I nodded. I'd returned to the Isley Wing, in the company of one of the other watchmen, before departing the museum. "The display case he'd broken into contained nothing but a few pots and an ostracon."

"A what?"

"The Egyptians used fragments of broken pots the way we use scrap paper," I explained. "To write letters, or jot down lists, that sort of thing. The Greeks called them *ostraca*. The word ostracize comes from this, because—"

"I'm sure it's fascinating, my dear," he interrupted with an affectionate smile, "but perhaps we could stick to the matter at hand for the moment?"

"Oh, er, yes. As I was saying, this particular ostracon was a letter from one priest of Horus to another. I wrote down the pertinent bit." I took out a bit of paper and read aloud. *"Should the need arise to again do battle with the forces of Nyarlathotep, I have concealed the location of the fane in the Valley of the Jackals."*

I looked at him expectantly, but he only frowned. "A...fane?"

"A temple or shrine," I explained.

"I see. Still, I don't understand why this is particularly important."

"The letter was never sent—why we don't know," I said. "Because it was found in the Valley of Jackals. In Nephren-ka's tomb. The site of Christine's excavation."

His gaze sharpened. "Christine's in danger."

"Presumably so." I stared down at our joined hands. "The thief's eyes...they reflected the light like an animal's. And he went on all fours, not like a man crawls, but more like a dog. I don't think he was entirely human. He *ate* part of the guard...and you said someone dug up and devoured a corpse, did you not?"

"Yes." He nodded slowly. "And this Nitocris is associated with jackal-like eaters of the dead. There must be a connection."

"I have to go to Egypt. Christine needs help—she wouldn't have sent the telegram otherwise. I just didn't want to admit it." I took a deep breath. "I'll miss you terribly."

Griffin gave me a puzzled look. "Don't be absurd. I'm going with you."

"But your business—what will become of it if you leave Widdershins for several months on end?"

"I doubt the inhabitants of Widdershins will run out of reasons to hire a discreet private detective any time soon," he said dryly. "It will be here when I return. Did you honestly think I'd let you travel all the way to Egypt, to confront something *Christine* can't handle, and not come with you?"

"To be fair, if Christine is having difficulties, it means the problem can't be simply shot or bludgeoned with a shovel," I pointed out, but my heart soared at his words.

"No doubt," he agreed. "But I have a few talents which may come in handy."

"True." I didn't want to argue, but felt I had no choice. "But what if word comes of your brothers while you're gone?"

"It's been over twenty-five years since I last saw them." His smile turned rueful. "A few more months will make no difference. Christine is my friend as well as yours, and I'm not about to abandon her." Drawing our joined hands up to press a kiss against my knuckles, he added, "Besides, I've cast my lot with yours, remember? Where you go, I go."

My ribs felt too constrictive around my heart. I leaned in and rested my forehead against his. "Thank you. First thing tomorrow, I'll explain to the director, and you can book our tickets for Egypt."

A bit over a week later, we took passage on the *Montcalm* from New York to London.

The tiny stateroom contained nothing more than a pair of berths designed for men much shorter than myself, and a sort of couch built directly into the wall below a porthole. Claustrophobic as it was, I spent as much time as possible in the little cabin, as the only alternative was mingling with the other passengers.

Had they been content to keep to their own business, I wouldn't have minded quite as much. But all of them wanted to chat, as if our brief consignment to a floating prison made us intimates. Griffin, of course, thrived in such an environment. By the time we disembarked, he knew every detail about each soul on board, from the porter to the captain.

The less said about our stay in London the better, and I gladly boarded the steamer to Port Said. Unfortunately, the heat grew as we traveled south. Our cabin became stifling, and at last drove even me out to seek a breeze.

Griffin and I strolled along the deck one evening after sundown. The stars shone out in their multitudes, and the half-full moon peered down from above. A great many other passengers took advantage of the cooler air on the deck, and a group of them hailed Griffin by name. He paused to talk while I continued on alone.

A woman stood near the prow of the ship, staring out over the dark water. Although difficult to make out the color for certain in the dim light, she appeared to dress in mourning black. It contrasted sharply with her flaxen hair and pale skin.

I tipped my hat to her politely, having not been introduced. As this was the quietest part of the ship at the moment, thanks to the group congregating along the starboard side, I took up position a respectable distance from her to wait for Griffin.

"Another who doesn't care for the crowds?" she asked. She possessed a deep, throaty voice and sounded as if she laughed a great deal.

"Er, yes," I said, surprised she had spoken.

"Forgive me if I disturb you," she said. "You're Dr. Whyborne, aren't you? Yours is the only name on the passenger manifest I've been unable to connect to a face. Please, let me introduce myself. I am Grafin Daphne de Wisborg."

From her American accent, I assumed her to be one of the many heiresses to find European husbands, my own sister among them. "I am. A pleasure to meet you, Grafin de Wisborg."

"Likewise." I expected her to bring up my father's name, or start chatting about her tour plans for Egypt, but instead she turned back to the view. "I believe Crete is somewhere to the north of us. In the deeps of the night, one can almost imagine Minos still in his palace, and the ghost of the Minotaur staring gloomily out as our modern ships pass by."

"Oh, you are a student of the classics?" I asked. Perhaps there was some intelligent conversation to be had on this dreadful boat after all.

"Yes. But this is the first time I've laid eyes on 'the wine-dark sea' as Homer put it. The history here…can you feel it?"

I nodded, surprised to find a sympathetic soul. "There is something to be said for crossing waters once sailed by heroes," I agreed. Some of whom were even…well, not like me, precisely. But who loved men without censure or fear, even if they had wives and children as well.

"And heroines." I could barely see her profile even with the moonlight, but I thought her lips curled into a bitter smile. "Minos is linked with the legend of the Minotaur, but it was his wife Pasiphaë whom the gods chose to as their tool to punish him. How did she feel, when her husband took away the child she loved despite its deformities and shut it away to go mad in the lonely dark of the labyrinth?"

A chill ran over my skin. "I never thought to consider the tale in such a fashion," I admitted.

"Of course not." Her tone implied she'd expected no better. Then she shook her head and laughed softly. "Forgive my fanciful talk, Dr. Whyborne. My husband died recently, and my thoughts tend to the morbid as of late."

"Of course. Quite understandable," I hurried to reassure her.

"I believe I shall retire for the evening. Good night, sir."

I bid her goodnight and watched her leave, the soft rustle of her black skirts melding with the whisper of waves against the hull. She made no move to speak to the other passengers, and I wondered if she had a traveling companion. Of course, in these modern days, it was no longer necessary for a woman to be chaperoned about like a child. But somehow she seemed very alone.

It was a state for which I possessed great sympathy. I glanced along the rail and spotted Griffin, still speaking animatedly with a small family. He knelt in front of a girl and used sleight of hand to appear to produce a coin from behind her ear. She clapped her hands in delight, and her brother begged for the same trick to be played on him.

Even at a distance, I could make out Griffin's smile. He would have made a wonderful father. Did he regret missing the opportunity? Did he hope the brothers he searched for might have children of their own, whom he could spoil? At moments like this, did he regret the life he'd given up by casting his lot with me, as he put it?

I walked slowly back down the deck. As I approached, he glanced up and turned his brilliant smile on me. "I think I'll retire, old fellow," I told him.

"I shall join you, as not to wake you later." He made his farewells, leaving the children pouting over his departure.

He seemed in a good mood when we returned to the cabin, but he was a consummate actor, and I feared he hid his sorrow and refused to let me see it.

Still, if he harbored regrets deep within, I could at least remind him our relationship provided certain advantages as well. As Griffin threw the bolt on the cabin door, I stepped up behind him and slid my arms around his waist, pressing a kiss to his hair.

"Mmm." He leaned back against me, stretching to lace his arms around my neck. The curve of his buttock pressed against my thigh, and his ribs flexed with breath beneath my hands. "Curse these cramped cabins. I can't wait to have you in a real bed again."

His words stirred my blood, as he no doubt knew they would. "How would you have me now?" I asked, pressing against him so he could feel my arousal against the small of his back.

"Naked and bent over the couch."

My cock showed approval for the idea, hardening fully against him. "I'd like that."

"Then get to it."

I let go of him and began to hurriedly undress. He did the same. The sight of his body seldom failed to arouse me, even after a year of beddings, and tonight proved no different. Trim but muscular limbs, broad shoulders, and well-formed member: he made my mouth water, just to look at him. A scar wrapped around his right thigh, a memento of his first encounter with the otherworldly, before we two ever met.

He kissed me, pressing his naked form against mine, the sear of his skin hot even in the overly warm cabin. He tasted of mint and brandy, and I sucked his lower lip into my mouth, worrying it lightly between my teeth. His hands roamed freely, shaping my back before cupping my buttocks and pulling me tighter against him.

"I want you," he growled into my ear. "I want to fuck you and make you come for me."

"Yes," I gasped. My breath quickened, and I ached with need for him. Pulling free of his embrace, I bent over and rested my elbows on the couch, naked and vulnerable and exposed to him. The wind through the open portal blew into my face, bringing with it a breath of coolness and salt.

"What a sight you make," Griffin murmured, trailing his fingers along the insides of my thighs, before squeezing my buttocks. "No one would ever guess you're such a wanton."

"You did," I whispered. My skin prickled in anticipation, and I resisted the urge to rub against the couch for relief. "Don't make me wait."

"Your wish is my command." I heard him fumbling with our baggage, but didn't move, instead staring out the open porthole. The moonlight mingled with star shine on the water, and phosphorescence edged the long swells. The heavy scent of the sea flooded the cabin, and I breathed of it deeply.

A slick finger pressed gently against my passage. I sighed and relaxed, welcoming the intrusion. My grip tightened slightly on the cushions of the couch as he worked me, sprinkling kisses across my back and shoulders as he did so. Had anyone else been in this position on the couch, staring out at the star-strewn ocean?

Griffin's back pressed against mine, his shaft hard against my crease. "Are you ready for me?"

The waves grew stronger, breaking against the side of the ship. Salt spray came through the open porthole and touched my lips. "Oh God, yes!"

The push and stretch of his cock drew a groan of sheer, animal lust out of me. He bent over me, his breath scalding against my back. His hand wrapped around my length, stroking me in time to his long, slow thrusts. The waves rocked the ship, and I gripped the couch more tightly.

"Yes," I repeated. Yes to all of it: his body in mine, his hand on me, the stars bright against the heaving blackness of the ocean. He nipped my skin gently, then harder, his movements growing more urgent. Every strike of his cock against the sensitive spot deep inside sent a new surge of pleasure through me, accompanied by the urgent tug of his hand on my member.

"Yes." The sea grew rougher, the steel hull of the ship moaning against the battering waves. "Keep going, please!"

"Ival." His voice went heavy and thick with need, trembling just on the edge. "Give your pleasure to me, love, do it."

I bit my lip hard, eyes closed and a private set of stars spangling the backs of the lids as my pleasure crested. My body clenched tight around him, and he let out a little cry, shuddering and shaking as he spent himself into me.

The sea gradually stilled and settled around us, the ship's roll growing gentle. "God," he murmured eventually, his lips against my spine. "You are a wonder to me."

His words made me smile. I wanted to curl up in his arms, heavy and sated, but nowhere in the cabin could accommodate both of us. "You are the wonder."

"You don't know yourself, my dear." He leaned in to kiss me. "I love you, Ival."

"I love you, too," I said. And hoped it would be enough.

Port Said offered as different a scene from the quays of Widdershins as I could have imagined. The heat, the swirl of colorful robes, the shouts in a dozen languages, combined to make my head spin. Scores of men and boys crowded the pier, shouting at the passengers in broken English as we disembarked.

"Donkey, *effendi!* To the rail station, yes?" one of the impertinent fellows offered, practically in my face. He stood almost as tall as me.

I took a step back. "No, thank you," I replied in Arabic. "I have arrangements already made."

He seemed surprised I'd addressed him in something other than English, but it worked to dissuade him, and he began yelling his offer at the passengers behind us.

"I don't see Christine, do you?" Griffin asked, tilting his hat to better shade his eyes against the glare of the sun.

"No." Had she encountered some delay? We'd been out of contact since a hastily wired telegram from England more than ten days ago. Anything could have happened since. "Let's get away from this crowd. I can't hear myself think."

It was much easier said than done. Everywhere boys and young men confronted us with offers to act as tour guides, donkeys to rent, or pleas for *baksheesh*. Our fellow passengers milled about, collecting their luggage and hiring porters from among the swarm of natives.

I glimpsed the Grafin de Wisborg in the crowd, a parasol shading her pale skin from the fierce sun. To my surprise, she snapped her fingers and issued orders in brisk Arabic. A number of strong-looking young men leapt at once to her command, and within moments, she and her luggage had vanished. Would we encounter her again at Shepheard's Hotel in Cairo? According to Christine, practically every foreign tourist lodged there, whether partaking in one of Mr. Cook's tours or on an excursion of their own, or at least came to enjoy the view from the famous terrace.

"Are you deaf?" yelled a portly man Englishman, his red face covered in a layer of sweat. "I want a coach! Now go get me one, or no *baksheesh,* understand?"

He berated a tall, slim Arab dressed in a summer weight suit and hat. A striking example of Egyptian manhood, his nose and mouth could have served as the model for one of the ancient statues of the pharaohs. "I understand you quite well, sir," he replied with an English accent. "But I fear I'm already engaged."

The portly man turned away in disgust. "It's true what they say about how lazy the natives are," he said in a loud voice to his wife.

The man he'd callously dismissed stiffened slightly, mouth tightening in anger. But an instant later, the expression vanished, smoothed away into a neutral mask. As he turned to scan the crowd, his gaze found me, and recognition flashed in his eyes. "Dr. Whyborne?"

"Er, yes?"

"Permit me to introduce myself. I'm Iskander Barnett, an associate of Dr. Putnam's."

I recalled his name from Christine's descriptions of her various adventures. I stuck out my hand; he looked vaguely bemused as he shook it. "Dr. Percival Endicott Whyborne—oh, you already know that, don't you?—and this is my traveling companion, Mr. Griffin Flaherty."

"A pleasure to meet you, Mr. Barnett," Griffin said, shaking his hand in turn. "Do you assist Dr. Putnam often?"

"Yes, I—"

"Oh good, Kander, you found them." Christine's familiar tones cut through the noise of the crowded dock. I turned to see her striding through the throng toward us. Her costume came as a bit of a shock. Although I knew she always adopted rational dress in the field, and had seen her in bloomers before in the course of our adventures, her working outfit proved even more radical than I'd supposed. The dusty tan trousers were quite mannish, and paired with a plain white shirt, tan vest, and coat. Her hat befit any explorer of the land, of whatever gender.

"Whyborne," she said crisply, thrusting her hand at me. "Good to see you."

I shook it more out of reflex than anything else. "Christine," I said, doing my best to convey I didn't appreciate her dragging me halfway around the globe without explanation.

"Griffin." She shook his hand heartily. "Excellent. I assumed Whyborne would bring you."

"What is this all about?" I asked, feeling I'd waited far too long for enlightenment already.

"I'll tell you in full later, away from these crowds," she said. "Now hurry it up, we don't want to be late for the train to Cairo."

"Christine!" I set my heels and folded my arms across my chest. "No. I'm not going another step until you offer me some word of explanation."

"Murder," she replied. "Murder most foul, as the bard says. Now stop being dramatic and find your luggage."

Chapter 5

The trip to Cairo took three hours by rail. I spent the time huddled against the window, staring out at this new land and wishing myself back in Widdershins already.

Many of the texts I'd translated referred to the red land and the black land—the inhospitable desert and the thin stripe of arable soil enriched by the yearly flood of the Nile. But never before had I truly realized the shocking contrast between the two. The verdant green of fields and villages gave way to barren desolation as abruptly as if some god had reached down from the sky and sundered them with the edge of a knife. A man could literally stand with one foot in each. The Egypt of maps might be a vast place, but in practical reality its width was less than some cities. Its length, however, stretched a thousand miles along either side of the life-giving waters of the Nile.

I wanted to demand more answers from Christine, but I suspected the murder she referred to contained elements she didn't wish to speak of in front of Mr. Barnett, let alone the other occupants of the crowded train car. As for my part, I certainly couldn't inform her of the warning letter, token, or inhuman cannibal maniac without Barnett and everyone around us thinking me deranged.

I'd brought the bulk of Christine's mail with me. She perused the letters as we rode, paying no heed to the rattling train, crying children, or overly loud tourists around us.

"What a bunch of rot," she said, scanning yet another one. "You shouldn't have bothered bringing them, Whyborne. Half consist of crackpot theories claiming the Ancient Egyptians came from Atlantis, and the rest of proposals of marriage."

"Proposals of marriage?" Mr. Barnett echoed.

"Fortune hunters," she replied dismissively. "For some reason, men seem to think I own the artifacts I've excavated, rather than the museum, and thus imagine me wealthy. And as I'm a known spinster, every layabout and drunkard seems compelled to write to me extolling his virtues and appealing for my hand in marriage. Look, this one even sent a photograph."

"A handsome fellow," I remarked. Mr. Barnett scowled but didn't disagree.

"I suppose." Christine eyed the photograph critically. "But still a fortune hunter. And I long ago realized marriage isn't for me anyway."

"What about when you considered marrying me?" I asked.

To my shock, Christine turned pink. "The situation was completely different."

"Of course she never bothered to consult me in the matter," I added to Mr. Barnett, who appeared somewhat concerned by this fact. As well he might, although if he'd worked with Christine as often as she said, I would have thought him used to her ways by now.

"How you do go on!" Christine exclaimed, her face growing even redder. Was the heat affecting her?

"If I may ask, Mr. Barnett," Griffin said, diverting the conversation. "How long have you been in Egypt?"

Barnett seemed surprised, but answered readily enough. "About eight years, now. Most people assume me a native, despite my accent."

"Fools," Christine dismissed them.

Barnett smiled, a bit ruefully. "My mother was Egyptian, my father an English diplomat stationed here when Egypt was still under the rule of the pashas. I was born in Kent and lived there most of my life. After my mother died, I decided to see the land of her birth. Once here, I never left."

Griffin nodded. "And now you work with Christine? I imagine it must be...interesting."

"Oh, do come out and say what you mean, Griffin," Christine exclaimed. "I have opinions and temper, neither of which I'm supposed to possess due to my sex."

"I said nothing of the sort."

"Well, it's true. And Kander is a saint to put up with me, I'll be the first to admit. How I'll get along when he finally leaves, I haven't the slightest idea."

"I have no intentions of leaving," Barnett assured her.

"Bah! You can do better than arranging food and transportation, paying bribes, and finding hotel rooms," she said, waving a dismissive hand at his protest. "Your skills are wasted—you should be planning your own expeditions."

Barnett seemed embarrassed by her praise, but clearly knew better than to demure. Instead, he asked to borrow one of the newspapers we'd brought from London, and buried himself in it. Griffin took out one of the awful dime novels he liked to read, and I settled back in my seat, hoping to catch a moment or two of sleep, although I doubted I'd succeed. We remained thus until two hours later, when the train at last pulled into Cairo.

Barnett took his leave of us at the station, tasked with escorting our luggage to Shepheard's Hotel, where we'd spend the night. Christine hired an open carriage, with the stated intention of visiting the site of the murder.

"Yes, what is this about a murder?" I asked testily, as soon as we were seated. "Or are you going to leave us in suspense for as long as possible?"

"Really, Whyborne, travel does make you rather peevish," she said. "That's exactly why we never married. Speaking of which, I can't believe you brought the matter up in front of Kander!"

"Why? If he's worked for you as long as you say, he must have noticed you're a madwoman."

Griffin cleared his throat. "The murder?"

The carriage lurched into motion. All around us unfolded the life of the city: tourists riding donkeys, women swathed in black robes and veils until only their dark eyes showed, men in colorful striped kaftans, vendors selling everything from water to sweets. Dung and incense scented the air, mingled with exotic spices.

Christine settled back, looking unusually pensive. "I arrived in Cairo last month, only to find a message waiting for me from Sayid Halabi, one of the most notorious scoundrels in Lower Egypt. He knows every tomb robber within five hundred miles. Or he did prior to being murdered."

"And you're angry because someone killed him before you had the opportunity to do it yourself?" I guessed.

"Not in Halabi's case. He made his start in the illicit antiquities trade, and I suspect he kept his hand in, but he grew to recognize the importance of applying proper science and excavation techniques. Not to mention he was quite aware his countrymen are paid mere pennies for antiquities which sell for thousands of dollars in Paris and New York." She scowled and gestured. "Look around you—most of these people are desperately poor, and it's even worse in the villages. Britain and France are like two doctors who argue over a dying man, but do nothing substantial to treat him. What Egypt needs is a decent system of education, especially for the women. If it were up to me—"

"Halabi?" I interrupted. Christine would go on for hours if given the chance to work up a full head of steam. I agreed with her, but I'd also heard the lecture a dozen times over, usually delivered at top volume in my office at the Ladysmith.

"Oh. Yes." She straightened her cuffs. "As I pay my workmen a fair price for the artifacts they uncover in the course of the dig, he began sending hints my way of various places the robbers knew, but of which archaeologists remained ignorant. I passed some along to those few colleagues I could trust not to utterly destroy the site. Petrie...well, never mind," she said at my look. "This time, my communication from Halabi was a bit odd. He said he needed to see me immediately, because he'd heard I'm searching for the Fane of Nyarlathotep."

"He was the god Nephren-ka worshipped, correct?" Griffin asked.

"And Blackbyrne and any number of other necromancers and persons of ill will throughout history," I replied.

The carriage lurched to a halt, while our driver screamed imprecations against a herd of goats blocking the road. I began to think it would be faster to simply get out and walk.

"Precisely," Christine said, seeming not at all perturbed by our lack of progress. "A god of *isfet*—chaos. No more evil force existed in Ancient Egypt. Legend has it Nephren-ka built a grand fane to the god somewhere in the western desert. A place of great magic, where he housed his most terrible secrets."

"And you want to *find* this place?" Griffin exclaimed. "After everything we've seen?"

A camel burdened with a sweating tourist waited directly beside our carriage, its handler adding his voice to the imprecations against the goats blocking the way. While the man was distracted, the camel thrust its head into the carriage and peered at me through eyes fringed with thick lashes. A soft nose, surmounted by an old scar, sniffed at my collar.

I pushed it gingerly aside, half afraid the beast might bite. It didn't, but it didn't move away, either.

"Honestly, you sound like Kander," Christine said, taking off her hat and fanning herself with it. "They said the same thing about Nephren-ka's tomb, which turned out to be nothing, didn't it?"

"Up until the point the Brotherhood stole one of Nephren-ka's scrolls and almost unleashed monstrous beings upon the earth," Griffin replied.

"Exactly. The tales are superstitious nonsense. The sort of thing spoken of around the fire at night, or by bored women locked away in the *harim*. Or, I dare say, in our own newspapers under the guise of headlines blathering about 'The Mummy's Curse!' in 50-point type. And...I'm in danger of losing the firman."

I sat up sharply, bumping my head into the camel, which now investigated my ear. "What? How?" The firman consisted of the right granted by the Antiquities Service—headed by the French—to legally excavate in a certain location. "You've more than earned the right to dig wherever you please, let alone in the valley where you found Nephren-ka's tomb!"

"If I were a man, you'd be correct." She stared off at the vendors waving carpets and trinkets at tourists, her posture rigid. "But certain colleagues have suggested to the Antiquities Service that my gender makes me unfit to continue long-term investigations, and the site should be given to them instead. There's also a hint of 'the girl has had her fun, but it's time to let the men in to do the real work.'"

She spoke lightly, but bitter anger darkened voice. I put a hand to her shoulder, and we exchanged a silent look. We had always understood one another, perhaps better than anyone else. Neither of us found it possible to adhere to society's expectations, but I liked to think we shared a sympathy of intellect which sealed the bond formed by our status as outsiders.

"It cannot be allowed," I said. "We'll assist you in any fashion needed."

"Thank you, Whyborne." She straightened self-consciously. "But we spoke of Halabi, did we not? As I said, he claimed to have a desperate warning for me. I came to meet him. No one answered my knock, so I let myself in, and found his study locked. I smelled blood even from the outside of the door. I summoned Iskander, and together we broke down it down. There wasn't a great deal left of the body we found."

"How horrible!" I commiserated.

"Quite. Much like the guard you wired me about, something had gnawed on the poor devil."

"And what did the police think happened?" Griffin asked.

"The police? Bah! They're utterly corrupt, not to mention incompetent." Christine glowered. "If a foreigner had died, the government would have no choice but to get involved. As it is Halabi's demise received only the most cursory investigation. Possibly someone paid bribes to keep it from going any farther. Or the mystery of how he died in a locked room roused too many superstitious fears. Either way, we'll receive no assistance from anyone else."

The carriage finally lurched into motion. At the same instant, my hat whisked from my head. Startled, I turned and saw the camel contentedly munching on it. "No! Wait!" I called, but now that the blockage had cleared, our driver seemed determined to continue forward no matter what.

"Do stop playing with the camels, Whyborne," Christine said. "We have more pressing things to attend to at the moment."

"I wasn't—my hat—" But the camel vanished behind a sea of carts and livestock. "Curse it!"

"Oh, do stop carrying on." The carriage passed a vendor displaying a large selection of the ubiquitous *fez*. Christine leaned out, tossed a coin to him, and snatched one up. "Here."

I took it gingerly. It was of red felt, with a black tassel, and looked like nothing I would ever willingly put on my head. "Christine..."

"Put the blasted thing on and quit complaining, man!"

I reluctantly obeyed. Turning to Griffin for his opinion, I found him doubled over in laughter.

"Quite f-fetching, my dear," he snickered.

My new fez perched atop my head, I slumped back against the seat and folded my arms petulantly over my chest. "I hate you both."

We left behind the busiest streets and delved into a veritable warren of crooked lanes and narrow alleys. Mud brick buildings with metal-screened windows lined the street, many with men sitting out front, smoking and watching our passage with curious eyes. As we rode, I showed the anonymous letter to Christine with its accompanying token, along with the one I'd taken from the cannibal's pocket.

"Nitocris, eh?" she mused, frowning at the letter I'd translated for her, as she didn't speak German. "Her cartouche isn't widely known. If this is the work of lunatics, they would be unusually well-informed."

"How well-informed?" Griffin asked.

"The throne wasn't one of the artifacts sent on tour with Nephren-ka. It's in a storeroom in the Ladysmith, undergoing restoration for display," Christine replied. "So I don't know how they would have seen it unless one of the restorers has gone mad."

"One of the library staff, I could believe," I said. "But they don't have access to the storeroom where the more valuable items are kept."

The carriage slowed as we arrived at our destination. A tall Egyptian squatted by the door. When he saw Christine, he rose to his feet in a single, fluid move. "Honored lady," he said in Arabic. "Will you not change your mind? This is no place for the living."

"Thank you for your concern." She held out a stack of folded banknotes. "I hope this will ease your conscience, should something untoward happen to us."

He accepted the bribe with aplomb and offered Christine a key. "Blessings of Allah upon you. You will forgive me if I don't linger. I have urgent business elsewhere."

"I'm sure you do," she said, taking the key.

"Who was he?" Griffin asked, once the man left.

"Halabi's brother-in-law. He inherited the house, but thanks to the manner of Halabi's death, everyone is convinced it's cursed or haunted or both. He can't give the thing away." Christine went to the door and tried the key. "The good news is no one has been inside since they removed the body. Which means if there are any clues as to what happened to him, they should still be within."

The house was built around an interior courtyard, with large rooms arranged to catch the breeze. Once, it had no doubt been a fine place to live, but now an air of neglect hung about it. Stains spotted the carpets, and the furniture had seen no polish in many a year. Once-bright paint faded and peeled beneath the harsh sun, and the trees in the courtyard looked to have died long ago.

"We found him in here," Christine said, opening a door. The hair on the back of my neck prickled. No doubt my unease stemmed from the fact I knew how the man died.

Dim light filtered through the ornate metal screen over the window, revealing a desk such as one might expect to find in any office back home. Had it been intended as a showpiece for Halabi's European clientele, or had he actually used it in his day-to-day business? Carpets covered every inch of the floor, muffling our steps. An odd, resinous incense lent a touch of fragrance to the air.

"I found him there," Christine said, gesturing to the desk chair, which lay overturned in a corner. Blood darkened the carpets beneath it, although the stains had dried and desiccated to the point little odor remained. She swallowed thickly. "I managed not to vomit until I reached the street outside."

It must have been a terrible sight indeed. I went to the desk and picked up the ledger laying on it. Given Halabi's involvement with the black market, I didn't expect anything clear to be written out, and my assumption proved correct. The items referred to were ordinary: pots, donkeys, even baboons. God—or Allah, in this case—only knew what any of it might have actually stood for.

A loose page slipped free and drifted to the floor. From the paper and the ragged edge, it appeared to have been torn from some other book and hastily stuffed into the ledger. But why?

Griffin picked it up. "It's in Arabic," he said, passing it to me. "Does it say anything interesting?"

The handwriting had a shaky, hurried quality to it, as if the dead man had scrawled this message at the last possible instant. "Nitocris has returned," I read aloud. "She seeks the Fane of Nyarlathotep. The Queen of the Ghūls has returned and will make a graveyard of the world."

Beneath the words were a charcoal rubbing, showing the outline of the same token I'd found in the pocket of a dead man.

Chapter 6

"Do you think it possible?" Griffin asked into the silence which followed. "The Brotherhood resurrected Blackbyrne, but he was only two centuries dead. Not…"

"Four thousand years," Christine supplied.

"If they had her body to render the essential salts," I said. "It wouldn't matter how long she had been dead."

"And who are they?" Griffin glanced back and forth between Christine and me. "Whyborne mentioned ghūls are some sort of flesh-eating monsters?'"

"They're creatures of Arab legend." Christine took the note from me and inspected it herself. "Evil things which feed on the dead. It's said they sometimes steal and raise human children."

"Do you think the man who attacked me at the museum could have been some sort of…hybrid?" Somehow the thought made the memory of his sharp teeth and animal eyes even more horrible.

"Who knows?" She tossed the note impatiently onto the desk. "Damn Halabi, couldn't he have just sent a long letter instead of insisting I meet him?"

"Indeed." I glanced around uneasily. "I suppose we have what we came for."

"Not entirely," Griffin said.

"What do you mean?" Christine asked.

"You said the man died here. There's only one door, and it was locked from within. How did his killer gain access?"

"Devil if I know."

Griffin's green eyes narrowed in thought as he studied the room. "Not beneath the desk," he murmured to himself. "Too much trouble to move." He paced across the room once or twice, then bent down, gripped one of the carpets, and flipped it back. The gesture exposed a wooden trap door set into the floor.

"Brilliant!" I exclaimed.

Christine clapped him on the shoulder. "I knew I did the right thing, asking you to come here."

"Whyborne almost left me at home."

"What?" She cast me a surprised look. "Why on earth would you do something so foolish? You aren't quarreling again, are you?"

"No! You didn't say to bring him." I scowled at her.

"Well of course I didn't. The director would have found a request for a private investigator rather suspicious, don't you think? The museum is financing your part of the trip, isn't it?"

"Yes, but this is my job." I looked around the room. "All right, *this* isn't. But Griffin has a business of his own, if you recall. Not everyone can go flitting about the globe."

"What case could possibly compare to this?" Christine asked. "Of course he'd want to come." Squatting beside the trap door, she grasped the iron ring and heaved it open. A cool blast of air rose from beneath. "At least the air is fresh. And there's a ladder."

Griffin regarded the trapdoor rather uncertainly. "Perhaps one of us should remain up here," I suggested.

Griffin shook his head. "No. Thank you for the attempt at kindness, my dear, but I cannot let this fear cripple me forever."

"Many have a touch of claustrophobia," Christine said with surprising diplomacy.

Griffin's mouth thinned. "It isn't claustrophobia. The incident which sent me to the asylum took place in a catacomb of sorts, deep underground. There was...a creature. It took my partner. When I reached him, nothing remained of his face save a bare skull...but he still screamed."

Christine went white beneath her tan. "Oh. How awful. I never knew the details...Of course, if you wish to remain here, Whyborne and I will be quite adequate to any exploration."

"No." Griffin crouched by ladder. "I won't stand by and watch the two of you vanish into the darkness."

I hated he felt the need to prove himself, but at the same time, I couldn't deny the pride which swelled my heart. "I'll find a lantern," I offered.

I expected to find a number of oil lamps, at least, but to my surprise the house seemed rather short on any sort of illumination. I finally located a single clay lamp on a shelf, in which only a small amount of oil remained.

I could have lit it with a word, but in deference to Griffin's feelings about my use of spells, I struck a match instead. Christine took it from me and went first. I followed, and Griffin came last.

The ladder was a crude affair, made of uneven lengths of wood lashed together, and it groaned like a querulous old man under our weight. Fortunately, it proved sturdier than it looked, and we reached the bottom without it collapsing under us.

The feeble light Christine held aloft revealed a small room and a hall leading away. Recessed areas pierced the three walls, each surmounted by an arched opening. Within them lay sarcophagi decorated with Roman-style carvings of faces and olive branches. The walls behind the sarcophagi displayed bas-reliefs featuring a very Egyptian Osiris and Anubis.

"Tombs," Christine said in surprise. "From late in Egypt's history—do you see the Roman influence, Whyborne?"

My heart beat more quickly with the excitement of discovery, and I leaned in to peer at the carvings. "Yes, I see. I didn't realize there were Roman-era catacombs beneath Cairo."

"Neither did anyone else." She pivoted slowly, redirecting the light of the lantern. "I take it back. Looters apparently knew." Indeed, the sarcophagus lids lay askew, and bits of linen wrappings were strewn about on the floor. The gleam of gold caught my eye, and I picked up a small scarab, winged in gold, which might have once been part of a necklace.

Christine took it from me. "This is twelfth dynasty. Far too old to belong to any of these burials. What the devil is it doing here?"

Griffin cleared his throat. "We're not really here to do archaeology," he reminded us.

I winced at the note of strain in his voice. "Of course. To business. Perhaps we can return later."

I held out my hand to him. He glanced reflexively toward Christine, even though she was well aware of our relationship. She noticed the look and rolled her eyes. "Oh, for heaven's sake, man. Don't be absurd."

He only shook his head, but took my hand. I squeezed his fingers and pulled him closer. He might feel the need to confront his fear of underground places, but I would not let him face it alone.

We followed the hall for a short distance. A few flakes of color still clung to the walls to indicate they had once been painted, but the passage of time had utterly obliterated any scenes or figures. The bits of linen strewn on the floor were joined by a jumble of old, animal-gnawed bones, faience beads, and broken jewelry. The air held a slight dampness to it, and I wondered if the Nile ever flooded these catacombs during the inundation, or if some underground river or aquifer flowed beneath us.

"Do you think this is where Halabi found his artifacts?" I asked, pausing to examine a canopic jar. The seal was broken, and any organs stored within either removed or turned to dust.

"No." Christine peered at the faint traces of a painting, but they were too light to make out. "Many of the objects he obtained originated in far earlier eras. Judging by the varying age of the debris left on the floor, though, he may have used it to store his ill-gotten gains. Perhaps we shall find an entire network of smugglers down here." She sounded practically cheerful about the prospect.

Sweat slicked Griffin's palm against mine, but his eyes stared determinedly ahead. "I'm very proud of you," I murmured, hopefully too low for Christine to hear.

He blinked and cast me a surprised glance. The ghost of a smile curved the corners of his mouth. "Thank you. It means a great deal, coming from you."

I didn't see why. Griffin had once called me brave, but I couldn't imagine how he would possibly think it. I feared everything: talking to strangers, leaving Widdershins, humiliating myself in public…the list went on and on. There was nothing for a man such as Griffin, who as a Pinkerton foiled bank robberies and chased down hardened criminals, to admire in me.

But he thought otherwise, mad as it sounded, and his belief made me want to be that man, the one he could admire. So I only gave his hand an encouraging squeeze.

A second hall intersected with the one we followed. Christine paused a moment, before shrugging and turning to the right.

This hall dead-ended in a single large room, and we stopped at the entrance and observed the contents with silent shock. Tomb loot of every sort lay jumbled on the floor and piled in the corners. Golden death masks, protective amulets, fragments of linen wrappings, rings, necklaces, canopic jars, all heaped together as if to line the nest of some gruesome magpie. Amidst the accumulation of grave goods stood stone couches in the Roman style, which formed a rough U shape around a low table covered with dark stains. Against the wall, behind the central couch, stone shelves held an assortment of scrolls and books.

"Damn you, Halabi," Christine muttered. "No provenance, no care taken to preserve anything. The fires of hell are too good for you."

"Some of this seems as if it's been here for quite a while." I pointed at a spread of beads on top of a sarcophagus, which must have once been sewn onto cloth, now rotted into nothing. "Far longer than Mr. Halabi's lifetime."

Griffin let go of my hand and stepped cautiously inside, careful to avoid the piles of artifacts. "What was this place? Originally, I mean?"

"A *triclinium,*" Christine replied. "Mourners would come here and hold feasts in honor of the dead."

"I see." He wiped one finger across the dark stains on the low stone table. "It's fresh."

I became very aware of the darkness pressing in from the corridor behind us. "Please say those are wine stains."

He shook his head. "Blood."

Christine and I followed him into the room, examining its contents. Most of the stone couches were without ornament, but the one at the head of the arrangement had a cartouche carved deeply into its surface. I bent down to read the all-too-familiar inscription.

"Nitocris," I said, and the hair on the back of my neck rose.

"Curse it," Christine murmured.

I turned my attention to the shelves. Here, at least, was a sort of order, proceeding from ancient papyrus scrolls, which looked likely to crumble to dust, to parchment scrolls, to bound books of vellum or cotton paper, no more than a few centuries old.

I picked up what appeared to be the most recent book, perhaps of seventeenth-century make, although it would take an expert in bookbinding techniques to be certain. The pages were crowded with densely inscribed Aklo, the same language the *Arcanorum* was written in.

"Hor-em-akhet was not meant as a tomb, but the priests may have concealed Nephren-ka's body below," I read aloud. "My ghūls will dig beneath it at the next new moon. If he is there, we will eat his bones and piss on his skull. Even if not, perhaps the priests of Horus will have concealed the key to the fane beneath the watchful eye of their god."

Christine let out a low hiss. "Hor-em-akhet means 'Horus of the horizon.' The ancients called the Great Sphinx of Giza by that name. Do you think…?"

I paged through rapidly. "It wasn't there. And the writer damns… her husband the pharaoh?" I looked up, saw blank surprise on the faces of my companions. "Perhaps this isn't the first time Nitocris has returned."

As my words faded into silence, the scrape of claws on stone sounded from the darkness beyond the small light of our lantern. I became painfully aware of our situation, in a hidden place beneath Cairo, where no one would ever find our bodies should something go wrong.

Christine handed the lamp to me and drew out her pistol. Behind us, Griffin did the same.

I pivoted toward the corridor and lifted the lamp to better illuminate the corridor. Its feeble, flickering light did little to penetrate the darkness, save to reflect in a pair of eyes set far too high off the ground to belong to an animal.

Christine let out an oath, and Griffin called, "Come forward, with your hands up!"

The eyes vanished, and nails clicked on stone, moving rapidly away.

"After it!" Christine shouted, and I obeyed automatically. Whoever—*whatever*—we'd disturbed fled like the very devil ahead of us. I raced after, lamp threatening to slosh hot oil everywhere. The madly flickering light snagged on bits and pieces of the creature's form, but refused to show me a whole. I glimpsed a reflective eye, the wide shoulders of a man, a muscular calf covered with matted brown fur.

The corridor opened up suddenly, the floor vanishing into the blackness of an oubliette. I stumbled to a halt, arms pinwheeling to keep myself from tumbling into the abyss. The lamp flew free from my hand, arcing like a falling star into the vast emptiness before us. I received the impression of an enormous well, with dozens of other corridors and tunnels intersecting it on a score of other levels above and below. The rotted remains of stairs clung to the inside of the well, mostly destroyed. Reflective eyes glared at me from farther down; the creature we'd chased clung to the ancient stone like a lizard on a wall.

The light went out, plunging us into darkness.

"Damn it, Whyborne!" Christine exclaimed from just behind me. Thank God she hadn't collided with my back; a fall into the well before us would have unquestionably been fatal.

The blackness of the depths surrounded us, utterly impenetrable. Griffin's breath caught hoarsely…and below, far below, there came the scuttle of claws on stone. Was it the creature we'd chased? Or did it have fellows?

I took a step back from the oubliette and bumped into one of my companions. "Excuse me."

"Never mind," Christine said. I heard the rustle of cloth. "Here. I always carry candles with me, in case the lanterns run low while we're in a tomb. Be a good fellow and light it, if you will."

She pressed the cylinder of paraffin into my shoulder. I took it with one hand, felt for the wick, then whispered the secret name of fire.

The light almost blinded me after the darkness. Just below us in the well, something growled.

The growl echoed...or did more than one creature do the growling?

I took a step back. "I suggest we pursue the better part of valor, and retreat to the surface."

"Agreed," Christine said reluctantly. "But let's return to the *triclinium*. The books may hold some vital clue."

I didn't dare remove the oldest scrolls, fearing they'd fall into nothingness at my touch. I took the books, however, and a scroll which seemed of early medieval origin. Lacking anything to carry them in, I cradled them carefully in my arms as we retreated to the ladder.

We encountered nothing further. But I couldn't help imagine what might lurk in the darkness behind us, and when the trapdoor slammed shut and we stumbled out into the brightness of the setting sun, I half-wished I could seal off the passage forever.

"What the hell was that thing?" Christine asked, once we reached the safety of the carriage and left the place behind.

I looked down at the books and scroll in my lap, remembering the words in Aklo. "A ghūl?" I suggested.

Christine cursed so foully our driver turned around to look at us in shock. "I can't believe we must seriously consider such a thing," she grumbled, ignoring the driver. "Monstrous eaters of the dead, resurrected sorceresses...when did our lives turn into a dime novel?"

"Let's say Nitocris has risen from the dead, and this isn't simply the work of some cult attempting to keep her memory alive," I said. "If she was Nephren-ka's wife, why would she have to seek out the fane? Wouldn't she already know where it is?"

"Perhaps he didn't trust her," Griffin suggested. "Men in this era certainly hide many things from their wives."

I resisted pointing out he ought to know, having carried on affairs in Chicago with a great many of those men. Christine scowled. "Perhaps. Perhaps he feared she would become a greater sorcerer than he."

"Has her tomb been located?"

"Not by modern science. But if she's been brought back from the dead, as you said, someone must have known where her body lay." Christine shook her head. "Well. I am certain of one thing, gentlemen. I'm not losing the discovery of the fane. Not to the men of the

Antiquities Service and certainly not to some undead sorceress."

Our carriage let us out in front of Shepheard's Hotel. Even a glance at the entryway proclaimed it British to the core. The lion and unicorn device surmounted the awning over the porch, and a military band in red coats performed in the garden. Dozens of people milled about on the steps, posing for photographs, brandishing postcards, or simply gawking at the famous hotel.

We'd made a brief stop in the market to purchase a basket to carry the books and scroll, so as not to call attention to ourselves. But as we mounted the steps, a man stopped and pointed at us. "Look! It's Dr. Putnam, the lady archaeologist! I recognize her from the papers."

"Damned tourists," Christine muttered, marching past the over-excited man without as much as a second glance. She didn't slow until we reached the lobby. "Wait here. I'll track down Iskander and see about your room. Best enjoy the chance for a decent meal and cold drinks, as I intend to leave for the site first thing in the morning."

"Just a moment!" I exclaimed. "Do I deduce your meaning correctly—*we* are to accompany you to your excavation?"

"Of course. Don't be daft, man," she said, taking the basket from me. "I'll have Kander put this with the rest of your luggage."

"Christine..."

She rolled her eyes. "You're far better at translation than I am, and since you've come all this way, I'm certainly not going to pass up the opportunity for your assistance."

"But..." I lowered my voice. "The murder was committed here! In town! And those catacombs...the fresh blood and the name of Nitocris...these books...surely we should remain here instead of traipsing out into the desert wastelands with you."

"She's looking for the fane, which is certainly not located in downtown Cairo." Christine lowered her voice even further. "I have an idea as to where to find an inscription which might lead us to it. But I need your help."

I couldn't argue, though I wanted to. I gloomily watched her depart, imagining tents and camels and who even knew what else. No baths, certainly.

Griffin clapped me on the arm, before leaving in search of a newspaper. I wandered aimlessly in the direction of the hotel terrace, drawn by the sound of the band. How long did Christine expect me to survive in the desert? Probably a scorpion would do me in before the end of the week.

"Dr. Whyborne?"

I turned to see my earlier thought, that we might encounter

Daphne de Wisborg at the hotel, had proved correct. She sat alone at one of the tables on the terrace. Her black mourning dress stood out sharply amidst the cream linen suits and pastel summer dresses of the other loungers, a crow amidst a flock of doves.

"Er, yes," I said. "I mean, a pleasure to see you again."

"The pleasure is mine." She nodded at my head. "Nice fez."

"A camel ate my other hat. I hope your sojourn in Egypt has been more pleasant."

"It has now I've found a friendly face." She gestured to the empty chairs at her table. "Will you join me?"

"I'm here with some, er, friends," I said, casting a look over my shoulder. Politeness dictated I make an offer. "I'd be pleased to introduce you, if you'd like."

"I'd like it very much."

I offered her my arm as a matter of courtesy, and she took it. A curious perfume rose from her skin: spicy as incense, rather than the floral scents normally preferred by women. I led the way back into the lobby. Griffin and Mr. Barnett stood to one side, while Christine spoke to an Arab. Or rather, she decried at the top of her lungs he charged extortionate rates for camels, and she could buy every beast in Cairo for less. He rather cheerfully yelled back his camels were the finest in all of Egypt, perfectly trained, and if she chose another seller she would soon find herself alone and dying in the middle of the desert.

As we approached, they seemed to reach an agreement, because money changed hands and the camel seller departed with alacrity. Christine turned and caught sight of me. "There you are, Why—"

The words died in her throat, and she swayed, her eyes locked on the woman beside me. As for the Grafin de Wisborg, she let out a soft cry and released my arm. Taking a step forward, she said, "Christine? I-I know you must be shocked to see me."

"Daphne?" Christine's face took on the color of old cheese. "But...I haven't...it's been ten years, at least..."

I'd never before seen Christine at a loss for words. Somewhat alarmed, I said, "Christine? Is Grafin de Wisborg known to you?"

"I'd say so," said the woman in question with a pale, hopeful smile. "Christine is my sister."

CHAPTER 7

A SHORT TIME later, we sat in a private room, a course of ox-tail soup on the table in front of us. Christine tossed back her first glass of wine as if she wished it were whiskey. Most likely she did.

The two sisters didn't resemble one another much, save for their dark eyes and square chins. Daphne was fair, without as much as a freckle, and her hair golden. Christine, naturally, was tanned from her time excavating, her hair dark and pulled back into a practical bun. But they both held themselves with pride, and I detected a similar fierceness in their expressions.

"What the devil are you doing here?" Christine asked with her typical lack of anything resembling tact.

Daphne toyed with her spoon, not having touched her soup. "My inquiries showed most American and English visitors stay at Shepheard's. If you weren't in the field yet, I thought it likely you'd stay here. And if you had already left, it seemed the best place to discover where I might find you."

"That isn't what I meant. What are you doing in Egypt? You haven't answered a letter from me in over a decade. Whatever do you want?"

I knew Christine had a falling out with her family when she chose to leave for the university rather than marry, but she'd never shared the details. She and her mother exchanged terse letters once a year around Easter. Apparently the rift reached even deeper with her sister.

Barnett looked pained. "Perhaps the two of you should speak

alone..."

"Not at all," said the Grafin de Wisborg. Turning her gaze to me, she added, "I should have recognized you from the papers, Dr. Whyborne—you're a great friend to my sister, aren't you?"

The idiotic society columns often linked our names. We served as one another's escorts during museum functions and various formal dinners with donors. By which I meant we mainly hid in a corner together and discussed the latest philological or archaeological theories.

"Er, yes," I said. Christine made no move to continue introductions, so I took up the task. "Grafin de Wisborg—"

"Please, you must call me Daphne."

I found myself unsurprised any sister of Christine's would disdain formality. I completed the introductions; Mr. Barnett asked us all to call him Iskander. Christine sat through the whole thing, eating her soup with an air of annoyance.

"You haven't answered my question, Daphne," she said when we finished our introductions.

Daphne sighed and dropped her gaze to her soup. "You're quite right to be cross with me, Christine," she admitted. "I won't deny it. My behavior has no excuse save for pride." She swallowed. "Three months ago, my...my husband died quite suddenly."

We all immediately offered our condolences. Christine looked surprised. "Mother didn't say. I would have expected her to at least wire me with such news."

"She doesn't know. I didn't...I couldn't bear to write the words." Daphne blinked overly bright eyes. "After years of marriage, I found myself a childless widow. In the depth of my grief, I saw how terribly I had isolated myself from those once closest to me. I realized family is the most important thing in the world, far greater than any small disappointment of mine."

Christine appeared as if she wished to object, but couldn't think how to with any grace. Griffin sat on my other side, nodding gravely. Iskander gazed down at his soup and bit his lip, a flash of white teeth in his dark face, quickly gone.

"I've followed your career," Daphne went on. "I knew you'd be here for the season. I should have written first, but I was too much a coward. After all this time, I feared you'd burn any missive from me unopened." Well, it did sound like something Christine would do. "I know we didn't part on the best of terms, but I've missed you. Please, Christine, give me a chance to be your sister again. To make amends and apologize for my long silence."

"I'm leaving Cairo tomorrow morning—"

"I know. I wish to come with you." Daphne held up her hand to forestall any objections. "I understand conditions won't be what I'm accustomed to. You will have no complaints from me, and should you hear one, you're free to send me back to Port Said immediately. I don't know what skills I have which may be of use, but I can cook, or wash clothes. I know a little of the hieroglyphs, and some hieratic—"

"You do?" I interrupted. "Oh, forgive me, I—"

"Daphne always possessed a genius for language," Christine said, a bit grudgingly. "Although I didn't realize you'd turned your attention to the hieroglyphs."

"I became interested when I learned of your find. It made me feel closer to you after all this time." Daphne smiled tentatively. "Of course, Wisborg was rather remote, and I couldn't get all of the scholarly journals, but I've read the work of Champollion."

Christine seemed a bit taken aback by this declaration. Griffin leaned forward in his seat. "Come now, Christine. Your sister is making a handsome apology. Surely you can meet her part way?"

Did his eagerness to see them reconciled stem from his hopes for his own family? Or his regrets, perhaps?

As for me, I didn't feel I could encourage Christine one way or the other, considering I would be thrilled if Stanford vanished out of my life for a decade. In all the years we'd known one another, Christine never indicated any particular feelings of loss over her family—quite the opposite. But perhaps the very fact she'd never spoken Daphne's name to me indicated her emotions ran deeper when it came to her sister.

Christine glanced at Griffin, then back to Daphne. "Very well. You may accompany us. Whyborne will judge your ability with the hieroglyphs—and I forbid him to be a gentleman about it," she added at my look of alarm. "If he says you're of no help to him, you'll work the screens and do any other tasks I ask of you."

Daphne's smile lit her face. "Thank you, sister. You won't regret this."

Christine downed the rest of her wine. "I'd better not."

I found myself unable to sleep that night.

Griffin and I took full advantage of our first night in quite a while in a real bed. And, it would seem, our last for quite a while as well. Ordinarily such activity would have been more than enough to relax me. Tonight, however, my mind refused to quiet.

Rather than wake him with my tossing and turning, I slipped out of bed, fighting my way clear of the mosquito netting around it. Pulling on a nightshirt, I crossed the room to the chair near the dresser. My pocket watch lay on the dresser, and I picked it up, running my fingers slowly over the familiar case. It occurred to me the picture inside had been taken on one of the last days Griffin could still claim his adoptive family. He had been happy, eating ice cream and riding the carousel, laughing at the antics of the seagulls and simply glad to be alive and in the sun.

I knew perfectly well why he'd spoken up over dinner, encouraging Christine to reconcile with her sister. He beheld in them the hope he had for himself.

What if he found his brothers? The chances they would somehow understand our relationship seemed slim at best. He'd chosen a life with me once, but despite all my efforts, I feared I wasn't enough. Our life in the shadows wasn't enough. How could I expect him to make the same choice a second time?

He was my rock. My soul. He'd added so much to my life, but I'd only subtracted from his.

I put aside the pocket watch. There was nothing to be gained from my maudlin thoughts, and if I couldn't sleep, I could at least do something useful. I lit a single candle and, by its light, located the basket containing the books and scroll we'd taken from the catacombs.

The bed creaked as Griffin rolled over. "Whyborne?" he slurred.

"I'm going to read a bit. Go back to sleep."

He mumbled something I couldn't quite make out, but his breathing evened once again. When I was certain he slept, I set myself to unrolling the parchment scroll.

The thing was hideously fragile, and the ink badly faded. A thorough examination would have to wait, but I could at least glance over a few lines. It was written in Greek, and yet the similarity to the much-later book in Aklo prickled the hairs on the back of my neck.

Now truly disturbed, I turned to the vellum book. Latin this time, perhaps thirteenth century. I scanned the pages, flipping back and forth, occasionally pausing to make out a difficult passage. Then finally I opened the most recent book in Aklo.

A short time later, I put the book aside and stared down at my hands. The three manuscripts came from vastly different time periods, and yet their similarities were striking.

"*The ghūls yet remember I called them forth from the dust...*"

"*...the Heart of Apep. Nephren-ka must have hidden it in his temple to that abomination Nyarlathotep.*"

"*...rumors of the Shining Trapezohedron. If the thieves had truly seen it, they would be dead...but the tale must have come from somewhere...*"

"*...with the knowledge of the Occultum Lapidem, I will have true power at last. All the secrets Nephren-ka kept from me. Then I will raise up my ghūls, and our feast will spread throughout the lands of man..."

Different languages, but did they all refer to the same object? All written by women who referred to Nephren-ka as their husband. All searching for the Fane of Nyarlathotep, or at least Nephren-ka's tomb in the hopes the secret might reside there.

Could the same woman have written all of these accounts, not to mention the even more ancient ones I'd been forced to leave behind? The Ancient Egyptians had gone to great lengths to preserve the bodies of the dead. Had Queen Nitocris been raised again, long after her death, perhaps by her loyal ghūls? And not just once, but century after century, each time thwarted in her quest?

Dear God. How powerful must she be, after so long? And how on earth were we to stop her if she'd been resurrected yet again?

The scrape of cloth against stone came from the direction of the window.

The gauzy curtains blew and waved in the night breeze, casting diaphanous shadows in the moonlight. For a moment, their movement confused my eye, until a solid shape slipped between them. A man, dressed in heavily embroidered robes, his head cloth wound in such a way to veil the lower half of his face. In his hand he held a knife.

"Griffin!" I exclaimed, leaping to my feet. At the same instant, a woman's cry of alarm sounded from nearby within the hotel.

Griffin flung back the netting and rolled out of bed. His sword cane rested in the umbrella stand near the door, but he'd concealed his revolver inside the dresser. As he yanked the drawer open, I cast about for something to hurl at the intruder.

Our attacker didn't advance on us, however. Instead, he waved his knife threateningly in our direction. "Abandon your search for the fane," he warned in oddly accented Arabic. "Or you will all die!"

Griffin's revolver gleamed in the moonlight as he brought it up. With one last flourish of the knife, the intruder retreated out the window.

"Stop!" Griffin ordered, running to the casement. From his curse, I took it to be too late. The fellow must be part cat to have climbed so quickly.

"I heard a woman cry out," I said, snatching up my dressing gown. The tread of running feet came from the hall outside. Griffin started after me, then swore again when he realized he was naked.

I left him to find his nightshirt. A number of men milled about in the hall, mainly foreigners but with some of the hotel staff mixed in.

The door to Christine's room stood open, and my heart seized with dread.

"Pardon me," I said, pushing my way through the crowd. "Out of the way, please!"

I found Christine inside the room, along with Daphne, whose own room lay on the same hall. "No, it was not a dream," Christine growled at the anxious man in front of her. I took him to be some sort of hotel official. "An intruder came through this very window—ask Daphne, she saw the fellow!"

The man looked unconvinced, but murmured something about instituting a search and alerting the authorities. When Christine transferred her gaze to me, he took his chance and escaped.

"You're a bit late, Whyborne," she said. "The blackguard has already escaped."

The crowd in the hall began to dissipate. A man laughed and remarked to his friend how easily women became frightened by fancies. Daphne's dark eyes blazed, and she drew herself up. "I came as soon as I heard Christine cry out. He was in the process of diving out the window when I entered. I didn't imagine it."

"Nor do we think you did," Griffin replied, having pulled on nightshirt and dressing gown in record time. "Unless Whyborne and I hallucinated a similar visitor."

Iskander appeared in the doorway, his face flushed. "Christine! Are you all right? I heard—"

"I'm quite fine, Kander," she assured him. "The lout came in through the window, but I routed him easily enough."

"She hit him with a lamp," Daphne said, pointing to the article in question, now rather dented.

"You aren't hurt?" Iskander crossed to Christine and put his hands on her shoulders.

I expected her to shake him off. Instead, she only repeated, "I'm fine. Truly."

"Did your visitor say anything?" Griffin asked.

Iskander seemed to recall our presence. He released his grip on Christine's shoulders and took a quick step back. "Say anything? What do you mean?"

"Someone invaded our room as well," I explained. "I happened to be unable to sleep and was sitting up when he came through the window." Thank heavens. Of course our intruder could hardly denounce Griffin and I to the world, for how could he without announcing his own guilt? Still, the idea of someone who meant us ill finding us sharing the same bed made my stomach churn with acid. "He warned us to abandon the search for the fane."

Iskander let out a shocked gasp. Christine nodded. "Mine did the same. Or started to, before I stuck him in the face."

"I don't...why would someone do such a thing?" Iskander asked bewildered.

"Clearly someone doesn't want us to continue our excavation in the Valley of Jackals," Christine replied. "Probably the same persons who killed Halabi."

Iskander frowned. "That's rather an assumption. These men didn't actually try to hurt you, did they? Just frighten?"

"There is a difference between killing a man with known connections to the black market," Griffin pointed out, "and murdering foreigners in Shepheard's Hotel. There isn't enough *baksheesh* in all of Egypt to convince the authorities to turn their backs on the latter."

"Exactly." Christine nodded. "Well, Daphne, are you certain you want to continue on with us?"

Daphne straightened, black eyes snapping. "Of course. I'm not one to easily frighten."

Christine grinned approvingly. "Ha! Good woman." Turning to us, she indicated the door. "Thank you for your attempt at assistance, gentlemen. I suggest you return to your own rooms for as much sleep as you can find. I doubt any of us will be troubled again tonight, and morning will come all too soon."

A heavy pounding on the door woke me a few hours later. I blinked sleep out of my eyes and sat up, feeling Griffin stiffen beside me. No light showed through our window; it wasn't even dawn yet.

"Whyborne!" Christine called stridently.

I muttered a curse. She'd have the guests to either side of us up if she continued to carry on. Staggering out of bed, I pulled on a dressing gown, while Griffin tugged the blankets up to his chin.

"Christine!" I hissed, opening the door a crack and glaring out at her. "What the devil are you about? The sun isn't even up."

"Well, it will be soon enough," she said. "Good gad, man, didn't you hear me last night when I said I meant to make an early day of it?"

"This isn't *day*!"

"Kander has already been up for an hour," she replied briskly. "Now wake Griffin and hurry up."

"I'm awake," he muttered from the direction of the bed, though he sounded no happier about it than I. Upon returning to our room, I'd told him what little I'd gleaned from my interrupted reading. As a result, we'd lain awake talking for several hours, although without much in the way of facts we did little but speculate with increasing wildness.

"Oh, good morning, Griffin," she called. "Well don't just stand there, Whyborne! Get a move on!"

I shut the door rather more forcefully than needed.

The night before, Griffin and I had unpacked only the absolute necessities. I mussed the second bed to allay any suspicions of the cleaning staff while Griffin washed and shaved, then made myself presentable while he gathered our things. In short order, we found ourselves on the hotel porch, shivering in the predawn chill.

The rest of our party had arrived before us, and stood with the camel seller of the night before and several camels. Daphne had put off her mourning, no doubt due to its impracticality, and dressed in a sensible shirtwaist, tweed skirt, and boots. Her only concession was a bit of black crepe swathed around her hat.

"Ah, there you are," Christine said cheerfully, when she spotted us. "Ready to ride out to the site?"

I froze. "You can't seriously mean to travel all the way out there on the backs of these...these creatures!"

"Of course I do," she replied. "Come now, Daphne, I'll show you how to mount up."

Handlers strapped our baggage to the camels, while I stood and stared at them. The things were far too large. In my opinion, nothing should be bigger than a horse. Maybe a pony.

"What about donkeys?" I suggested desperately. "There are plenty of them about."

Christine snorted. "Because you'd look like a fool with your feet dragging in the sand to either side of the poor little thing. Now stop complaining."

She selected one of the beasts and issued a sharp command. It knelt immediately, going first to its front...elbows, I supposed, before lowering its hindquarters. She demonstrated the use of the saddle to her sister. Iskander adjusted the stirrups for her, and a moment later the creature rose in reverse order, back legs up first. Christine didn't seem at all perturbed by this tossing about.

"But...they spit, don't they?" I asked helplessly.

"Only if you upset them," Iskander replied. "They're actually very gentle chaps, as long as they're well treated."

One of the handlers had already assisted Griffin to mount. Clearly, everyone else intended to ignore my objections to this barbarous mode of transportation. As I stood trying to come up with some new argument, hot breath blew against the back of my head.

"The devil!" I spun around, just in time to save my fez from the lips of the perpetrator. The beast stared at me reproachfully, and I noted a distinctive scar across its nose.

"Of all the camels in Egypt, you had to hire this one!" I exclaimed in horror.

"What on earth are you going on about?" Christine asked. "Mount up, and be quick about it."

The handler caused the creature to kneel, although I noted its eyes remained fixed on my hat. "You're not getting this one," I told it with a scowl. "I lose quite enough of them on my own, thank you very much."

I took its return blink to indicate it only waited for the right moment of opportunity to strike again.

Chapter 8

Under other circumstances, the trip to the excavation site would have been pleasant, at least in the beginning. We left the fertile fields along the Nile behind, and crossed over into the red land—the land of the dead, according to ancient belief. Of demons and jackals, ruled by the god Set, the slayer of his brother Osiris.

The pyramids of Giza glowed in the early light of the sun, well off to our right but still breathtakingly huge. I'd never thought to see them myself, but the weight of age and grandeur upon them made my heart stir. I'd heard climbing them was a popular activity for tourists, but at this early hour, their imposing sides lay bare.

"Most impressive," Griffin said.

Being naturally more inclined to physical activity than myself, Griffin took to camel riding with relative ease. I'd accepted the advice of the camel-wrangler assisting me and left the reins slack, but Griffin practiced guiding his own mount, and eventually drew it back to ride beside me. I wondered what he would look like in the flowing robes of a Bedouin. From there, I imagined him dragging me off to some opulent tent and having his way with me.

I shifted and winced; this ride was already uncomfortable enough without adding to it. "It is," I agreed.

"Worth leaving Widdershins?" he teased.

I wished we were alone. I would have liked to stand with him and take in the sight, our arms around one another. "Yes."

"Good." He smiled at me, green eyes flashing.

Daphne rode a few camel-lengths ahead of us. Although she didn't seem like an accomplished rider, she sat very straight in the saddle, staring off at the pyramids as well. I felt a sudden sympathy for her. I might be unable to embrace Griffin, but at least I had him here with me. Did she think of her dead husband at this moment, or did the grandeur of the ancient past distract her from her recent loss? I hoped for the latter.

As the ride stretched on, my fascination with the landscape faded. The sun grew far too bright and hot for this early in the day. Daphne clearly felt it too, wilting in her saddle despite the shade of her parasol. The gait of the beast under me became no more comfortable, and by the time we stopped for a brief lunch, I reeked of camel and ached in places I didn't even know existed. Sand on the blowing wind worked its way into my clothes, and a film of sweat made my skin itch. Dismally, I wondered how long it would be before I could have a proper bath again.

"Almost there," Christine said, pointing at a low line of jumbled cliffs rising to the west of us.

I took a long drink from my canteen; the water possessed an odd taste. Having seen the water sellers in Cairo with their goatskin bags, I thought it best not to enquire as to the flavor. As I wiped sweat from my brow, Griffin indicated with a motion of his head I should follow him. Wondering what he wanted, I trailed after while he approached Christine and murmured something to her.

"Daphne, could you help Kander unpack lunch?" she called. As her sister moved to obey, Christine and Griffin drew close, and I joined them.

"What's this about?" Christine asked.

"The tracks," Griffin said with a nod at the barren desert.

Christine and I exchanged a blank look. "Tracks?"

Griffin beckoned to us, leading us a short distance from the camels. "Here," he said, pointing to a disturbance in the sand. "And here. We've been following them for a while now."

"Jackals, probably," Christine replied. "They're all over the place."

"That's what I thought as well. Except sometimes the tracks are of something going on all fours…and sometimes on two legs."

A chill pricked the back of my neck, even through the heat of the day. "The ghūls are making for the necropolis as well, just as Halabi said." I glanced at Christine. "I took a brief look at some of the writings we removed from the catacomb. They're more journals than anything, all written by women who seem to command ghūls. All searching for the Fane of Nyarlathotep for some sort of magical item, or perhaps items. The Shining Trapezohedron was mentioned."

"The what?" Griffin asked.

"The alchemists referred to it as the Occultum Lapidem. The secret stone."

"Impossible," Christine exclaimed. "The fane was lost to antiquity, but the pharaoh who succeeded Nephren-ka razed the pyramid where the stone was kept to the ground."

"Did he?" I countered. "Or did he merely claim to have done so? How many rulers have exaggerated their victory over an enemy?"

"You have a point. I've read inscriptions which make a disorganized retreat sound like a triumphal procession," she admitted.

Griffin frowned. "Forgive me, but I still have no idea what either of you mean."

"According to legend, the Lapidem was some sort of gem which granted visions," Christine replied. "Or enlightenment, or some such rot. Occult knowledge, I would guess, although of what sort I couldn't say. Nephren-ka supposedly found it as a young man, while hunting on the banks of the Nile. At any rate, his father, brothers, and any other obstacles between him and the throne died in short order thereafter, under very mysterious circumstances. Nephren-ka became a powerful sorcerer, did a great many horrible things, and eventually went mad and died."

"What should we tell the others?" Griffin asked.

"Nothing for now. They'd think us insane if we began ranting about ghūls." Christine started toward the camels. "We'll have to stay on our guard and hope to foil our enemies with vigilance. For now, we'd best get back to the others, before they start wondering what we're up to."

After lunch, the cliffs drew rapidly closer, until they loomed above us. Eventually, Christine's camel topped a sand dune, and she drew it to a halt. "Here it is, Daphne, gentlemen," she said as we crested the rise behind her. "The Valley of the Jackals. Site of the necropolis of Nephren-ka."

Up close, it became clear the cliffs consisted of a wild tumble of shattered rock and wind-carved crevasses. Directly ahead of us, the heights split in two, as if the same hand which divided the red and black lands had struck here as well, this time in fury. Deep shadow cloaked the narrow cleft, and the wind blowing through it sent up an eerie moan like a man in pain.

"How on earth did you find this place?" Griffin asked in amazement. "It certainly doesn't look very promising."

Christine's smile took on a certain smugness. "Years of work, my dear fellow. Most of my so-called colleagues scoffed at the very idea

Nephren-ka was anything more than a legend handed down from the time of the Old Kingdom. But I proved them wrong." The satisfied smile lapsed into a scowl, and I knew she thought of the threat to her firman.

"You did," I said. "And you'll prove them wrong again, when you discover the fane."

She nodded firmly. "Quite right. Come along."

We passed into the gap, cool shadow falling over us. Daphne straightened, as if just being out of the sun for a few moments revived her. I felt much the same.

It didn't last. The narrow walls soon pulled away to either side, forming a long, wide valley hemmed in by the twisted cliffs. The section nearest us consisted mainly of undisturbed sand and stone, although men worked hard in the distance. As we rode, Christine gestured to the open space around us. "The village of the workmen who constructed the tomb stood here," she said. "I hope to investigate this part of the site in the future, in order to learn more about the ordinary folk—the master stone cutters, the men who hauled those stones into place with the strength of their backs, even the bakers who fed them."

Looking about at the scene of utter desolation which surrounded us now, I could barely believe life had once flourished here, even on a temporary basis. I was accustomed to the sea, to green lawns and lush trees. In my student days at Miskatonic, I'd once viewed the moon through a telescope. Its surface had seemed no more alien or desolate than this landscape. But humans had survived here before, so I suspected I wouldn't succeed in trying to convince Christine the place was utterly uninhabitable.

The valley beyond narrowed slightly, and a line of weathered pillars and effigies of the gods lined the gap, as if guarding something. All of them faced west, toward the tomb, rather than out away from it as might have been expected. Beyond them, a narrow canyon ran off the south. "The tomb is at the dead end of the wadi," Christine said, gesturing to the canyon. "As the area has already been thoroughly surveyed, we set up camp there."

Beyond the canyon, the valley floor teemed with movement. Lines of robed men worked at moving tons of sand, their voices lifted in song. A maze of ramps, ropes, and scaffolding occupied the steeper areas. Beyond them, a second line of towering statues stood—or lay, in the case of those toppled by time—along the western entrance to the valley. These also faced inward, and I remembered what Christine once said about the tomb. The design of its traps seemed intended to keep something in, rather than tomb robbers out. On the other side of the statues crouched the half-tumbled remains of a wall of some sort, with a gap in it. A lone statue stood beyond, this one gazing out into the vast empty desert beyond.

As we approached the dig site, an Arab came to greet us. "How is the work coming, Khaled?" Christine asked, and I recognized the name of her *reis*, who directly oversaw the workers.

"The work goes well, *sitt*," he replied, giving us a curious glance before turning his attention back to Christine. "The men themselves... less well."

Christine commanded her camel to kneel and swung off its back to face him on a level. "What do you mean?"

"A jackal took a child in the night. It stole her through the window where she slept." He glanced uneasily at Christine. "There are whispers it was the work of an *ifrit*. I've reminded them Allah protects the faithful from demons, but..." He shrugged helplessly.

I held my breath, waiting for an explosion which never came. Instead, Christine's expression grew grave. "Whose child?"

"Young Ahmed, *sitt*. It was only a daughter, but...well. He is taking the loss very hard."

"Kander, get everyone settled," she ordered. "Khaled, take me to Ahmed at once."

As Iskander led us away, I looked back over my shoulder. Christine stood with a young man, his shoulders bowed as if beneath a great weight. They seemed to be speaking quietly, from what I could tell.

"That was rather odd," I remarked, once we passed well out of earshot.

Iskander gave me a surprised look. "What do you mean?"

"Christine." I gestured vaguely. "I thought she'd react a bit more strongly to, well, unrest." In truth I'd expected her to deliver a blistering lecture on the evils of superstition.

Iskander frowned. "The men don't always know what to make of her, it's true," he said, his voice polite but with a chilly edge. "But she's worked hard to win their complete loyalty."

"I'm aware she pays them a fair value for every artifact found, to keep down theft—"

"She doesn't pay them fairly to keep down theft," Iskander snapped. "She pays them fairly because she sees them as human beings worthy of dignity, not savages who should be grateful for whatever scraps are thrown their way."

Heat suffused my face. "I-I didn't mean..."

"I'm certain Whyborne intended no offense," Daphne said, coming unexpectedly to my defense.

Iskander passed a hand over his face. "Forgive me. I shouldn't have spoken harshly."

I couldn't help but recall the man on the Port Said docks, bellowing at Iskander as if his Egyptian blood made him a servant by default. "The fault is mine," I said. "I spoke poorly. It's only...well, you may not have noticed, but Christine has a slight temper."

Griffin smothered a snort—not very successfully. A wry grin reluctantly curved the corner of Iskander's mouth. "It hadn't escaped my attention," he said dryly. "And I don't mean to suggest she doesn't employ it frequently. But she isn't without heart."

I nodded. "I know."

He looked away sharply. "Yes. I rather suppose you would."

What on earth did the man mean? Christine and I were friends, but surely he didn't intend to imply anything more.

"I look forward to getting to know her again," Daphne said. "It's been so long, we're practically strangers to one another now."

We entered the wadi to find our camp. A large fire pit, no doubt used for cooking, sat nearest to the valley. Close by stood a small table, surrounded by chairs. Beyond waited three tents, strung out along the canyon wall to give at least an illusion of privacy to the inhabitants. A few men squatted in the shade, rising to their feet and coming to assist as we approached.

Our camels halted and we dismounted. I did my best not to wince openly, but Griffin cast me a sympathetic look, so apparently I didn't succeed.

"The men return to the village at night," Iskander said, once we secured our camels. "It will only be the five of us. Daphne, I believe Christine mentioned she would share her tent with you." He gestured to the first tent. "The next is mine, and accommodations have been set up for you gentlemen in the farthest one. I trust you don't mind sharing?"

My cheeks heated, although of course it was a reasonable question, given Iskander had no way of knowing the truth about us. "Er, no. Not at all."

"Excellent."

The men finished placing our trunks in the tent and left. Griffin led the way inside, and I followed reluctantly. A pair of narrow cots, a camp table, a lantern, two chairs, and a bowl and shaving mirror comprised the only furnishings. The air within was only slightly cooler than without, and I thought longingly of ocean breezes and brisk winter air.

"Is there anything else you require?" Iskander asked from the open flaps.

"What sort of watch do you usually set?" Griffin inquired.

Iskander frowned slightly. "We don't."

"After the attack at the hotel and the tragedy at the nearby village, perhaps we should."

For a moment, I thought Iskander appeared troubled. Then he shook his head. "A jackal carried off the infant—horrible, but not unheard of. As for the men at the hotel, I suspect we've seen the last of them."

"Do you?" Griffin asked coolly.

"They attempted to frighten you and Christine, not do you any real harm. No doubt a prank of some sort, pulled by a rival archaeologist. I shouldn't worry about it."

"Of course," Griffin agreed. "If you'll excuse us, we'll get settled here and join you shortly."

Iskander departed. I stepped closer to Griffin. "You don't trust him," I said in a low voice.

Griffin glanced at me in surprise. "I gave myself away?"

"Not to him, I think. But I know you."

His mouth curved into a smile. "Indeed you do, my dear. And I would not precisely say I don't trust him. After all, he doesn't know there are occult forces loose in the world, as we do. And yet, I find his assurances no one will follow us a bit…glib, shall we say, given the amount of concern he evinced last night. Not to mention, I can't help but feel he's concealing something from us."

"I see." I didn't want to believe it, but I couldn't argue with his reasoning. "What shall we do?"

"I could be wrong," Griffin said, staring out the open flaps to where Iskander assisted Daphne with her things. "But I think we'd do well to keep a close eye on our Mr. Barnett."

CHAPTER 9

ONCE WE SETTLED our baggage, we went down to the dig site itself. Christine spotted us and beckoned me over. "This is where you'll work, Whyborne," she said, gesturing to the ruined wall. Workers had uncovered most of the southern stretch, but they still labored to excavate the northern half. "I suspect this is where our long-ago priest of Horus left his inscription."

I nodded. "Very well."

"Before you begin, let me show you something," she added, gesturing to the statue beyond the wall. She led the way through the gap and we all circled around to view it from the fore. A human-headed god stared defiantly out at the desert, his fists held up to his chest. One gripped what appeared to be a serpent, but the other fist was empty.

"This is Heka. You could call him a god of magic," she said.

I stared up at the empty fist. "There's a hole, as if he used to be holding something."

"Usually Heka is depicted holding two staffs in the shape of snakes. The symbol of magic in Ancient Egypt. Snakes represented chaos, and what is more chaotic than changing the very laws of the universe?"

"You're starting to sound like Griffin," I muttered.

"Whatever was there, it's been missing since antiquity," Christine went on. "But I thought you would find it interesting. As I said, Whyborne, your job is the wall. Griffin, you can work a camera, can't you? Why don't you take some photographs of the hieroglyphs? Iskander has a dark room jury-rigged in the tomb, so we can develop them later if needed. Daphne, you'll assist me on the screens."

We started on our assigned tasks. True, I hadn't relished the thought of coming here, or the travel which brought us. But when I stood before the half-fallen wall and found myself viewing the handiwork of the ancients...the discomfort seemed worth it after all.

Of course I'd translated finds before. Ancient papyrus, which threatened to crumble to dust if handled too roughly, or the delicate cartouches carved into the base of amulets. Even the lines of hieroglyphs inscribed upon the statues shipped back to the museum. All of it had filled me with wonder.

I was no poet. There was a reason I translated the words of others, rather than create my own. But to stand upon the shifting sands, to smell the dry, dusty scent of the ancient desert, to know thousands of years ago another soul stood in this very place, touched me. I could not help but wonder if we would have understood one another, the unknown scribe and I, if any of our passions overlapped. Or if we'd be as alien to each other as I generally found the people of my own time.

And to read these signs, which no other had seen in millennia, since the shifting sands covered them over! Even when newly inscribed, the vast majority of those who gazed upon them would have done so without comprehension. To decipher their meaning, to hear in my mind the voice of the man who composed them...

"A scribe would have sketched the hieroglyphs on the stone," I said, laying my palm gently on the sculpted rock. "Next the stone-workers came after and chiseled out the rough shapes. And last a master would put on the finishing touches and create a work of art to last the ages."

Griffin stood close to my side, examining the timeworn inscriptions. "I would have thought Christine would handle this part herself. Surely she's fluent in hieroglyphs."

"Because she's an archaeologist?" At his nod, I said, "Not necessarily. Some excavators can't read them at all and hire someone such as myself to translate."

"Oh?"

"Yes." Unable to resist the chance to explain a bit of my work to him, I said, "The various symbols stand for sounds. This hieroglyph shaped like an owl is simply the equivalent of our letter *m*. It has nothing to do with an owl."

Griffin nodded his understanding. "So the owl would be grouped with other hieroglyphs to form a word."

"Exactly. Which sounds simple enough, but context plays a part. If I see the hieroglyphs for the word bull, does it literally mean a bull, or is it a sacred title of the pharaoh pictured beside the inscription? Or is it part of an obscure name?" I gestured to a symbol which looked something like a flower. "And of course there are still differences of opinion on how certain of the older or lesser-used hieroglyphs should be read. Plus there are variations on the hieroglyphs themselves—the direction the animal or human ones are facing indicates which direction the inscription should be read, for example. Or the animals might be drawn without legs to symbolically keep them from leaving. The carvings are often very worn, and it isn't always obvious at first glance what the case might be."

"So it's a bit of a puzzle," Griffin said.

"A bit. Did I mention they only wrote consonants? No vowels?"

Griffin laughed and held up his hands. "All right. I'm duly impressed."

"I'm sorry," I said, rubbing at my neck self-consciously. "I didn't mean to lecture. This must be terribly boring for you."

"Quite the opposite. What would Christine have done in the ordinary course of things, without you here?"

"Done a rough translation herself, then saved the rest of it for her arrival back in Widdershins. The portable objects I'd examine directly, and the walls via photographs and sketches. Most of the time, there isn't any urgency associated with such translations, of course."

"A good thing we came, then." He nodded at the wall. "Besides, I love watching you work. You are in your element here, and it is a magnificent thing to see."

I flushed. "You're speaking nonsense."

"Not at all. Your passion is something to behold, my dear. No matter what outlet it is directed into." His smile turned sly. "I find myself longing for nightfall."

"You're a devil," I muttered, removing my notebook from my pocket to give me something to do with my hands.

"But a charming one."

"And far too cognizant of the fact." I offered him a smile of my own. "But I don't mean it as a complaint."

"Then I shall not take it as one." He leaned in close, on the pretext of setting up the camera. "But perhaps I will take you tonight."

The tips of my ears grew hot from something other than the sun, but I cast him a playful look. "Really? From your earlier comment, I assumed you wished to be the outlet into which I directed my passions."

He laughed. "And you call me a devil."

~ * ~

By the time the work ended for the day, exhaustion settled into my bones, and I could do nothing but think longingly of the cot in our tent. At my request, the men set up a makeshift shade for us to work beneath, to shield us from the direct sun, but even so, the heat had sapped my strength.

Once the workers departed for their village, we retired to the wadi where the camp lay. A few servants lingered: the cook and a helper, who would soon leave for the night as well. "I'm hungry enough to eat a camel," Christine declared.

"We won't be, will we?" I asked.

"Chicken from the village," she responded. "I'm going to wash up."

Unlike her sister, Daphne looked exhausted, with dark circles beneath her eyes. I felt rather bad for her; clearly the sun had taken its toll. "I'd thought we might discuss some of the inscriptions after dinner," I said, "but if you'd prefer to put it off for tomorrow, we can."

"No." She roused herself. "I'd like to look at your notes tonight, and you may judge my abilities."

We went to our tents to wash up as Christine suggested. Griffin allowed me to go first. When I finished, I stepped outside. The western wall of the canyon cast a blue shadow over us, and the cloudless sky took on a curious bronze tint. As none of my other companions had yet emerged from their tents, I strolled a short distance deeper into the wadi.

The tomb entrance lay at the end, according to Christine, but I didn't wish to hike far enough to start sweating again before dinner. Instead, I studied the reddish rock formations, the tumbled boulders and shattered cliffs. God, this place was desolate. The dry air seemed to suck the very moisture from my lungs. How could anything live here?

I paused and rested against a boulder. This was enough exploration for one night. Hopefully, dinner would be edible, or at least not too offensive to a palate unaccustomed to the local spices.

"Whyborne," Iskander Barnett called.

I started badly, having not heard his approach. He stood a few feet away, a wicked-looking knife in his hand.

Dear heavens, Griffin had been right! Before I could react, Iskander drew his arm back to throw the knife. "No, wait!" I cried.

The knife struck the boulder only inches from my hand. With a shout of alarm, I hurled myself to the side. Iskander scooped up his blade, and I backed away. "S-stay back!"

He pointed the knife at me. "You almost put your hand on it," he said nonsensically.

"I...what?" For a moment, I hadn't the slightest idea what he meant. Then I noticed the rather large scorpion skewered on the end of the blade.

"Oh...oh!" The man must think me a complete idiot. Curse Griffin for putting ideas in my head. "Th-thank you."

"You're welcome." But he didn't smile, and his dark eyes remained grave. "This is an unforgiving land, old chap. Those who fail to tread cautiously soon cease to tread at all."

Dinner proved to be less challenging than I feared, the boiled chicken perfectly edible and the side dishes served out of cans. Despite my exhaustion, I slept poorly. The desert nights were far colder than I'd expected. Griffin and I discreetly moved our cots together and huddled beneath our blankets. At least we didn't have to worry about cleaning staff; no one here would wander into our tent without permission, either at night or during the day.

I'd washed as best I could the evening before, but as camels carted in all our water, we had to make do with using as little as possible for anything other than drinking. The dry air caused my skin to crack abominably, and discomfort left me tossing and turning. The yelps and howls of jackals sounded intermittently throughout the night, usually right when I reached the verge of sleep. Ordinarily they wouldn't have bothered me, knowing the creatures were scavengers and unlikely to attack a healthy adult. But I couldn't help but think of the strange tracks Griffin had spotted and remember the missing infant.

Did the stories of ghūls stealing children to raise as their own contain any truth to them? Certainly the intruder at the museum had appeared less than human, with his animal eyes and teeth. Did a jackal take the infant, or was it possible ghūls even now suckled her as one of their own in some night-blasted catacomb?

Christine agreed to Griffin's suggestion of setting a watch, and I spent the last few hours before dawn huddled near the campfire, silently cursing the desert, Nephren-ka, Egypt, and Christine in succession. Every time the wind blew or the camels snorted, my heart began to race, and I braced for an attack from monsters which never came. By the time dawn broke, my mood was less than ideal.

I cradled a cup of coffee in my hands, while the early-rising Iskander prepared a breakfast of porridge. Christine emerged from her tent looking positively refreshed. "Good morning, Whyborne," she said cheerfully. "Really, stop glowering. Your face will stick."

I bit back the curse which leapt to my tongue. "You're correct. It is morning," I said, with a pointed glance at the pale east. "Barely."

She greeted Iskander before turning to me, her manner oddly hesitant. "May I speak with you? Privately?"

The request caught me by surprise. "Of course."

She led the way out of the wadi, stopping only when we overlooked the expanse of the main valley. "You have siblings," she said. "A brother and sister."

"Yes."

"Your relationship with them isn't very good, correct?"

"You already know this." I eyed her closely. "Is this to do with Daphne? Did you quarrel last night?"

"No. Not at all." Christine removed her hat and turned it around and around in her hands, as if examining the brim. "It's only the unexpected nature of her reappearance in my life."

I hadn't drunk enough coffee for this. "Were you close as children?"

"I...don't know, really. In some ways, I suppose. We shared a great deal by default, being close in age. I remember..." She bit her lip, and for a moment I thought she wouldn't continue. "I remember the two of us lying awake, listening to our parents scream at one another. I'd roll over and look at her, and see the whites of her eyes in the moonlight. Afraid. But we never talked about it during the day. One didn't acknowledge unpleasant things, you see. A lesson we learned very young."

I could picture it with a horrible clarity. Of all my other complaints concerning my family, at least my parents kept any quarrels private. "I'm sorry. I had no idea."

"Of course you didn't." Christine's fingers crushed the brim of her hat. "Mother saw things in the war...she'd disguised herself as a man and signed up to fight, you see. No one ever caught on, although of course she couldn't apply for a pension afterward without risking discovery. She tried to put the past behind her, marrying our father and becoming a respectable lady. But she couldn't forget, so she turned to drink."

"A great many veterans of the war did." Not Father, thank heavens, but the horrors of the battlefield ruined more than one life. "It was very brave of her to enlist. I see where your courage comes from."

Christine smiled thinly. "I suppose. And it wasn't all terrible. Mother taught me to shoot. And to drink whiskey."

"Yet she wished you to marry and settle down?"

"It was what she did." Christine shrugged. "I bring this up because Daphne didn't fare as well as I. She was always more sensitive, I suppose. Once, when we were girls, I found her stabbing herself in the thigh with a hatpin. She couldn't tell me why, only it made her feel better for a little while. And we never spoke of it again. If she continued to do such things, she hid it from me."

How terrible. "But you fell out eventually."

"Yes." Christine seemed to realize she'd mangled her hat and straightened it with a sigh. "Our Uncle Leopold died. He was a confirmed bachelor—I'd guess he shared your inclinations, although no one ever said as much. At any rate, he knew of my interest in academics and made me his sole heir, something I only discovered at the reading of the will. I took the money and left immediately. But you must believe me—I would never have abandoned Daphne to that house if I thought she hadn't a way out already. She was engaged, and the wedding date only a month later. I left with a clear conscience!"

Obviously something had gone wrong. "What happened?"

"The wretched fellow broke off the engagement." Christine scowled at her hat, and I half expected it to burst into flames from the heat of her anger. "Or his family forced him to, I've no idea. Well, as soon as I found out, I sent a letter suggesting Daphne join me. But did she write back or accept the offer? Oh no, she would rather moon over the lout. Mother passed along the message Daphne's heart had broken beyond repair, and the fault was mine for causing a scandal."

I winced, in part because I doubted Christine's letter had been entirely tactful. Or at all tactful. If Daphne truly loved her fiancé, a brusque missive from Christine wouldn't have been well-received.

Of course it wasn't Christine's fault the fellow possessed no spine, but I doubted the young Daphne had seen it that way. "She must have consoled herself eventually, as she married the graf."

"Hmm. Yes." Christine's glare eased into something more wistful. "I've asked about him, but she hasn't said much. I suspect she viewed marriage as a way to escape the turmoil at home, and when she couldn't have the man she wanted, she took whatever options remained to her."

"Perhaps. But she doesn't seem terribly unhappy. I haven't spoken with her much, of course, but she appears to have found her footing in life." Certainly it was difficult to imagine the bold woman I'd encountered as a young girl hurting her body to ease the pain of her soul. "It may be her loss is too fresh to speak of yet. Whatever the case, she seems eager to reconnect with you."

"Exactly. Which is the point of all this." Christine slapped her hat against her trouser-clad thigh. "I know I'm not responsible for what happened all those years ago, but I can't help but feel some...well, some guilt. Having spoken with her again, I find I'd like to do right by her. To be her sister again. But I'm not entirely certain how to go about it."

"And you're asking me?" I raised an eyebrow at her. "The person who got into a fight with his brother over Christmas dinner?"

"You did?" She laughed. "Well, I'm certain he deserved it. And yes, I'm asking you. You're my best friend. Who else should I ask?"

Her words warmed me. "I'll do my best to give you an answer, then. Daphne did extraordinarily well last night when I presented her with some translations to test her abilities."

Christine looked pleasantly surprised. "Oh?"

"Yes. I'm shocked she's had as little time to learn the hieroglyphs as she says—her talent must be natural."

"Or there wasn't much to do in the wild mountains of Wisborg."

"Certainly a possibility," I agreed. "Either way, I think she'll be of great help to me. She seems determined to earn her place, from what I've seen."

Christine nodded. "Yes. She worked hard on the screens yesterday, although I'm certain she can't be used to such physical activity."

"She chose to reach out to you, by offering to assist in your work." I rescued the mauled hat from Christine's hands. "That alone is surely an indication she wishes to make amends for the past. It may not be entirely easy—naturally the two of you will quarrel at times. But in this, I must agree with Griffin. You have the chance now for a relationship perhaps even better than the one you shared as children. Take what she offers, and...I don't know. Think of what you might offer her in return." I held out the hat. "Companionship, for the moment, and work to keep her mind from her mourning."

"Yes, yes, you're quite right." Christine took her hat and placed it squarely back on her head. "She's not brought up her long-ago fiancé yet. Do you think I should...?"

"No," I said hastily. If any tender scars yet remained from the incident, better not to have Christine be the one to poke at them. "Let her broach the subject. And be...well. Understanding. Don't apologize for your actions, but show her you can see her side of things as well."

"But—"

"Christine." I gave her a pointed look. "You asked. So listen."

"Oh, very well." She sighed. "With any luck, she's over the young idiot after all this time. But we're all fools for love at least once."

"Indeed."

"We should probably get back to breakfast." She started toward the camp, then paused. "Thank you, Whyborne."

"You're welcome. It's what best friends are for."

She smiled broadly. "Quite right. Come along."

We strolled back to camp in companionable silence. As we approached the cook fire, Iskander glanced up. For a moment, his fierce, black eyes locked on us, burning with some strong emotion. Then he looked quickly away, like a man in pain.

What was wrong with him? Christine didn't seem to notice, heading for the tent she shared with Daphne, far more of a spring in her step than earlier. I made for my tent, hoping for a shave before breakfast. But as I pulled open the flaps and ducked inside, I felt Iskander's hot gaze boring into my back.

CHAPTER 10

OVER THE NEXT few days, we settled into a routine of sorts. Despite our fears, we saw no sign of either robed men or ghūls. No new attacks on the village came, and nothing disturbed our night watches.

Although I ordinarily worked alone, I found Daphne to be surprisingly good company. Perhaps the nature of the work put me more at ease than I usually felt in such a situation, as the hieroglyphs created a common ground between us. As I'd told Christine, the woman had a genius for them, suggesting some rather intriguing possibilities as to the interpretation of some of the disputed signs.

A group of workers continued to uncover the northern section of the wall, and we labored slowly behind them, translating what they uncovered the day before. There was also a second locus of activity nearby, where a team of men worked to build the scaffolding necessary to hoist one of the fallen statues upright again. As a result, Christine frequently passed by, usually bellowing orders at the workers.

"She was always like this, you know," Daphne said one morning, after Christine departed again.

I tried to think of a tactful way of putting it. "Decisive?"

"That's one word for it," she agreed with a chuckle. Despite what Christine had told me of her youthful melancholy, the Daphne of today seemed a cheerful sort who laughed often. "Shall I sketch the hieroglyphs?"

"Please do." Although we had photographed them already, the sketches might capture details missed on the plates, and would provide us a reference while we worked in the evening. "I hope I don't give offense, but you said Christine inspired you to study the hieroglyphs?"

Daphne pursed her mouth slightly, her pencil already moving across the paper, copying the ancient signs. "In a way. Wisborg is a lonely place, high among the Carpathian Mountains. In some ways, nothing has truly changed there since medieval times. There was little in the way of intellectual pursuits."

I cringed inwardly at the thought. I didn't enjoy society, generally speaking, but at least life in a civilized town allowed me access to as many books, newspapers, and journals as I might wish. "It sounds very lonely."

She cast me a surprised glance, as if I'd sensed more than she intended. "Yes. It was, at times." She bent her head over her sketch. A strand of golden hair worked its way free of her bun, and tumbled across her cheek. "Even there, though, we heard of the great discovery. The tomb of the Pharaoh Nephren-ka, dismissed as a mere myth by the scientific establishment, now proven real by my own sister. The name was familiar to me—I'd come across it in a book. My husband had an old and extensive library, you see."

"What happened to it?" Oh dear, how must I sound? The poor woman had recently been widowed, and here I was salivating over a library which might have been handed off to some relative. "I mean, er..."

She laughed. "No need to conceal your intellectual zeal. The library is still intact and in my possession. If you ever visit Wisborg, I would welcome the opportunity to show it to you. There are some very rare volumes which I believe you would find of interest."

"I'd like that." Thank heavens she hadn't taken offense.

"Of course. As I said, I grew interested in Christine's unparalleled triumph. I sent for various journals, texts, anything which might help me learn more of the history and language. The hieroglyphs in particular fascinated me."

"And your reunion with Christine?" I asked cautiously. "You feel it's going well? You may tell me it's none of my business, of course."

She paused to compare her sketch with the hieroglyphs. "I'm very satisfied with my visit."

"I'm glad. I know Christine wished to make amends for the past years of silence." That sounded good, didn't it? Helpful, without betraying the fact Christine had spoken to me of family secrets?

Daphne glanced about as if to make certain no one else stood nearby. "May I ask...you and my sister. Are you...?"

I took me a moment to catch her meaning. "Good Lord, no!" I exclaimed, my face burning. "Christine is my friend, and I hold her in the highest regard, but I assure you there is nothing more between us."

Daphne laughed. "Don't blush—I'm a modern woman and a widow besides, and would hardly have been shocked. But it's good to know there's nothing between you."

"Is it?" I asked. Had she thought me a cad, and was glad to find out otherwise?

Her smile offered me no clues. "Very good indeed," she affirmed, before turning back to the wall and leaving me to my confusion.

"Whyborne!" Christine called to me later the same afternoon. "Come take a look at this, will you?"

I sat cross-legged on the sand, peering at some of the hieroglyphs near the base of the wall. The priests who erected the structure certainly had been a wordy bunch, although thus far the inscriptions mainly consisted of prayers to make sure Nephren-ka remained in the underworld.

At Christine's summons, I rose to my feet, wincing as stiff muscles protested. Daphne and I both drooped in the afternoon heat, even beneath our canopy, and today she seemed even paler than usual. "Come with me," I suggested. "Perhaps we'll catch a breeze."

It seemed unlikely, but she seized on the excuse, and together we climbed out of the dig and followed Christine to the sorting tables. The tons of sand removed by the workmen all had to be carefully sifted, to make certain no small artifacts were missed. As a result, groups of small items covered the tables, each cluster labeled as to the part of the site where it was recovered. Bits of broken pot predominated, followed by dozens of faience beads and amulets, and the occasional random bit of detritus such as a broken bronze pin.

Griffin stood by one of the tables, fanning himself with his hat. Dust from sifting coated him head to toe, and he'd set aside his coat and rolled up his shirtsleeves to his elbows. He gave a quick smile upon spotting me, but his mind seemed on something else.

Iskander came to look as well. "What did you find?"

Christine indicated the longest object on the table: a tarnished metal rod, perhaps a foot in length, and cast in the shape of a hooded cobra. "A magician's wand. I suspect it once fit in the statue of Heka."

"Oh!" My heart quickened. Was it merely a prop, or had some ancient sorcerer actually used it? "May I?"

"Go ahead," Christine said.

The metal felt startlingly cool despite having lain the blazing sun. The surface bore etched scales, barely detectable against my fingers. As I turned the wand in my hand to examine its curving body, it almost seemed to move and shift. An optical illusion of some sort, no doubt. A pair of red gemstone eyes regarded me, and an odd tingle began in my palms.

The breeze I had hoped for suddenly blew up. It whispered against my skin, then gusted as it grew in strength. Sand stung my cheek, and Iskander's hat went flying. The various canopies meant to shield us from the sun cracked and snapped, ropes singing in the gust.

The thunder of my pulse obliterated everything else. Sand. Dust. Could I try the earth spell again, with this? Would it let me—

Griffin yanked the wand roughly from my hands. I blinked in surprise, as the wind died around us. His hat had blown away. Shouts and curses echoed from the dig site, aimed at the miniature sandstorm, which unexpectedly enveloped the valley.

Griffin's green eyes went wide, and his brows arched with a worry he couldn't speak aloud. He didn't have to. I knew his thought. The freak wind at Christmas, and now this?

But it wasn't my doing. It couldn't be.

I turned hastily away from him. No one else noticed, being too preoccupied with the loss of hats. At least my fez had stayed firmly attached to my head.

Christine swore furiously. "Blast—there's sand all over the sorting tables and everything's disarranged. Get it back in order while I make certain nothing blew over at the excavation."

She strode off toward the workmen, who still milled about like a bunch of ants stirred up with a stick. Not meeting Griffin's gaze, I began brushing aside sand and reordering the artifacts. Daphne joined in beside me, bending to pick up a blue faience amulet which had rolled off the table.

"Ah!" she cried, snatching her hand back.

"What happened?" Did something bite her?

"The amulet. It burned me." She held out her finger, displaying reddened skin. "Hot from lying in the sun, no doubt."

Iskander picked up the little amulet. "Wepwawet," he said, gazing at Daphne instead of the small figure. "The wolf-headed god who guards the dead. It's cool now."

He held it out to her, but she shied away. "No, thank you. Once is enough," she said. "I should put water on the burn."

When she departed, I met Griffin's eyes again. The serpent wand had been oddly cold. Now an amulet of colored paste grew fiery hot one minute, before reverting to its ordinary temperature the next.

What the devil was happening?

That night, Griffin and I waited until Christine took her turn at watch, before slipping out of our tent. She sat near the fire, her rifle propped beside her chair, the golden light outlining the contours of her face. When she spotted us, she arched a questioning brow, but didn't say anything aloud.

Griffin motioned for her to join us. Taking up her lantern, she did so, and the three of us walked down the canyon toward the valley. Jackals barked and howled beneath the bright stars. Their cries disturbed me. Were the creatures calling out tonight mere animals, or something far more horrifying?

"What is it?" she asked, once we'd gone far enough to be out of earshot of the tents. "Is something wrong?"

"Not exactly. Daphne and I had a breakthrough in our translation this evening."

Christine's eyes widened. "You've discovered the location of the fane? Why didn't you say so earlier?"

"Well, no," I said apologetically. Her expression darkened; the threat of losing the firman must hang heavily over her. "And I don't think Daphne realized the significance of what we translated. Why should she? It must sound like nothing more than some ancient myth to her."

"What did you find?"

I glanced around uneasily, although who I thought might overhear us in the deserted night, I couldn't say. "Confirmation."

"I take it from your tone it's nothing to our good," Griffin said. The moonlight cast silvery shadows across his face, washing away the color of his eyes and tie.

"When is it ever?" Christine asked. "Out with it, Whyborne."

"Give me a moment." I took out the notes I'd brought with me, shuffling through them. "I'll summarize, rather than bore you with a great deal of hyper-ritualized talk. One of the more interesting characteristics of the wall, to me at least, is many of the inscriptions read more like execration texts. Curses," I explained at Griffin's puzzled look. "Many necropolises bear such inscriptions, but they're always aimed at those who would disturb the dead. Tomb robbers, for the most part. But these threaten Nephren-ka himself, promising terrible things will happen to him should he...well, should he return to the world of the living."

Even in the moonlight, I could tell Griffin paled. "Is he likely to?"

"I don't think so," I replied. "Nephren-ka was a necromancer, it's true, but as far as I know his mummy hasn't started lurching about."

"Yet," Griffin muttered.

"Go on." Christine poked me in the side. "What about the fane?"

"As I said, I've yet to find any clues as to where its location might be. But there are inscriptions discussing an object which Nephren-ka kept within. Do you recall what I said about the journals? That Nitocris, assuming she truly wrote all of the journals, was searching for the fane because of the Occultum Lapidem? The earliest works referred to it as the Heart of Apep, and that's what appears on the wall."

In the desert beyond, jackals yipped and howled. The wind moaned softly over the cliffs, and coolness touched the back of my neck.

Griffin shivered, as if he'd felt it, too. "So, according to the journals, Nitocris suspected the Lapidem was hidden in the fane. And wanted it. Why?"

I shrugged. "I don't know for certain. Occult knowledge, according to her writings. Something about the cities becoming feasts for her ghūls. Death on a massive scale. But there's something more."

"Of course there is," Christine muttered.

"Apparently the stone has some sort of guardian spirit connected to it. A daemon of the night, according to the inscription, which of course tells us nothing about its true nature. If the proper rituals aren't observed when the Lapidem is used, the daemon will come forth—from where it doesn't say—and kill everyone in the vicinity." I looked up from my notes. "Which means if we locate the fane and reach it before Nitocris, we must be very careful indeed, lest we become the daemon's next victims."

CHAPTER 11

THE NEXT NIGHT, I woke suddenly, my heart pounding in my chest. Griffin lay peacefully beside me on our joined cots, both of us dressed in our nightshirts against the chilly night air. Did a dream wake me? I recalled no nightmare, but a sound would have waked Griffin as well.

What time was it? Would Iskander soon come to rouse Griffin for his watch with a soft call through the closed tent flaps?

God, it was quiet. The wind had died, and even the jackals had fallen silent. I was acutely aware of my own breath and heartbeat, of Griffin's, and of a sense of creeping unease.

A woman screamed.

I all but fell out of the cot. Griffin jerked to wakefulness, and I heard him groping about, but we had no time to find matches. Fixing the location of the lantern in my mind, I whispered the true name of fire.

It burst into light. For once, Griffin didn't complain. A few seconds of fumbling at the ties holding the tent closed, and we were out into the night air and racing toward the women's tent.

Our lantern must have shown through the canvas side, because Christine called, "Whyborne? Griffin? Is that you?"

"It's us! Are you all right?" I replied.

"For the most part. Come around the back."

Confused, I did as she said. A long and savage slice marred the canvas, as if someone had hacked through the tent with a knife. "Bring your light here," Christine ordered.

I pushed through the sliced canvas and entered the tent. An overturned cot lay just inside, and Daphne crouched beyond, cradling her arm. Blood stained the nightgown billowing around her.

Christine swore at the sight. She also wore only her nightgown. I fixed my attention on the carpets strewn about to make a floor. My feet ached where I'd stepped on rocks without any shoes, and I became painfully aware my nightshirt exposed far too much of my legs for modesty.

"What happened?" Griffin asked, as Christine crouched beside her sister to inspect the wound.

Daphne held her arm out steadily, revealing a slice which surprised me by its shallowness. From the quantity of blood, I'd imagined she'd taken a much deeper blow. "I woke up suddenly—I'm not sure what disturbed me," Daphne said.

"I did the same," I said. "Something brought me up out of a sound sleep, but I'm at a loss to say what."

"Daphne's cry woke me," Christine admitted. Griffin nodded.

"Perhaps it was but a coincidence," I said. "Please, go on."

Daphne winced as Christine rinsed the wound. "The next thing I knew, I heard an odd sound, like cloth ripping. I sat up, wondering if I might be dreaming—and a figure appeared, looming over me. He dressed in robes like the man who broke into our hotel room, and he brandished a knife. I flung out my arm—I think he meant to murder us in our beds!"

Griffin looked around. "Where is Iskander? Isn't he supposed to be on watch?"

Christine went pale. "Oh no."

"Go," Daphne said. "I'm quite all right."

Christine didn't need to be told twice. The three of us ducked back out the rent in the canvas and hurried toward the dim glow of the campfire, which had nearly burned out. There was no sign of Iskander.

"Damn it," Christine said, and her voice shook slightly. "Kander! Where the devil are you?"

A low moan came from the direction of the valley. Christine snatched the lantern from my hand and charged forward, heedless of the stony ground. We ran after her. "Christine, wait!" Griffin called. "I have my revolver!"

She stopped abruptly and dropped to her knees. For a terrible moment, I thought the assassin had attacked her as well. Then I saw her crouched beside a prostrate form.

"Kander? Speak to me, man!" she cried, shaking him roughly.

Iskander groaned. Griffin and I hurried to assist, and soon we had him sitting up. He put one hand to the back of his head, blinking sluggishly. "Christine?"

"Yes, it's me. Are you hurt? For heaven's sake, speak up!"

"Give the man a chance, Christine," Griffin said.

Iskander squinted at her, then at us, confusion clear on his face. "What...what happened?"

"An intruder cut his way into our tent," Christine replied, sitting back on her heels. "He tried to kill Daphne."

Iskander closed his eyes. "Sod it. It's my fault. Please, tell me she's all right."

"She's fine, save for a cut on her arm. The intruder got away, damn the luck. But what of you?"

"Indeed," Griffin said, sitting back on his heels and watching Iskander closely. "What are you doing all the way out here?"

The dim light rendered Iskander's expression difficult to read. "I was sitting my watch. I thought I heard something, so I walked out to be certain."

"With no light?"

Iskander frowned. "I brought a candle. I don't know what happened to it—I probably dropped it among the rocks. I thought a jackal made the noise, and I meant to scare it away. Something hit my head, and I don't recall anything further."

Griffin nodded. "I see. Head wounds are dangerous. You should let one of us examine it."

"No need, really." Iskander tried to stand, and Christine moved to help him. "There doesn't even seem to be any blood. He must have only struck a glancing blow."

"Daphne glimpsed her attacker," Christine said. "One of the fiends who came to the hotel. As they failed in scaring us off, they now must mean to kill us instead. You were lucky to be spared."

Iskander's mouth tightened, but he didn't disagree. "No doubt. Perhaps they only see me as a servant."

"The more fools they," Christine replied.

Iskander ducked his head. "I...I don't think I'm up to finishing out my watch."

"Of course," Griffin said. "Whyborne and I will take turns for the rest of the night."

"Good idea," Christine agreed. We'd reached the tents; she turned to Iskander. "Are you certain you're all right?"

"I'm fine." He offered her a tired smile. "A bit of headache powder will set things to rights."

"As you say."

When Iskander returned into his tent, Griffin said, "Perhaps you and Daphne should take our tent for the rest of the night, rather than sleep in one with damage to it. Just give us a few minutes to dress and set things to rights."

"Thank you, gents. I appreciate the gesture. We'll sew it up tomorrow." Christine handed the lantern to me and made for her tent. The soft glow of the lantern we'd left inside showed Daphne's outline against the canvas, sitting alone and very still.

Griffin caught my hand and drew me after him to our tent. As soon as the flaps closed behind us, I whispered, "You don't believe Iskander, do you?"

Griffin shook his head, his face grim. "No. Not in the slightest."

"Christine," Griffin said over breakfast the next morning, "you do realize Whyborne and I still haven't seen the actual tomb yet. Surely you don't mean to have made us come this far without a viewing?"

I'd spent the rest of the night first huddled in front of the fire while Griffin scoured the area for tracks, then slumped against him, drifting in and out of a faint doze. My eyes felt scratchy and I wanted nothing more than to collapse for a few hours of sleep. Certainly I didn't have the slightest desire to explore a tomb. But I suspected viewing the tomb wasn't what Griffin truly had in mind.

"Oh, I suppose you're right," she said. "My apologies. I'll be happy to give you the grand tour this evening."

"I would like to spend the evening working on translations," I said quickly. "As usual. Can't we take a little time this morning, before work gets underway?"

Christine seemed to finally realize we wished to speak with her alone. "Oh, very well, but it will have to be a quick look and nothing more."

We left Daphne and Iskander to tidy up breakfast and made the short hike to the dead end of the wadi. The tomb entrance gaped open, its square mouth surmounted by heavily carved bas-reliefs, and impenetrable darkness within.

"This was under tons of rubble, when we found it," Christine said, gesturing to the entrance. "The ancients filled the wadi up nearly to the cliff tops for a good twenty feet back."

"Impressive," Griffin allowed.

"Yes." She stopped at the entrance and leaned against the carven lintel. "Now, what did you want to speak about?"

Griffin and I exchanged a look. Perhaps the question would sit better coming from me. "How well do you know Iskander Barnett?"

Christine straightened and crossed her arms over her chest.

"Quite well. Better than I'd claim to know anyone other than you, Whyborne. Why?"

"Aspects of his behavior have struck me as odd," Griffin said. "I'm certain he's hiding something. And last night, he acted like a man who'd read about concussions in dime novels, not actually suffered one."

Christine dropped her arms. "Don't be absurd. You can't seriously be accusing him of—of what? Plotting against us? Trying to kill my sister?"

"I didn't say anything of the sort," Griffin protested. "Perhaps he merely tried to cover up a lapse of his own—"

"Ridiculous!" Her eyes flashed fire, and she took a step toward him, her hands clenching. "Kander would never do such a thing! Next you'll be accusing me of wrongdoing."

"Christine—"

"I refuse to stand here and listen to this baseless slander!" Squaring her shoulders, she stomped away from us back down the wadi.

"Well, that didn't go quite as well as I'd hoped," Griffin said.

"Let me speak with her." I left Griffin and trotted after Christine, catching up with her quickly.

She shot me a glare. "I suppose you're on *his* side."

I wanted to point out she wasn't being rational, but feared she might respond to such an accusation with her fists. Instead, I said, "How long have you been in love with Mr. Barnett?"

Christine froze mid-stride. All the color drained from her face. "Don't be ridiculous," she said, her voice far quieter than her usual bellow.

"I'm not." I folded my arms across my chest. "We've been friends for years. I may not be the most observant fellow, but give me some credit for knowing you." When she didn't respond, I said, "Do you remember the day in my office when you forced me to admit becoming enamored of Griffin?"

A tiny smile twitched the corners of her mouth. "And this is your revenge? You're more sly than I gave you credit for."

"Iskander doesn't know, does he?"

She sighed. "Of course not. He's my friend and my assistant, but I'm not so deluded as to think he'd wish anything more."

"Why not?" I asked, then cursed myself. I wasn't here to encourage her, merely to point out her lack of clear thought when it came to the man.

She rolled her eyes. "Dear heavens, *look* at me."

Her clothing was creased and dusty, but so was everyone's after a week in this place. I could make no harsh judgment of her hat, given my fez, and the sand and rock meant regrettable boots for us all. "Because of the trousers?" I asked, confused.

To my surprise she laughed. "You truly have no opinion when it comes to women, do you?"

"Well, no," I admitted. "But you're changing the subject."

"It's a sore subject." Her smile wilted, became rueful. "I'm no great beauty and never have been. Daphne was the one admirers showered with gifts, the one with the full dance card and a string of beaus on a leash. I was never jealous of her, exactly..." She caught my skeptical look and relented. "Oh very well, I was terribly jealous. We were both young and foolish, as is common for persons of both sexes at such an age."

"I won't disagree."

"Few would. But I made my choice when I left for university. I accepted I would live and die a spinster, but at least I would do it on my own terms." She shrugged. "I only considered otherwise once, after I met you and realized I wouldn't have to worry about depriving some other woman of your company. Truthfully, you're the only person I've met who I could imagine tolerating for the next forty years."

"Except perhaps Iskander?" I suggested softly.

"Oh, who knows? It doesn't matter anyway." She flung up her arms in a gesture of defeat. "And if you meant all this to show I'm not entirely unbiased when it comes to him, you're right. But I know the man, Whyborne. He would never betray us, no matter what Griffin thinks." Straightening her hat, she turned determinedly back toward camp. "Enough of this nonsense. There's work to be done."

I remained where I was and watched her stride away. A few minutes later, Griffin joined me.

"Did you talk sense into her?" he asked.

"You know how loyal Christine is to her friends," I said. "She's adamant Iskander can be trusted."

Griffin's lips tightened and he shook his head. "For all our sakes, I hope she's right."

The day stretched out painfully long, thanks to my lack of sleep the previous night. Iskander insisted he had recovered enough to return to work, a look of confusion on his face when Christine glared daggers at Griffin upon the announcement. For his part, I thought Griffin rather put out with her as well. No doubt he felt she should have at least considered his instincts might be correct. As a result, they didn't speak a word to one another over either lunch or dinner, directing all their comments at me instead, a situation which quickly grew tiresome.

As a result, I escaped to the tent and my task of translating as soon as I possibly could after dinner. "Griffin and my sister seem to be having a bit of a quarrel," Daphne observed when she joined me a few minutes later. We generally spent the evening comparing our translations and looking over her sketches. Normally, I tied back the tent flaps so as not to cast any possible aspersions our propriety, but tonight I'd forgotten in my agitation.

"Yes," I said. "They're both strong willed. Thus when they disagree, neither wants to admit to being in the wrong."

"What are they arguing about?"

"Oh, er, I'm not sure." I didn't want to accuse Iskander without better proof, and I certainly wouldn't betray Christine's confidences. "Some silly dispute over the sifting tables no doubt. Shall we get to work?"

I laid our notes and the photographs Iskander had developed on the folding camp table. Daphne took her usual seat next to me and leaned over. I sat back to give her room.

"Do you believe there's anything to it?" she asked.

I blinked. "To what?"

"This?" She gestured to the notes in front of us. "Do you believe Nephren-ka knew secret things? I don't mean the absurdity spouted by the theosophists or the so-called mediums who recall past lives as Egyptian princesses." Her lip curled in scorn. "I mean...other things."

Should I lie? Tell her no, I didn't believe any of it? I'd never stood by while a madman read aloud from one of the scrolls found within the very tomb behind us, and opened a gateway to the Outside?

But to what end? To protect her? I recalled the argument with Griffin, when I'd said Mother was no child, to be coddled. Daphne didn't strike me as a fool. Surely she deserved the respect of an honest answer. "Yes. I do."

She turned her attention from the papers and to me, but without sitting back in her chair. It put her face uncomfortably close to mine, and I wondered if I could scoot my chair away without causing offense.

"I thought as much." Her voice was deep, throaty, and something I couldn't name burned in her dark eyes.

"You, er did?" Had I done or said something to indicate it? I couldn't recall.

She breathed deeply. "Even in the midst of this desert, you smell of the sea," she whispered.

"I...do?" What on earth did she mean? Did I need to change my cologne?

"Yes." She glanced down, then up at me through her lashes. "I was glad when you told me I don't have to compete with Christine for this."

I opened my mouth to ask what she meant. At the same moment, she leaned forward and kissed me.

CHAPTER 12

I FROZE IN utter shock. She tasted of the coffee we'd had with dinner, and something else, something musky and dark and completely unlike Griffin.

Her tongue slid through my open lips, and I jerked back. Unfortunately, my chair sat on carpets piled over sand, not hardwood, so the effect of my motion was to tip me over backwards.

My legs caught the table, sending it over with a crash. I wound up flat on my back, with my shoes in the air. My fez rolled lazily away and came to rest against my cot.

Face burning, I stumbled to my feet. "Are you all right?" Daphne asked in obvious concern as she reached for me.

I tried to back away, but she gripped on my coat—and seemed to be trying to divest me of it.

"Fine!" I exclaimed, frantically trying to remove her hands from my person. "I just, er, I…"

"What?" she murmured, taking a step forward for every step I took back. "Neither of us have any obligations. I'm a widow, not some swooning girl who doesn't know anything about pleasing a man."

"I'm sure you're quite good at it," I assured her, prying her fingers from my coat. "But I—I well—I can't!"

Freed, I bolted out of the tent. The campfire burned nearby, but I didn't dare show my scalding face. Instead, I hurried up the wadi toward the tomb. Griffin called after me, but I pretended not to hear him, walking away as quickly as possible without actually breaking into a run.

I stopped outside the tomb entrance, collapsing against the stone. Dear heavens, had I somehow led Daphne to believe I had a romantic interest in her?

"Whyborne?" Griffin called, and I started badly. He appeared around the last outcropping of rock, and the lantern in his hand revealed his concern. "What's wrong?"

"N-nothing," I replied. What would he think? Surely he wouldn't imagine I'd done anything to encourage Daphne, would he?

"You seem rather upset for 'nothing,'" he said. Setting the lantern on the ground, he took my hands. "Did the hieroglyphs say something terrible?"

"What? Oh...no. No."

"Then what?"

"Er..." I didn't wish to confess it, but in truth I had no choice. "Daphne...kissed me."

I glanced up worriedly, only to find the lout struggling to suppress...laughter?

"Curse it, Griffin!" I snatched my hands away. "It isn't funny!"

"Not to the poor woman, I'm sure," he agreed.

"You're an utter swine."

"Me? You're the one who leaves a string of broken female hearts everywhere he goes. Poor Miss Parkhurst, Amelie, and now Daphne—"

Miss Parkhurst? What on earth was the man nattering about? "That's utterly absurd," I snapped, embarrassment giving way to annoyance. "I don't appreciate your attitude at all."

Griffin's amusement failed to abate. "I'm sure you don't. Now tell me—what happened?"

I related the whole embarrassing story to him. He shook his head. "Well, you might have found a better way of handling things, but you did nothing wrong. And neither did she. If she seems discomfited tomorrow, apologize and give her some excuse. A love back home, or high morals, or whatever seems expedient."

"I hope you're right. We've enough tensions in camp without adding to them," I said glumly.

"Indeed. Now let's return to the fire, unless you intend to hide up here all night."

"I'd prefer it."

"I'm sure you would," he said, clapping me on the arm. "But eventually Christine would come to see what the matter is, and you wouldn't want that, would you?"

He had a point, so I followed him back to camp. Thankfully, by the time we returned, Daphne had turned in, claiming a headache.

Christine and Iskander gave me curious looks, but I ignored them both in favor of retreating to the tent. I put away the notes and the folding table, and dragged the cots together as usual. But I left a foot or two of space between them tonight, and sank down on the edge of mine, lost in thought.

Griffin came in shortly thereafter. He gave the arrangement of cots a curious look, but refrained from commenting until he'd done up the ties on the flaps and removed his shoes, coat, and vest. After shuttering the lamp too low to throw our silhouettes on the sides of our makeshift domicile, he came and sat beside me. "Are you well?" he asked.

I shrugged. "Just thinking."

"About what?"

He'd keep asking until I gave in. "That you find the idea of anyone else wanting me amusing."

Griffin caught his breath sharply. "Ival, I never—"

"You would have laughed aloud if a man kissed me," I cut in.

"You're wrong."

"Why do I doubt it?"

He caught my jaw in his hand, tilting my head to face him. "You shouldn't. I would be quite upset if you went about kissing other men."

My heartbeat quickened slightly. "You'd laugh at me," I whispered, because I feared it was true. "You'd say no one else could possibly want—"

He cut off my words with a kiss: hard and hot and demanding. I yielded to it, clutching him, because of course I was right, and he could be secure knowing no other would look at me twice.

But when he broke off the kiss and leaned his forehead against mine, he growled, "You have no idea, do you? You were so cold and aloof when I met you. Frozen, and I wanted nothing more in the world than to thaw you, to uncover the fire I knew you hid inside. And I was so damned glad we weren't in Chicago, or New York, where I'd have to compete with half the city to catch your attention. And now that you've found yourself, your confidence, your power...you could snap your fingers and have a mouth on your cock, without any effort at all."

The thought was ludicrous. "You're speaking nonsense," I murmured against his lips.

His hands tightened on my upper arms, almost hard enough to bruise. "I'm not. How you burn, bright enough it almost blinds me. But I can't look away."

His words made no sense. So I said the first, foolish thing which came to mind. "She said I smell like the ocean."

Griffin stiffened slightly. "I don't like anyone being close enough to notice," he said into my ear, his breath hot against my skin.

"It's true?"

He breathed deep. "You smell like a clean wind off the sea. Like salt and ambergris." His hand trailed along the line of buttons on my shirt. "Like home. Like every good thing in this world."

I pressed my lips against his hair. "Griffin..."

"Would you have? If you'd been kissed by a Donald rather than a Daphne."

"Would I what?"

"Have kissed him back."

"Don't be absurd," I said.

"I'm not." His eyes were dark, the irises thin rings of emerald around his pupils.

I drew in a ragged breath...then let it out and snapped my fingers.

He cocked his head to the side, before understanding transformed his features. "There is your answer," I said as he reached for the buttons on my trousers. "There is one mouth I want. How convenient its owner is here and amenable."

He made a show of it, undoing the buttons one at a time, rubbing against me like a cat and mouthing me through the thin cotton of my drawers. I closed my eyes and shivered in delight, biting back a gasp when he slid his mouth down around me.

It was hot and warm and borderline heavenly, and all I could do not to make some louder sound. After a few minutes, though, I gently pushed him away. "Take off your clothes."

I extinguished the lantern and we both stripped, nothing but warmth and skin in the darkness. The cots were forgotten when he pushed me back on the carpets, kissing me hungrily, his cock leaving a slick trail on my belly.

"I'd never laugh at the thought of sharing you," he whispered into my neck, his lips hot against my skin. "But if you need to...to find out if there's more...to experiment, or find something I can't give you, I'd endure it. For you. For your happiness."

"What? No!" I drew away, startled. How had he reached such a conclusion? "I love you."

"I know. Which is the only reason I could bear to risk your finding someone else a better bed partner," he said softly, even as his hands traced my skin with lines of fire. "Because I trust you'd always come back to me."

I'd thought he found the idea someone else would want me absurd, but it seemed as though he felt the opposite. I'd no idea he'd ever considered I might not be happy with our arrangement. How could I convince him of his misapprehension?

I rolled us over; my shoulder clipped the cot, and I winced. "Stay put," I ordered softly, pressing him down against he carpets. He did as ordered while I rummaged in the packs, coming up with the small jar of lubricant.

I slicked my fingers even as he drew up his legs, eager and wanting. Even as a half-glimpsed shadow, he made my cock stiffen with need to drive in deep. "I'm not here because I want something else," I said, pressing my fingers into him, probing for the spot which would make him writhe and beg for more. "I'm here because you undo me, utterly, and always have. I was yours for the taking from the first."

He shuddered and sighed around my fingers. "I feel greedy, keeping you to myself," he whispered. "If I took you to one of the decadent clubs in Chicago, there would be a line of men begging for the chance to fuck you."

I rather doubted it. Whatever Griffin saw in me, no else seemed to have ever noticed. My life before him had been one of wretched loneliness, and I hoped, desperately, I hadn't dragged him down with me. I feared his decision to remain with me increased his sense of isolation, where I found only belonging.

"They'd be sorely disappointed," I said. I draped myself over him, kissing him softly, the hard line of his member like a bar of hot iron against my belly. "I'm yours."

"I know." He framed my face with his hands. "Now fuck me, Ival, before you drive me mad with wanting."

I certainly wasn't going to argue. Taking up position, I worked into him slowly. I wished we could risk some light. I loved to watch his face when we made love, the way his kiss-swollen lips parted, his eyes hooded with desire as he watched me in turn. Wished, too, we dared do more than whisper, so I might hear him beg and moan for more.

The tent still held the heat of the day, and sweat sheened my skin. I closed my eyes against the darkness and tilted my head back, all my concentration on the places where we touched: his feet against the back of my thighs, his hand gripping my shoulder, the slickness of his member against my stomach as he stroked himself. Most of all, the tight heat of his body around my shaft, the muscular ring gripping me with every thrust.

"Harder," he whispered.

I gave him what he asked for. His fingers clenched my shoulder, and the tempo of his hand on his cock sped up along with his ragged breathing. God! I wanted to hear him cry out; I wanted to shout his name to the heavens. Instead I bit my lip hard, struggling to hold back the edge of need, until he arched under me. Hot spend hit my chest, and he clenched tight around me. I shuddered and thrust again and again, until it became too much, and I spilled inside him.

When I could move again, I went to the washbasin, returning with a cloth soaked in tepid water to run over Griffin's skin. He sighed in contentment, then sat up and stretched languidly. Again I cursed the enforced darkness, which deprived me of the sight of his well-developed torso. How long would we be trapped here in this wasteland? Perhaps I could convince Christine to let us return to Cairo for a few days, where at least we'd have a real bed and walls we didn't have to worry about casting shadows against.

We pushed the cots together, pulled on our nightshirts against the possibility of some emergency calling us forth, and curled up beside one another. Griffin took my hand and pressed a sleepy kiss to my knuckles. "I'm not trying to push you away from me," he said softly. "Quite the opposite. I worry since you were inexperienced when we met, you might wonder what you may have missed out on. I don't want to share you with anyone, but I want to lose you even less."

"Where do you come up with these absurd notions?" I asked, with a touch of exasperation. "Is this about Daphne? Because I assure you—"

"I know you have no interest in women, my dear." Which wasn't as much a given as it might have seemed. Before we'd met, Griffin had slept with women on more than one occasion, although he did not prefer it. He and I were not made exactly the same; whatever part of my brain or body caused me to desire men had rendered me utterly insensible to feminine charms in a way that he was not.

"It's merely something which crossed my mind as of late," he went on. "I have no wish to hold you back. And if you say it's a foolish worry, I'll think no more on it."

"It *is* foolish," I replied. Tiredness gripped me, and I found myself suppressing a yawn. "I assure you, I find our intimate relationship to be most, er, fulfilling. Among other things."

"I'm glad." He might have said more, but the long day caught up with me. I slipped into restless dreams in which I ran down the corridors of an endless tomb, looking for something I could neither name nor find.

CHAPTER 13

BREAKFAST WAS PREDICTABLY awkward. I tried to greet Daphne normally, but ended up stammering the words. As the five of us ate, she turned to Griffin and said, "I thought perhaps I'd like to take another turn on the screens today."

"Of course," he said amiably. At least he was too much the gentleman to make a teasing remark about assisting me, although I'm sure a number of them passed through his mind.

For their parts, Iskander and Christine both appeared puzzled. Neither of them said anything at the time, and I hoped the matter might be dropped and put behind us.

The hope proved futile, of course. As we prepared for work, Christine joined Griffin and I in front of the wall. "What on earth is going on, Whyborne?" she demanded. "Have you and Daphne argued over your translation?"

"No, and keep your voice down," I said, glancing about. Fortunately, only Griffin stood close enough to overhear.

"Well, what's wrong? Tensions are normal in a situation like this, isolated from civilization as we are, but it's best to get them out in the open before they have a chance to fester."

There was no way around it. I explained the situation to Christine as delicately as I could, given Daphne was her sister. When I finished, Christine rubbed her chin thoughtfully. "Hmm. I'll just tell her you're a eunuch."

"Christine!" I exclaimed.

"Well, I can't lie and say you've a woman waiting back home," she pointed out. "What if she wants to visit me in Widdershins? Or even move there? When this mysterious other woman failed to appear, she'd know I'd made the whole thing up."

"Surely you can think of something better than my being a...a..."

"Impotence. It would be more believable, anyway."

"Christine!"

"Oh honestly, Whyborne, don't put up such a fuss. I swear, you men have your entire egos tied to the functioning of a few inches of flesh."

"More than a few," Griffin said with a smirk. I buried my face in my hands and wished the mummy's curse were real and might strike me down immediately.

"I don't want to know, and implore you not to say anything further," Christine responded.

"I thought nothing shocked you."

Christine snorted. "Whyborne is my brother, by choice if not by blood. I wish him all happiness, but have no desire to know any details."

"Would you both please stop talking?" I begged. "Tell Daphne I'm dead. Over here. Killed by apoplexy thanks to the two people closest to me. Perhaps she can speak a phrase from the Coffin Texts over my corpse."

"Good gad, you're so melodramatic," Christine exclaimed. "Have it your way. I won't say anything."

"Thank you."

Christine departed, and I tried to turn my mind to work. Although Griffin's assistance was useful on occasion, in truth, his complete lack of knowledge of hieroglyphics meant he had little to offer besides working the camera. Perhaps I could apologize to Daphne and convince her to return. If only I'd handled the situation better in the first place. Surely there must have been some way I might have demurred with a kind word or a witty remark, which would have left her at her ease. Instead, I'd bolted out of the tent as if fleeing a dangerous animal. My behavior had been abominable.

"You know," Griffin said, pulling my attention away from my meandering thoughts, "this trip has given me great hope."

I looked up in confusion. He rested against the scaffolding of our canopy, coatless and with his shirtsleeves rolled up to expose his strong forearms. The Egyptian sun had called forth more freckles than ever across his nose and cheeks, and his green eyes gleamed in contrast to his browned skin.

"What do you mean?" I asked, bewildered.

Griffin glanced in the direction of the screens, although we couldn't see them from our position. "Seeing Christine and her sister reconcile, after many years of not speaking to one another."

"Oh." Did he hope he might find some similar reconciliation with his parents?

"And not just this trip. Your family makes me feel perhaps, if I do find my brothers, there might be some chance."

"My family?" I asked in surprise. "Are we talking about the same people? Stanford and I loathe one another. Father barely tolerates my existence."

"That isn't true." Griffin picked up his canteen from where it rested nearby and took a long drink. "When your father needed an investigator to go to Threshold, he invited me to *dinner*. Not a business meeting in an office. Dinner with the family. He and your mother asked me to Christmas. Although your brother is an ass, I'll admit."

My head spun. "Father and Stanford—the Brotherhood—they would have killed you!"

"True," he said, not looking at me. "But I believe they didn't suspect the nature of our relationship at the time."

My head ached. I took off my fez and ran a hand through my hair. Under the rough conditions of camp life, it had become even more rebellious than usual. "Perhaps you're right," I said reluctantly. It seemed bizarre my family could be a source of encouragement for anyone else, as they'd been nothing but misery for me. "As for your brothers, we'll simply have to hope they don't belong to any murderous cults."

Griffin smiled. "And who knows? It's possible one or even both of them share our inclinations."

And if they didn't? If he found them, only to be confronted with the same choice his adoptive family gave him? I would do anything for him, but how could I ask him to go through the same pain a second time? I turned back to the wall to conceal my expression. Griffin worried about keeping me happy, but it seemed clear to me I'd already failed in doing the same for him.

"Whyborne!" Christine shouted from. "Griffin! Away from the wall, gents—we're about to start hoisting the statue!"

At least it would be a distraction from my thoughts. Worried my notes might blow away, I returned briefly to the tent and placed them with the earlier pages Daphne and I had worked on. Then I rejoined Griffin, and we took up position where we could safely observe the work.

The statue in question was a larger-than-life representation of

Bast, who, in her cat form, cut the chaos serpent to bits with her claws. Over the last week, the workmen had dug out beneath and around the statue to put in place a cradle of ropes attached to a system of pulleys. Now they prepared to undertake the Herculean task of levering it back into the position it occupied so many centuries ago.

"It is quite a sight, isn't it?" I asked. The ancient statue in its web of ropes, the men taking their places, ready to wrest it back to a place of honor. Christine strode back and forth, making last minute checks and shouting orders. Iskander hovered nearby along with the *reis* Khaled.

"Indeed it is," Daphne said from behind me.

I started and turned to find her coming up behind us, a parasol shading her pale skin from the sun. "Imagine how this place must have looked when new, the masonry intact rather than worn by time, the statues wearing bright coats of paint," she went on.

"Agreed," I said. Griffin pretended to be oblivious and remained standing beside me. When a cough failed to dislodge him, I sighed and turned back to Daphne. "Forgive me if I gave offense yesterday," I said in a low voice.

Her cheeks turned slightly pink. "I should be the one asking for forgiveness," she replied stiffly. "You must think me very forward."

"Not at all! It's only I'm unused to receiving such, er, compliments. And I fear I'm not at liberty to return them." There. That sounded vague enough, I hoped.

"Khaled!" Christine bellowed. We all returned our attention to the work. "I think we're ready to begin."

Khaled stepped in and began to issue the orders to the work crews. Although the process had been carefully planned, the prospect of moving a hundred-ton statue was not without its dangers. Most of the workers bent their backs to this task, but a few manned the pulleys to keep an eye out for any jams, and others moved in and out of the scaffolding, alert for any crack of wood or other sign of failure.

Apparently satisfied, Khaled signaled the workers to start. Lines of sweating men began to pull on the ropes. Some had stripped to the waist in the heat, and the sight of their muscles bulging with effort was impressive indeed. They sang to coordinate their movements, and the sound of their voices echoed from the heights around us.

It seemed almost impossible the statue of the goddess might rise from its long slumber, and yet within moments, it began to slowly, ponderously inch its way upright. Most of the sand had been removed from its surface, but a few trickles poured down over the sides. Christine shouted encouragement even as she hurried to inspect the statue, to make certain no cracks formed from uneven distribution of the weight. Its shadow fell across her.

"Christine!" Iskander shouted.

There came a loud crack, as of a whip, followed by several more in quick succession. No, not a whip—ropes breaking beneath the strain.

The scaffolding groaned. More ropes snapped as the weight of the statue depended from fewer and fewer points. Time itself seemed to slow, the ends of the ropes snaking through the air, the men pulling on them stumbling back and falling onto each other as the tension suddenly vanished from their line. The statue began its slow, inevitable return to the ground. Christine stood beneath its shadow, one hand instinctively flung up to ward off the tons of rock rushing toward her. I cried out her name, but she was too far away. I could do nothing to save her.

Iskander caught Christine around the waist. Half-lifting, half-dragging her, he hurled them both out of the statue's path. They rolled across the rocky ground in a tangle.

The statue of Bast smashed into the ground with such force it vibrated through my shoes. An enormous cloud of dust exploded from beneath it, and the world changed to panicked chaos. Men cried out in alarm, some running toward the statue and some away. My heart lurched in my chest, and I sprinted toward the scene. For a moment, the dust cloud obscured my vision and clogged my nostrils. Coughing, I held my arm over my mouth and nose, trying to breathe through the cloth to filter the dust. Where was Christine? Had Iskander knocked her aside in time, or did the stone flatten them both?

There! As the dust began to drift away in the desert wind, I spotted the outline of her hat. She sat on the ground with Iskander, half-clinging to his coat, while he gripped her upper arms. Although coughing and choking, neither made a move to stand, and I feared they'd both been injured.

"Christine!" I cried.

She jerked away, freeing herself from Iskander's grasp. He hurriedly dropped his hands, but they shook as he wiped them on his trousers.

"Thank God Iskander acted so quickly!" I said, my voice shaking with relief. "Are you all right?"

"Never mind!" she exclaimed impatiently. "What about the statue? Is it damaged?"

Griffin caught up with me. "She must be fine if she's inquiring about the statue."

"Have you ever met Christine? If it had crushed her in half, she'd use her dying breath to make certain it remained in one piece."

Although I spoke lightly, my voice trembled. God, the call had been a close one. If Iskander hadn't acted with such swiftness, she would have died right here in front of us.

Khaled bellowed at the workers, cursing them for their carelessness, while Christine examined the statue. "Blast it!" she shouted. "There's a crack—see, here. What the devil went wrong?"

A murmuring came from some of the men, and I caught the Arabic word for curse. Predictably, this did nothing to improve Christine's mood, and she loosed a long string of blistering oaths.

"I suppose that's as good evidence as any she's unharmed," said Daphne, who joined us to watch.

"Indeed," I agreed.

As the dust continued to settle, Griffin went to look over the statue as well, before picking through the tangle of ropes and broken wood. At one point he bent down and inspected one of the snapped ropes.

I watched him, wondering what he might be about. Eventually, he left off, strolling back up to me with his hands stuffed in his pockets. Daphne still regarded her sister with an expression of worry, so I fell in beside Griffin and walked with him. "Well?" I asked.

"One of the ropes was half-sawed through." His expression beneath the brim of his hat turned grim. "Not enough to break immediately. It held just long enough for the statue to start to rise."

"When it would be most dangerous."

"Exactly. I suspect several others were cut through as well. It wouldn't take many before the weight grew too great and brought the whole thing crashing down." He shook his head. "A warning. An attempted murder in the night. And now sabotage which could have killed any number of unfortunates."

"Yes." I glanced over my shoulder to where Iskander stood, staring at the ruin of tackle and wood. "But surely this clears Mr. Barnett. Unless he is the world's finest actor, he genuinely feared for Christine's life."

"I agree," Griffin said slowly.

"But?" I asked, sensing something unsaid.

Griffin's green gaze met mine. "But his warning to Christine came *before* the ropes broke."

Some good came from the disaster. Daphne forgot her embarrassment in the worry for her sister and returned to her old, cheerful attitude toward me. I was glad for it, both for the work and our growing friendship. Still, there was little for any of us to be happy about that evening, and after a silent meal, I said, "I'm going to return to my translation. Daphne, will you assist me?"

"Of course," she said.

"At least some progress might be made today," Christine muttered, jabbing her fork rather more forcefully into our meal of spiced lamb than the tender meat required.

Once at the tent, I started to untie the flaps, which I'd secured against the constant wind sweeping in and scattering our things about. Only the ties already hung loose. I must have forgotten to retie them in my haste to join Griffin earlier.

Pushing aside the canvas, I ducked inside. Paper crinkled beneath my feet, and I stopped to let my eyes adjust to the shade.

Only Daphne's presence restrained me from loosing the oath which leapt to my lips at the sight which greeted me. My notes, Daphne's sketches, all our hard work, lay violently ripped into tiny pieces and scattered about the floor.

The others came running in response to Daphne's exclamation of horror. Christine swore, and Iskander put a hand to his face in a gesture of despair.

"Everyone out," Griffin ordered. "You too, Whyborne."

"What? Why?" I asked through the haze of shock which began to give way to rage. All of our work, the hours we'd spent carefully making notations and corrections, all gone!

"Perhaps something can be salvaged," Christine said, trying to push past me. Griffin, however, turned on her sharply.

"I said back! All of you!"

Christine stared at him in shock, then obeyed along with the rest of us. "Hold the tent flaps open and get some light in here," Griffin said.

When we obeyed, he carefully picked up his sword cane and held it with the weighted head away from him. Standing in the center of the tent, he examined every inch visually, slowly pivoting around. Other things had been tossed about as well: our clothing lay in crumpled heaps, and our bedding hung half-off the cots. After a few moments of thought, he approached my cot and went down on one knee. Holding the cane out as far as he could from his body, he slid it beneath the gap between floor and covers.

Something long and thin lunged out. Griffin jerked back. The hooded cobra hidden beneath the bed whipped into a coil, head poised to strike again.

Chapter 14

Griffin swung the cane and brought the heavy end down on the poor thing's skull with a muffled crunch. Its body snapped about in death throes, but there was no question he'd managed to kill it.

My heart felt as though it would burst from my chest. "Griffin! Did it bite you?" I cried, rushing to his side. I wanted to throw my arms around him and hold him tight, but our audience prevented it. I settled for grasping his shoulder.

"No—it struck at the cane, as I'd intended," he said, a bit shakily.

"How did you know?" Daphne asked from the entrance to the tent. She sounded torn between admiration and horror.

"Our enemies clearly don't care who dies here," Griffin replied.

"Do you think it's the same man who cut through the tent and attacked Daphne?" Christine asked.

"It seems likely."

"But why?" Daphne asked. "Who would want to kill us? We've found no gold or jewels, no valuable artifacts which could be sold on the black market, at least not for enough money to murder us over. It makes no sense."

"Agreed." Iskander wiped his forehead with his handkerchief. "After this, I, for one, could use a stiff drink."

"Excellent suggestion," Christine said. "Daphne, will you help Iskander pour? We'll be along in a moment—I want to take a look at something."

Once they left, I took the opportunity to give Griffin a quick embrace. He patted my arm. "I'm quite well, my dear."

Christine crouched down and inspected the dead snake. "Hooded cobras are the most deadly serpents in Egypt," she said quietly.

"I would have certainly trodden on it when I moved my cot tonight." I shook my head. "The poor thing. I wish we hadn't had to kill it."

"Better it than Griffin," Christine replied, rising again. "Or you. Blast it all."

"There's something else," Griffin said. "I inspected the ropes on the statue. At least one of them was partially cut."

Her eyes widened—then narrowed in anger. "Damn it. I've spoken to Khaled about the men—some of them are new." Christine chewed her lip. "It must be one of them. I'll have him fire them tomorrow. It's unfair to any who are innocent, but I won't take chances with our lives. The next question is what are we to do now your notes are destroyed?" Christine gestured to the torn scraps of paper. "This is quite the setback, no two ways around it."

I picked up a crumpled strip of paper and stared down at it for a long moment. Heat grew in my chest, and I wished I had the person responsible for the destruction in front of me.

"I recall a great deal," I said. "The work isn't wasted." I met their gazes. "I'll labor night and day to recreate the inscription—and to carry the translation farther and unlock the secret of how to locate the fane. These attempts almost cost me the two people I care about most today. I won't let whoever is behind them win."

I sat at the table long into the night, reworking everything I could from memory. Daphne helped, and between the two of us I thought we'd at least made a good start. I managed to catch an hour or two of sleep before my turn came at watch. But as I sat shivering in the predawn darkness, jumping at every sound, my mind brooded over the events of the day.

Christine and Griffin had both been in jeopardy, and what had I done to save them? Nothing. I'd merely stood by while Iskander rescued Christine, and Griffin faced the dangerous serpent by himself. Useless.

The familiar weight of the *Arcanorum* tugged on my jacket pocket. If the dire hints and warnings were true, if Nitocris had somehow returned from the dead and even now raised an army of ghūls, we needed every advantage we could get. Surely I should try to master the earth spell again.

And the wand we'd found. What if it truly was the tool of ancient sorcerers? Could it give me some aid now?

I left the fire and crept as stealthily as I could to the crates packed with artifacts. We stored them here in the wadi, as a way to put them under guard, lest some enterprising thief decide to make off with them during the night. Fortunately, I'd made note of the wand's lot number, and found the crate with relative ease. Getting to it proved another matter, as it had a second crate stacked on top of it.

The crate was damnably heavy, and although I managed not to drop it on my feet, I made more noise than I'd wished in heaving it off. I froze and listened for a moment, but there came no sound from either inside or outside the camp. Even the jackals had fallen silent.

Fortunately, the crate hadn't been nailed shut for transport yet, as Christine still hoped to see if the wand fit the Heka statue when the opportunity presented itself. Straw cushioned and separated the artifacts, but luckily the wand lay neatly on top. When I lifted it from its bed, the firelight caught in its ruby eyes, and for a moment its curved body seemed to move and shift within my grasp. As before, the metal felt oddly cool, although at least this time I could attribute it to having been packed away from the rays of the sun.

I took my lantern and the wand, and headed toward the open end of the wadi. This way no one—or no *thing*—could slip past me and into the camp while I worked.

My previous failures to direct the earth spell involved breaking stone. But perhaps stone was too ambitious. Could I affect sand more easily?

I found an area where the wind had piled a heap of sand near the entrance of the wadi, against a sudden outcropping. Setting the lantern carefully aside, I crouched on the periphery of the forming dune. My mouth had gone dry, and I wished I'd brought my canteen.

Holding the wand in both hands, I pressed the tip of its tail against the earth and pointed the hooded head at the stars. For a long moment, I listened to only the sound of my own breaths, measured and slow. Calm settled over me, tinged with a familiar sense of excitement.

Uncertainty ruled every other part of my life. I worried over everything: making a fool of myself at the museum, damaging my relationship with Griffin, failing to live up to the expectations of those I loved.

But this...this was different. No wonder I half-feared it.

I began to whisper the words of the spell. The wand shivered in my hands, growing slowly warmer against my skin. I repeated the spell again. Had some grains of sand slipped down from the dune? Due to the wind, or the spell?

I spoke the words a third time. The sand definitely moved now, shifting and sliding, as if something stirred from beneath it. My heart pounded, and a laugh of delight escaped me—

"Whyborne! What are you doing?"

I stumbled to my feet. Griffin stood behind me, his face lit from beneath by my lantern, his expression aghast.

Damn.

"Er..." Would he believe I was just out for a walk? But no, one look at his face told me he'd seen far too much to believe anything but the truth. "I'm testing the wand," I said. "With a new spell."

His brows drew together sharply. "Curse it—"

"I'm not doing anything wrong!" I broke in hotly.

"If you believed that, you wouldn't have snuck out here alone, where no one could see you!"

"And you're spying on me." I folded my arms across my chest, almost striking myself in the face with the wand as I did so. "You're supposed to be asleep, not sneaking around, as you put it."

"A noise woke me—no doubt when you moved the crates." Blast. "And you're changing the subject. You know how I feel about this."

"I know you're completely irrational when it comes to magic," I said through gritted teeth.

He flung his hands up. "It's not irrational to worry about you!"

"Yes, it is!" I dropped my arms in exasperation. The wind stirred, blowing through the canyon and ruffling Griffin's curls. "Time and time again, the spells from the *Arcanorum* have saved our lives. But you insist upon pretending they're inherently perilous, or dangerous to me in some way—"

He stepped forward and seized me by the arms, his fingers digging into my flesh through coat and shirt. "The dweller *did* something to you!"

The wind died away. "What?" I asked. "You're speaking nonsense."

"Am I?" He let go of me and stepped back. "The tree at Christmas. The wind which came up when you found the wand. Just now."

"The dweller did nothing permanent to me!"

"Then maybe it awoke something already there!" he shouted back.

I gaped at him. How dare he make such baseless allegations? "You're accusing me of having powers I don't possess." I gestured wildly at the valley beyond. "We're in the desert, Griffin! The wind blows here! You're taking natural occurrences and twisting them around to be my fault somehow. Well, I won't have it!"

"Whyborne—"

"No!" I snatched up my lantern and stomped back toward camp. "I'm sick and tired of you acting as though I'm barely any better than

Blackbyrne or Nephren-ka. As if one or two spells make me a sorcerer."

He stalked after me. "You're being reckless! You know nothing at all about the wand in your hand, and yet you obviously felt no hesitation when it came to using the accursed thing! Did you even *think?*"

We reached the edge of the camp. I turned around. "Yes, I thought. I *thought* I wouldn't just stand by while assassins try to kill Daphne, and you and Christine almost die, and God only knows what else! I thought I'd at least try to save us!"

The flaps on Christine's tent flew back, and she stuck her head out. "What the devil are you two arguing about?" she yelled. "The rest of us are trying to sleep!"

"Nothing," Griffin growled back at her.

"Since Mr. Flaherty apparently can't sleep, he can finish out the watch," I said stiffly. "Good night to you all."

Gripping the wand tightly in my hand, I marched back inside our tent and let the flaps fall closed behind me. Griffin didn't follow.

Dawn found us an unhappy group. I woke to the memory of my argument with Griffin, and it left me seething through my morning ablutions. Christine was put out with both of us for waking the entire camp, and dark circles showed under Iskander's eyes. Breakfast conversation remained at the barest minimum, with Griffin and I sitting on opposite sites of the table without looking at one another. By the time we made our way down to the site, we were all in the blackest of moods.

"The men are late," Iskander observed with a worried frown.

Christine scowled, but said, "Give them time. Perhaps there was some delay."

Daphne and I went to our wall. I feared she'd ask me about the quarrel with Griffin, but she seemed more concerned about the missing workmen.

An hour later, it became clear there was no delay. The workers simply weren't coming. Nor had anyone sent a runner to explain why.

"Curse Khaled—I thought better of him than this!" Christine exclaimed, tearing her hat from her head and flinging it to the ground. For a moment, I thought she might stomp on it in her frustration. "What the devil is wrong with him?"

"Shall I ride to the village and find out?" Iskander offered.

"No. I'd better do it myself. And I want you to stay here and guard the site, in case...well. In case."

Iskander's frown deepened. "Someone should accompany you."

"I can," Griffin suggested.

"No. You don't speak Arabic." She waved a hand at me. "Whyborne, you come along. Daphne, stay here and work on the blasted wall inscription. Griffin, help Iskander guard the site."

No one argued further—given her mood, no one dared. But as she strode off toward the camels, I jogged up behind her. "Why do you really want me to come?" I asked.

"Because if ghūls are involved, I want your particular sort of expertise."

"Ah. That makes sense."

"Of course it does." She ground her teeth fiercely. "Curse it! If word gets out my workmen have deserted me, it will be taken as proof a woman can't manage a site."

I winced but couldn't argue. "We'll simply have to convince the men to return."

Iskander readied the camels while Christine and I grabbed canteens for our brief trek, and Christine fetched her rifle from her tent. I sincerely hoped she wouldn't need it.

Iskander gave me the same demon-possessed camel as I'd ridden before. It lunged at me, teeth nearly closing on my fez, but I'd expected the maneuver and managed to duck away in time.

"No! Bad camel!" I told it. "Christine, do you not feed these creatures?"

"Do stop playing around and mount up, Whyborne," she ordered.

I mentally cursed both her and the camel, while Iskander persuaded it to kneel. The devilish creature didn't seem to have any interest in *his* hat, of course. Within a few minutes, my camel trotted after Christine's, with me clinging to its back.

The village lay a few miles east. Christine claimed its location in the red land proved the main occupation of the menfolk had been tomb robbing from time immemorial. She further insisted missing the tomb of Nephren-ka despite its proximity had damaged their professional pride to the point they'd given up looting and turned into honest workmen. I had my doubts. Not of their honesty or loyalty, but of her reasoning.

Once we cleared the valley, she reined in her camel to ride beside me. "All right, out with it. What did you and Griffin argue about last night?"

I didn't really wish to discuss it. But she would only badger me until I told her. "Griffin's usual lack of anything resembling reason when it comes to the spells from the *Arcanorum*. I tried using the wand we found as a sort of...I don't know. Amplifying device, I suppose. And it worked!"

"Really? Do you think the priests of Horus were sorcerers?" she asked. "Now there would be a paper. Unfortunately, it would get us both laughed out of the scientific world."

"None of which is my point. Griffin can't seem to understand I'm doing what's best. I'm trying to help! But he refuses to see it."

Christine sighed. "Such an attitude would be annoying," she agreed. "Although I suspect he's motivated by worry for you."

"And do *you* enjoy it when others express concern over your chosen field of study, and suggest you'd be better off staying at home for your own safety?" I asked triumphantly.

As I'd expected, she immediately scowled. "You're absolutely right. Griffin should trust you more. Shall I speak to him for you?"

Oh dear Lord. "No," I said hastily. "I can handle this. It's just he's so...so frustrating!"

Thankfully, the village came into sight, cutting short our conversation. As we drew closer, I received my first glimpse of the small settlement. It struck me as a wretched place indeed, with tiny hovels of packed mud, roofed only with cornstalks. They clustered around what appeared to be a central common area. Women cooked over open flames, and I wondered their concealing veils didn't catch fire. Thin dogs and naked children ran about in a filthy tumult.

As we approached, the women withdrew. The men, who had been sitting about smoking, gathered into a crowd. I recognized many of them from the site. Their expressions mingled shame and fear, but the beginnings of anger as well.

We halted. No one offered to take our camels, or to invite us inside, which even I knew was a profound breach of Egyptian etiquette. How often had Christine spoken of the hospitality shown by even the poorest man when a visitor appeared at his door?

"Where is Khaled?" Christine asked into the silence.

There came a shuffling, and Khaled appeared from one of the houses. He seemed utterly downcast and wretched, his eyes directed to the ground in front of him.

Christine said nothing further. She merely waited, keeping him fixed with her sharp gaze. Any man would have crumbled beneath it eventually, and Khaled proved no exception.

"An *ifrit* took Ahmed's daughter," he said unhappily. "I know you don't believe in such things, but it's true. I saw the creature with my own eyes."

Chapter 15

"**What happened?**" Christine asked, watching Khaled intently.

"It stole into my own house last night." His mouth tightened. "I woke and saw the thing standing over my youngest son, ready to snatch him up. It went on two legs and was the size of a man, *sitt*, but it was nothing human. It had a jackal's ears and face, teeth and fur."

Christine let out a hiss. "Is your son all right?"

"Yes. I cried out, and it tried to escape through the window. But Ahmed and some others have stayed watchful since the girl vanished. Together we killed it and threw the body into a pit far from here."

Damn. The ghūls threatening us was one thing. But the children of the village…it could not be allowed to continue.

"You are an honest man," Christine said at last. "I believe you when you tell me you saw this thing. But surely such *ifrit* are creatures of darkness. If you come to the site during the day and—"

"No!" Fire flashed in Khaled's eyes. "This thing almost took my son! It was a warning. The will of Allah is for us leave the ancient dead to their rest. We will work no more in the Valley of the Jackals."

For a moment, I thought for certain Christine would erupt into a curse. Her eyes flashed, and her nostrils flared. Then she nodded once. "Very well, Khaled. You may sit here and rot. I'm sure there are still brave men to be found in Egypt."

She turned her camel and urged it into a gallop. Mine, of course, bolted after, and I could do nothing but cling to the saddle and try not to fall off. Fortunately, she slowed enough for my camel to catch up once we passed out of sight of the village.

"I'm sorry," I said.

She ground her teeth. "I thought Khaled was above this sort of thing. Blast those ghūls!"

"The villagers only wish to protect their children," I protested.

"Don't you think I know that? But this isn't some conceit of mine, Whyborne! You said yourself that in her journals, Nitocris speaks of gaining untold power if she is able to locate the fane and take the Lapidem."

I shivered, recalling some of the more descriptive passages. "Of turning cities into graves for her ghūls to feast on. Yes."

"What if she's the one behind the attempt to murder Daphne, the sabotage on the rigging, the cobra, and the destruction of your notes?" Christine went on. "Or her agents, at least. The message in German warned us; Halabi warned us. We've seen her token too many times to dismiss it. What if she wants to drive us from the dig site so she can have free rein of it for herself? If she does, if she finds the Lapidem and its secrets of occult power, then no one will be safe."

I threw myself into my work, Daphne laboring feverishly beside me. When Christine and I returned with the bad news, I'd seen yet another sign of their sisterhood in Daphne's unexpected show of temper. She'd flung her cup of coffee violently aside, the china shattering against the rocky desert floor. Along with the cup, she'd hurled imprecations against the natives, railing at their superstition and foolish fear.

"Don't be absurd," Christine snapped back, clearly at the end of her patience. "There are idiots everywhere. The European and American presses print endless rubbish about the mummy's curse and every other sort of nonsense. I daresay we'd be in the same blighted straights if we excavated in the midst of London or New York."

Not unsurprisingly, this helped the temper of neither woman, and soon both fumed. I'd hoped our work would provide an outlet for Daphne's frustrations, but Christine thwarted even this. Griffin and Iskander sifted the last of the fill, and with no one else to supervise, Christine hovered over Daphne and me, questioning our translations and interrupting every train of thought.

"Christine," I finally said through clenched teeth. "Do you wish this wall inscription translated or not?"

"Of course I do!" she exclaimed. "What the devil do you think?"

"Then," I went on, as calmly as possible, "please leave us to it, before our work is interrupted by a death."

"A death?"

"Yes. Yours or mine."

Christine glared at me, but took my meaning and left. With a sigh, I turned back to the wall, to find Daphne watching me with a bemused expression.

"You handle her well," she said.

"Say instead I am used to interruptions, knocks on the door at inopportune hours, and a complete lack of any sense my office is meant for work, rather than a room where one adjourns to complain," I replied.

"Do you love her?"

"What?" I blinked at Daphne in shock. "I already said there's nothing between us, did I not?"

"Which is not at all the same question," she observed shrewdly.

How to answer her, without betraying myself? I remembered the phrase Christine used in reference to her uncle. "I'm a confirmed bachelor," I replied, "and as delightful as your sister is, she has not swayed my opinion."

Daphne snorted. "I shouldn't think so. Forgive my curiosity—it was merely a question."

Without Christine's infernal interruptions, the time passed swiftly. What the others did during those hours, I confess I had no idea, being too immersed in the thrill of discovery. Daphne and I crouched side-by-side, alight with excitement and arguing spiritedly over various interpretations.

We finished by dinner, and took our places with a sense of great importance around the fire afterward. "Well?" Christine asked, obviously having caught our mood.

Daphne nodded to me. "Dr. Whyborne, I believe the honor should be yours," she said.

I flushed lightly, not usually enjoying being the center of attention. And yet a part of me couldn't help but relish it at the moment. "Er," I began, clearing my throat. "I believe we've translated everything which is to be found on the unexcavated portions of the wall. As you recall, the priests of Horus—"

"Yes, yes, get on with it!" Christine interrupted.

I shot her an annoyed glare. "Yes," I said forcefully. "At any rate, according to the inscriptions, if the statue of Heka is struck by the spear of Horus, a map showing the location of the fane will somehow be revealed."

"The spear of Horus?" Griffin frowned over his cup of coffee. "Some object which must be found before this map can be uncovered?"

"No," I said. "Although one might think so from a literal

translation. But the weapon is metaphorical. Lightning is the spear of Horus, and the thunder following after the cry of anguish from his great enemy Set. Who, by the way, is a chaos god, much like Nyarlathotep."

"What does this imply?" Iskander asked. "The wand we found earlier—it would fit in the statue's hand?"

"I suspect it would," I agreed, not looking at Griffin when I spoke. "And lightning would strike it, and reveal the map in some fashion."

Iskander shook his head. "Let's hope this is only some fancy of the ancients. Storms here are infrequent at best, and what are the chances of lightning hitting a particular statue in all the vastness of the desert? If the story is true, I fear we'll never locate the fane. Nor will anyone else."

"Yes," Christine agreed, meeting my eyes. "A damned shame, isn't it?"

Deep in the night, Christine and I sneaked out of camp during her watch, leaving everyone else sleeping. We said nothing until we'd exited the wadi and crossed the deserted site to the wall.

"Well?" she asked. "I assume you're confident you can cast the spell."

I nodded. I'd retired shortly after dinner, claiming exhaustion, which was true enough. But instead of taking to my bed, I examined the *Arcanorum*. In truth, I'd wanted to try the lightning spell for some time, but hadn't been able to think of any way to do so within Widdershins in safety. Or without Griffin finding out.

Fortunately, it possessed elements familiar from the spells I'd already mastered. Lightning was a bridge of sorts, between the sky and the earth. Able to manipulate both wind and sand, I felt confident of success.

"It may take a few tries to get the wording and such correct," I cautioned her. "And there is the matter of concentration, especially with a new spell. Don't distract me."

"I would never distract you from your work," she said. I rolled my eyes and made no reply.

We stopped before the great statue of Heka. The entire thing was larger-than-life, eight feet high and set on a plinth, which raised it another two feet. "Be careful not to damage the stonework," Christine said.

"I won't." I stepped up onto the plinth, the wand in one hand. Half holding my breath, I stretched to fit the tail of the serpent into the empty space of Heka's grasp.

It seemed to settle in like a creature returning to its den, fitting better than it should have given the shape of the wand and the simplicity of the hole bored in the statue. Where my fingertips rested lightly against the cool stone, I detected a sort of vibration deep within, almost beyond my ability to sense.

Well, *something* had happened, anyway.

Allowing myself a triumphant smile, I stepped back to the ground. Before I could say anything, however, the light of a lantern appeared in the direction of the wadi.

What would we say if the lantern-bearer proved to be Iskander or Daphne? That we'd suddenly decided to test our theory about the wand in the middle of the night? But before I could think of an excuse, I recognized Griffin's familiar gait and outlines.

"Come to supervise?" I asked when he joined us.

"If I can't talk sense into you." He looked from me to Christine. "I don't want to fight."

"Then perhaps you should return to the tent," I suggested.

"Damn it, Whyborne, listen to me for five seconds!" His green eyes snapped in the lantern light. "The two of you are rushing ahead, without even considering the consequences of your actions. Has it occurred to either of you that whatever is concealed within the fane should be left there?"

"You're just upset because I'm learning a new spell," I broke in. "Admit it."

Griffin's eyes darkened with annoyance. "I don't care for that aspect of it, you're right. And the very fact it takes a sorcerer—"

"Scholar."

"No!" He grabbed my lapels, as though he meant to shake me. "You're a sorcerer, Whyborne. Whether you'll admit it to yourself or not doesn't change the truth. It just makes things more dangerous."

"What do you want us to do, Griffin?" Christine asked. "Run back to Widdershins with our tails tucked between our legs? Leave the site for Nitocris? She's surely a sorceress, and even if she can't call down lightning personally, I'm sure she could find someone else to do it for her."

Griffin's face eased into a neutral expression. "We could dynamite the wall. Destroy it, to prevent anyone else from ever locating the fane."

We stared at him utterly aghast. How could he even suggest such a thing? I'd spent my life studying the past; his suggestion of eradicating it felt like a betrayal.

Christine regained her power of speech first. *"Dynamite* it?" she asked. "This necropolis is an irreplaceable window onto the past. What will you propose to blow up next? The sphinx? The pyramids?"

"The museum?" I added. "Will you burn the books in the library because someone might use them for harm? Must I guard against you flinging the *Arcanorum* into the fire some night?"

"Don't tempt me," he muttered. "Very well. I see neither of you will be dissuaded. At least allow me to *supervise*, as you put it."

"You could just go back to bed," I pointed out.

"No, I can't. In case you haven't noticed, I'm worried because I care for you." He glanced from me to Christine and back again. "Neither of you have ever abandoned me. If I can't turn you from this course, my only choice is to see it to the end with you."

"I...oh," I said, disarmed by his words. I wanted to embrace him, but didn't feel quite up to it in front of Christine. "Thank you."

"I cast my lot with yours, if you recall. I may not always be happy with the direction you take us, but it does not change what I said."

"Then let's get on with it!" Christine exclaimed. "Men always make such a cursed drama of every little thing."

I shot her a glare but decided she had a point. The things I wished to say to Griffin would be better spoken beneath the blankets, anyway. "Move back from the statue, if you please. I don't want either of you to inadvertently be struck, should the lightning fork."

"And what about you?" Griffin asked.

I didn't really have an answer, other than it was a risk which had to be taken. Since I doubted such a reply would improve his attitude, I pretended I hadn't heard. I took out the *Arcanorum,* glanced over the words one last time, then tucked it back in my pocket. Taking a deep breath, I set my feet firmly and raised my arms to the sky.

I could sense the wand, its gemstone eyes watching me. Waiting to see what I would do. But no, that was a ridiculous fancy. I couldn't allow myself to get carried way.

The calm of certainty settled over me, and all other thoughts dropped away one at a time. The million stars above echoed the million grains of sand beneath my feet. The whisper of my breath was the soft sigh of the wind; the blood moving invisible through my veins the echo of underground rivers hidden within the earth. I was the world, and the world was me.

And my will would shape it.

I spoke the words without conscious volition, as if the universe itself decided this moment the one to say them. Nothing happened, but I felt neither disappointment nor surprise. I recited the incantation a second time. My pulse quickened, and the wand watched me with gemstone eyes.

I spoke again. A metallic taste filled my mouth. The fine hairs on my arms lifted. Something was happening.

I could do this. I could call to the earth and sky and have them answer. I could sing to the stars, to the sand. All the daily indecision, the nagging uncertainties accumulating in my gut as I muddled my way through life, fell away. I stretched my arms higher, fingertips reaching for the heavens, something inside me reaching out as well. Calling.

Commanding.

I shouted the words with all the air in my lungs, forcing the sky and the wand and the sand to do my bidding. And they answered.

A titanic crack of lightning split the air, leaping from the cloudless sky to strike the wand. Half-blinded and deafened by the bolt, I threw my head back and laughed aloud. It worked! I was Zeus and Thor, striking with the fury of the storm. I wanted to sing with the joy of it. I wanted to grab Griffin, drag him back to the tent, and make love to him the rest of the night.

"Did anything happen?" Christine asked, striding past me to the statue.

Well, of course she didn't appreciate my accomplishment. Griffin, on the other hand, stared at me with a slightly stunned expression on his face, his lips parted in an unconscious gesture of desire.

At my heated look, he seemed to remember himself, swallowing and shifting his stance. "We should help Christine."

He was right, and there would be plenty of time later tonight. Still, it took me a moment to compose myself.

Christine's bellow helped kill the last of my ardor. "Whyborne! Look here!"

Griffin and I hurried to join Christine at the base of the statue. A small compartment had opened in the midst of a block, which before appeared perfectly whole and smooth.

Christine crouched in front of the compartment. "Hold the lantern for me," she said. "See if you can't shine the light on whatever's inside."

Only one object lay within. Christine reached inside and carefully drew out a stone palette thickly inscribed with hieroglyphs.

I peered over her shoulder to scan the inscription. "This seems to be a fairly straightforward set of directions. I'm not certain what the illustration is intended to depict, but this should guide us to the fane."

Christine rose to her feet, an expression of triumph transforming her features. "Good show, Whyborne. We've done it. We'll mount an expedition as soon as possible. My reputation will be made, and we'll keep the Lapidem out of Nitocris's hands."

"You're wrong," Daphne said.

I started badly, having heard no steps or seen any approaching light. Lifting the lantern, I illuminated her slim form, the flames lending false color to her pale skin and hair. Iskander knelt at her feet, his face gray with fear, restrained by the taloned hands of the ghūls on either side of him.

"What?" I said through numb lips. The scene made no sense. Daphne couldn't be in league with Nitocris and the ghūls. It simply wasn't possible.

But she drew a knife from her belt and held its edge against Iskander's throat. "The map, Christine," she said calmly. "Or I'll cut his throat and you can watch him die."

CHAPTER 16

"D-Daphne?" Christine asked in bewildered horror. "Wh-what are you doing?"

"I'm holding a knife to Mr. Barnett's throat," Daphne replied, as calmly as she had discussed our work before. "As to what I'm going to do next, it entirely depends on whether or not you give me the map."

I found my voice. "You...the ghūls...you knew?" I stammered.

"Of course, Dr. Whyborne." Her lip twisted, revealing her white teeth. "Just as I divined your true nature. A pity you didn't prove more amenable. I would have made a valuable friend."

"What the hell are you going on about?" Christine demanded. She started forward, but Daphne pressed the knife against Iskander's skin. A drop of blood traced the contours of his throat, and Christine froze.

"Not a step closer, unless it's to hand over the map," Daphne warned. Any lingering doubts vanished. It was apparent she would cut Iskander's throat without hesitation.

How did I misjudge her this badly? How had I worked beside her day after day and never guessed?

"You've allied with the ghūls and betrayed your own sister," Griffin said. He'd gone pale beneath his tan, but his voice held steady. "Why? What did Nitocris promise you?"

"Promise me?" Daphne gave him a feral grin. "She didn't need to promise me anything. I am Nitocris."

Dread began to seep past my shock. "That's not possible. She was human. Nephren-ka's chief wife, and even if she's been brought back from the dead, it would have been a bodily resurrection..."

But that had been an assumption on my part, hadn't it? Based on what Blackbyrne did with the spells from the tomb. I didn't even consider any other possibilities.

"I'm disappointed in you," she said, shaking her head in mock-sadness. "But you're right about the first part. Nitocris was human. A powerful sorceress and Queen of Ghūls. But her husband the pharaoh feared her strength. He hid his secrets from her, and when that didn't prove enough, he murdered her. But he didn't know she'd already made certain arrangements with those from Outside."

The hairs on the back of my neck tried to stand up. If any part of Nitocris truly lingered Outside...whatever came back couldn't be human. Not any more.

"Do you know, I owe it all to you, Christine," she said, a mocking edge to her voice. "If not for your decision to dig here, I would never have delved into the legends. Never read the name of Nitocris. But I did. I studied the blackest of books, things which would make your hair curl to even hear the title spoken aloud. And I learned. Her husband tortured and abused her, just as that pig the graf did to me."

Christine's lips parted, but no sound came out. Anger flashed in Daphne's eyes. "Oh, don't look shocked, sister. Shall I speak of the beatings, the chokings, the cruelty, stuck in a moldering castle far from any help? And what help would come to defend a wife against her husband? No court, no man, would ever lift a finger."

Christine found her voice. "Daphne, no—"

"I read the books. I heard her whispering from the other side of reality. The Queen of the Ghūls, banished to the Outside. But not forever. Just a few simple things would bring her back. To defile the bones of my husband's forefathers, the bastards who gave him life, locked away in the tomb beneath the castle." Daphne's mouth twisted into a snarl like a feral dog's. "I almost vomited when I first tasted their rotted flesh, but in time it grew sweet. And Adolph himself, of course. His death opened the way. We drank his blood once she joined me, ate his newly cold meat to sustain us."

Christine turned white as a corpse herself. "Daphne, this isn't you speaking. This isn't—"

The façade of calm shattered. "And how would you know?" Daphne snarled. In the flickering light, she looked utterly deranged, and the drops of blood on Iskander's brown skin grew to a trickle. "You *left!* You left me at home and ruined my only means of escape. Do you really think I wanted to *reconcile* with you? This was my fallback plan. I'd hoped to find the secret hidden amidst the treasures at your museum. But my agent failed."

I swallowed tightly. "He would have anyway. The ostracon didn't give the location."

"And Halabi?" Griffin asked. "You killed him before he could warn Christine."

"He was one of mine. Taken as a child and raised in the catacombs under Cairo. My ghūls were the only family he ever knew, but he chose to betray us." She shrugged negligently. "None of which matters now. The map, or Iskander dies. Your choice."

"H-How do I know you won't kill him anyway?" Christine asked, her voice rough with strain.

"This is how," Griffin said. The cold click of his revolver sounded loud in the night air. "Let Iskander go, or I'll put a bullet in your brain."

"Will you?" Daphne stared challengingly back at him. "Will you really kill Christine's only sister before her very eyes?"

Griffin made no reply.

"All right." Christine said. "The map for Iskander. But betray the deal, and I'll gladly shoot you myself."

"Now that, I can believe," Daphne said with a feral grin. "Bring the map to me."

Christine swallowed hard, but her steps remained firm as she slowly approached the Ghūl Queen. My mind raced, and I tried to think what to do, how to stop this and save Iskander both. But no plan came to mind—any attack on Daphne or her minions would end with Iskander dead.

Once Christine came within arm's reach, one of the ghūls released its grip on Iskander and held out a taloned hand. Its jackal-like maw gaped, betraying a lolling tongue and fearsome teeth.

"No. Let Iskander go first," Christine ordered. "Do so, and I'll swear I'll give you the map. You know I don't make promises I don't keep"

Daphne's black eyes glittered like the shiny backs of beetles. "Very well."

She removed the knife from Iskander's throat, and the ghūl clutching his arm sent him sprawling across the sand. At the same moment, its companion lunged forward, snatching the palette from Christine's grasp.

Iskander and Christine both stumbled back. She put a steadying hand to his arm as he scrambled to his feet beside her. "I'm glad we finally had this chance to talk, Christine," Daphne said. "But I have more important things to attend to now. Goodbye."

She turned and walked away into the night, the darkness swallowing her almost instantly. There came the sound of claws on the sand, and a host of eyes replaced her slim figure, reflecting the light of the lantern like those of animals.

The pack of ghūls drew closer, growling low. Griffin leveled his revolver, and Christine her rifle. Iskander drew a pair of knives, like the one he'd used to kill the scorpion our first day here.

I lunged at the statue of Heka, scrambling onto the plinth. The ruby eyes of the serpent wand glittered at me. I stretched up to grasp it—I couldn't leave it—

"Whyborne, we have to retreat!" Griffin shouted.

My fingers scraped the etched metal scales, and for an instant I feared the wand wouldn't come loose. Then it popped free, and I tumbled back, almost on top of Griffin.

Christine fired, and the oncoming ghūls shied. "Now, go!" she ordered.

We sprinted through the gap in the wall and toward the heart of the valley. Behind us, the ghūls sent up a chilling series of barks and howls. How long could we outrace them?

"Retreat to the tomb!" Christine shouted back over her shoulder. "At least there they won't be able to come at us from all sides!"

We raced through the excavation site. The light of the moon cast a maze of confusing shadows from the scaffolding. My foot caught on a rope or stone, and I sprawled heavily over the sand on my belly. I rolled over onto my side, just in time to see a ghūl rushing at me on all fours, its maw gaping open.

"Ival!" Griffin shouted.

I flung up my arm to hold back the slavering jaws. Its hot breath ghosted over me, and I braced myself against the puncture of teeth through my flesh.

Before the jaws could close, a knife sprouted suddenly from between its eyes. It collapsed heavily on top of me, limbs still twitching.

Iskander stood there, his eyes narrowed in concentration, his hand still poised from throwing the knife.

I shoved the stinking carcass off. Griffin took my arm and pulled me to my feet.

"Thank you!" I gasped.

Griffin shoved me in the direction of the wadi. "Go, go!"

He and Christine paused to fire off shots. Two ghūls fell, and the rest scattered, although their shapes still showed in the clear light of the moon. More crawled down from the tumbled northern slopes. God, how many were there?

We took advantage of the momentary retreat to put as much

ground as possible between us and the ghūls. As we passed through the camp, I snatched up a spare lantern from our dinner table. Despite my long legs, I wasn't much of a runner, and Christine and Iskander soon passed me. Griffin reached for me, but I shouted, "Keep going! I'll take rear guard!"

I stumbled several times on the rocky surface of the canyon floor. The walls began to close in on either side as we neared the blind end. I thought I glimpsed shapes moving on the edges of the cliffs high above.

"Look out—they're right behind you!" Christine shouted. Griffin stopped dead, and I almost collided with him.

"No!" I gripped his arm with one hand. Three of the beasts were almost on us. Their teeth gleamed in the night, and their rank musk fouled the air.

I flung the unlit lantern at them with all of my strength. It shattered, splashing oil on the tightly packed creatures. The lead one jerked back, pawing frantically at its eyes.

I called out the secret name of fire and put the spark to their oil-soaked fur.

The things went up like torches, their screams so horribly human I froze in horror. The burning ghūls thrashed, momentarily forming a blockade against the others coming up the wadi.

"Come," Griffin said, his hand closing firmly on my wrist.

The entrance to the tomb appeared at the very end of the canyon, gaping like a dark mouth. A ghūl leapt down from the rocks above it, but Christine shot the thing, and it thudded to the ground dead.

We scrambled into the narrow entrance, and Christine and Griffin took up position to either side. "How much ammunition do you have?" Christine asked him.

"Only the five shots remaining in my gun" Griffin's expression betrayed his worry. "I've no idea how many of them there are, but if they keep coming, we may find ourselves overwhelmed."

"I fear you're right," Christine agreed. "Look."

Dark shapes prowled up the wadi, some of them clambering amidst the tumbled rocks. They paused at the remains of their burned brethren, and the crack of bone and wet rip of flesh drifted to us.

"They're *eating* the bodies," Iskander gasped. What the poor man thought of all this, I couldn't even imagine. At least he hadn't collapsed into a gibbering heap.

"Can we go deeper into the tomb?" Griffin asked. "Is there a door or something we might blockade against them?"

"They have human intelligence—what if they trap us inside?" Christine countered.

I stared at the approaching ghûls. The narrow canyon at least acted like a funnel, trapping them.

Could it funnel something else as well?

"Get back," I said. "I have an idea."

"Whyborne?" Griffin asked. But Christine grabbed a handful of his coat and dragged him away from the tomb entrance.

"Whatever you have in mind, do it," she ordered.

I had nothing with which to draw a sigil. But Griffin believed I no longer needed to, and perhaps with the assistance of the wand, I could prove him right.

Stepping to the entrance of the tomb, I stared down at the ghûls. They no longer ran but loped steadily, their eyes glowing the sickly greenish-white of corpse candles. Jaws gaped, revealing teeth stained with blood and the ragged flesh of the ghûls they'd just devoured. Some came on all fours and others on two legs, their golden-brown fur matted with the filth of the grave.

I lifted the wand in my hands. Once again, I formed the conduit between sky and earth. I chanted the words, felt the world respond like a well-trained dog coming to heel. Forces gathered, the air growing heavy. The ghûls lifted their snouts, snarling at me as the first eddies of wind stirred their dirty fur.

Perhaps one of them realized what I intended. It let out an angry bark, which might almost have been a command. The pack surged forward, breaking into a gallop. They closed in on me, their breath hot and foul.

I shouted the command, and the universe obeyed. Wind screamed down the canyon from my position, the narrow cliffs funneling it into a wrathful hurricane. A great wall of sand rose with it, blasting the ghûls. The roar of the gale quickly overwhelmed their cries of pain, and their glowing eyes vanished behind the great billowing cloud of choking dust.

I lowered my arms slowly, my heart pounding. Had it been enough?

I sensed Griffin behind me, his revolver at the ready. The wind died, and the dust cloud slowly cleared. The wadi stretched empty before us.

"They've retreated, at least for now," he said. "But we'd best stay here until dawn, in case they're still lurking about."

"Good show," Christine said, clapping me on the shoulder. "Quick thinking, Whyborne."

"Thank you," I said, feeling rather pleased with myself. I turned to go back inside the tomb, and found Iskander staring at me with an expression of utter shock. His gaze shifted to Christine, to Griffin, and back to me.

"Pardon me," he said, "but would someone please tell me what the bloody hell is going on?"

After what seemed like endless hours of darkness, we left the tomb with the sunrise. The eastern sky glowed pink as the inside of a shell, the air clear and cool. The only traces remaining of the ghūls were the chewed bones of those we'd killed.

Iskander stilled looked dazed, as well he might. The three of us spent much of the remainder of the night explaining things to him. The existence of the occult, the ghūls, and a bit of our previous brushes with horrors from beyond. Not to mention my own arcane abilities. Truthfully, he'd handled it far better than I would have expected. Or perhaps the poor fellow was still in shock.

The wind I'd summoned had the unfortunate effect of damaging the tents and blowing over our table and chairs. As we walked among the debris, Christine said, "I can't believe this. Why would Daphne *do* such a thing?"

I winced. Poor Christine. To have learned their entire reconciliation had been nothing but a sham must wound both her heart and her pride. "I'm sorry. I know you must be feeling hurt."

"I'm feeling *angry*," she snapped back. "How could any sister of mine be so stupid as to go and get herself possessed by some—some monstrous entity from the Outside?"

"Do you think she spoke the truth about her husband?" I asked hesitantly.

"Of course. Don't be naïve. But why didn't she write to me and ask for help?"

"I doubt the graf allowed her to," Griffin said. He straightened one of the chairs which had blown over. "In my time with the Pinkertons, I once tracked a man who'd fled west after murdering his wife. When her family hired the agency to bring him to justice, she hadn't contacted them for four years, and they even lived in a nearby town. She had no friends, and her children were kept equally as isolated. Their oldest son attested his father would fly into a jealous rage upon seeing his wife speak even to another woman. If Daphne's husband was of the same ilk, her long silence may not, in fact, have been by choice."

"Oh." The stricken expression on Christine's face hurt to see.

How had Daphne felt, living in an isolated castle with a violent savage for a husband, cut off from any source of help? Had she believed she'd escaped the pain of her parents' house, only to find herself in an even more horrid situation? Surely after years of such suffering, the hint of escape offered by the blasphemous books she'd read must have seemed a godsend.

Then I remembered her description of eating the dead of the family crypt, and my stomach turned. Had she even been sane by then?

"We'll save her," I vowed. "I don't know how, yet, but we'll save her and send Nitocris screaming back into the void."

Christine's expression eased back into one of confidence. "Yes. Yes, of course we will. You'll find something in your book."

Iskander seemed more doubtful. "Daphne is gone," he pointed out. "Fled across the desert with our only map. How do you even propose to find her?"

"That many ghūls had to leave tracks," Griffin said. "If we hurry, I believe I can follow their trail."

"I spotted some of the camels wandering loose in the valley—they must have panicked last night." Christine put her hands on her hips and surveyed the camp. "At least the ghūls didn't eat them. We'll need to round up the camels and gather supplies for what might be a long trip."

Turning to Iskander, she said, "Kander, this is beyond your usual job description. You didn't sign up for fighting ghūls, let alone striking out across the desert with no idea how many days' journey lies ahead of us. I won't blame you if you wish to return to Cairo."

He straightened his shoulders and lifted his chin. In the morning light, he looked like Ramses or Amenhotep, incongruously dressed in a modern suit instead of folded linen. "I'm with you, Christine. Always."

She smiled and clapped him on the arm. "Good man. You can help Whyborne gather our things here in the camp while Griffin and I find the camels."

Chapter 17

A FEW HOURS later, we left the site behind.

We could carry enough water for a week, which meant if the fane didn't lie within four days of the necropolis, we would have to turn back. The very possibility our journey might last so long made me wish for the security of life in a tent, let alone anything more civilized.

As I checked over the saddle on my camel, the ridiculous beast began its usual attempts to eat my fez. I pushed its big head aside, reflecting I'd best get used to keeping a close watch on my hat, since I'd be in close quarters with the camel for the next several days at least.

"What's its name?" I asked Iskander. "The camel, I mean."

Iskander shrugged. "It doesn't have one, as far as I know. Call it whatever you want."

"Daisy," I decided, after a quick glance to confirm it a female.

"What an absurd name for a camel," Christine said as her mount heaved to its feet.

"Daisy and I don't care," I replied loftily. We also ignored the roll of Griffin's eyes.

We departed shortly thereafter, riding past the statue of Heka, which kept watch on the western desert. The land of the dead lay in the west, according to legend. Perhaps it was no accident Nephren-ka built the fane in that direction.

Griffin rode in the lead, pausing occasionally to dismount and inspect the ground. The red lands were harsh and uncompromising, a barren waste of sand and rock. Even so, as he'd said, a large group moving together could not help but leave signs. The ghūls supposedly shunned the light of the sun, but was it a preference rather than a necessity? If they only had the night hours to travel, could we catch up with them before they reached the fane?

I had far too many questions and not nearly enough answers. Particularly since I'd promised to somehow save Daphne.

Daphne. God. Had there been some sign, some clue, as to her true nature? She'd thoroughly fooled us all. Not even Griffin suspected. Perhaps I should have wondered more when the amulet of Wepwawet, guardian of the dead, burned her. But I'd already been thrown off by the strangeness of the wand, and put it down to something similar.

She'd seemed...normal. I'd *liked* her, her intelligence, her sense of humor.

No wonder she'd shown such mastery of the hieroglyphs. They recorded the native tongue of the creature possessing her. I have should have questioned further, should have asked exactly how she'd come about her knowledge, precisely what journals she'd read. But there had seemed no reason. How could I have guessed her competency came from such a terrible source?

How must Christine feel about all of this? She sat straight in her saddle and betrayed no signs of weariness or grief, save for a slight tightness around the corners of her mouth. Was she truly as composed as she seemed? Doubtful. Especially after hearing the truth about Daphne's life in Wisborg.

Had it been purely Daphne's decision to look into the stories of Nitocris, or had more sinister forces motivated her? The legend had lingered suspiciously long for someone who died four millennia ago. Nitocris's name, carved on the stone couch in the catacombs below Cairo, dated more than two thousand years after her death. The journals seemed to indicate she had returned from the Outside more than once. Possessed other women, led her ghūls, and...what? Died? Been defeated in some way?

Nephren-ka's necropolis and its secrets had been lost, deliberately obliterated from history. If he murdered Nitocris well before his own death, she wouldn't know where he'd been buried. Egypt was a vast place; she had spent centuries in fruitless search for tomb and fane, returning through the veil again and again.

And now what she desired finally lay within her grasp.

"I don't understand something," I said aloud. "We assumed from the beginning Nitocris wanted to keep us away from the necropolis in order to have the site to herself and discover the location of the fane. But in reality, she used us to find the map."

"Yes, yes, no need to rub it in," Christine snapped.

I held back a retort. I'd probably be testy as well, if I'd just discovered my sister had turned into a flesh-eating maniac. "So who were the men who attacked us at the hotel? Who tried to kill Daphne? Who sabotaged the ropes, destroyed my notes, and left the cobra in our tent? All of those attacks were aimed at stopping the excavation, which was the last thing Nitocris wanted."

"I wondered the same thing," Griffin said with an approving nod in my direction. "I thought to bring it up around the campfire tonight, but we might as well hash it out now. Unfortunately, there's only one conclusion."

Iskander looked alarmed. "What do you mean?"

Griffin gazed at him coolly. "There is more than one force at work here. Someone else is bent on stopping Nitocris. And if they think we're her allies, even unknowingly so, they won't hesitate to kill us."

That evening, I found myself wishing I'd never complained about the tents. We brought two smaller tents with us, but it took too much time to set them up and take them down without need. Instead, we spread our blankets on the sand and pillowed our heads on our saddles. My skin itched from dried sweat and dust, and I smelled no different from Daisy. No water could be spared for washing or shaving, and I wondered how long I could endure it before going mad.

Despite the horrid conditions, I immediately fell asleep due to my exhaustion. The rocking gait of my camel filled my dreams. I held the *Arcanorum* in my hands, searching desperately for something to save Daphne. But none of the words made sense, and I realized with horror I had forgotten how to read.

I jerked awake. The night was cold and silent, save for the rustling of the camels. The millions of stars glittered overhead like staring eyes. My throat ached with dryness and my eyes felt gritty. I sat up and took a small swallow from my canteen.

Griffin sat watch, his back to the glowing embers of the camel dung fire. "Bad dream?" he asked sympathetically.

I nodded. Sleep seemed impossibly far away now. I joined him at the fire, sitting close enough for our shoulders to touch. He smelled of sweat and camel, but so did I. Thank heavens I had him with me in this awful desert. I couldn't imagine what I would have done otherwise.

As I relaxed and the dream faded, weariness crept cautiously back. Perhaps I dozed sitting up, because my eyes jolted open when Griffin's shoulder tensed.

"What is it?" I asked.

"Movement," he murmured. "To the west."

From the direction of the deeper desert. The direction Daphne had fled.

The camels snorted and shifted restlessly, but we'd hobbled them to prevent their wandering. I became acutely aware of every beat of my heart, every half-held breath. At first, nothing stirred to disturb the endless waste of sand. Then came a shadow, slinking from one dune to the next. Another followed. And another.

"Damn it." Griffin scrambled to his feet. "Wake up! To arms! To arms!"

Christine and Iskander scrambled out of their blankets. We'd all slept in our ordinary clothes and with our weapons at hand. Snatching up her rifle, Christine ordered, "Whyborne! Stoke the fire."

I hastened to do as she asked. Although rocks partially shielded our camp, we remained vulnerable to attack from three sides. Iskander drew a pair of knives and stood watching the north for any ghūls circling around. Christine and Griffin took up positions facing west and south.

As the fire leapt up, I cast about for something I might use as a weapon. Nothing presented itself, save for the wand.

It had certainly been useful before, when summoning the wind. But now? There was no wadi to funnel the wind into a gale; I might inconvenience the ghūls, but I doubted I could drive them back. Could I do something with the sand? Or fire? Or—

An eerie howl split the night. There was no time left to dither about, so I snatched up the wand.

The crack of Christine's rifle put an end to the howl. Shapes loped out of the darkness, eyes glowing like pallid fire. The sick stench of rot tainted the clean desert air, and my stomach tightened.

Iskander's knives flashed orange in the firelight. With a howl of his own, he met a charging ghūl. One blade slashed across its face; when it reared back on its hind legs, he stabbed the other into its heart.

Griffin fired, catching a ghūl through the shoulder. Its blood sprayed, black in the moonlight. Two more charged him. He shot one in the face, but the other darted around him and came at me.

My mind automatically went to the first spell I'd ever learned. Thrusting the wand out in front of me, I called out the name of fire and hoped the ghūl didn't rip my arm off.

The wand writhed, the serpent's head flashing red-hot even though the metal against my hand remained cool. Flames burst into being, wreathed around the gemstone eyes and flared hood. I flailed at the ghūl; the wand shuddered as it struck flesh. Skin sizzled against the hot metal, accompanied by the smell of burning hair. The ghūl shrieked and scrambled back, clawing at its seared shoulder.

"Whyborne!" Griffin yelled. I twisted about, only to find the muzzle of a ghūl leering practically in my face. I tried to swing the wand, but the ghūl slammed into my chest. I struck the ground hard enough to drive the wind from my lungs. I lay stunned and gasping for breath, the moon bright in my eyes.

Then the ghūl loomed over me, cutting off its light.

Clawed hands came down to either side of my shoulders, and its weight settled on my legs, trapping me. A demoniac grin split its muzzle, growing larger and larger, until its jaws gaped to reveal rows of teeth. Hot, fetid breath gusted into my face.

I jammed the wand into its gaping mouth even as it lunged to bite. Teeth scraped and broke against the metal, a terrible sound. I spoke the name of fire. Flesh sizzled, and the creature tried to scream past the rod of heated metal in its mouth. It flailed madly on top of me, and something hissed and popped inside its skull. A cry of disgust escaped me, and I thrashed, trying to shove its weight aside.

Griffin kicked the ghūl savagely, rolling its dying body off of me. He'd dropped his revolver and held the sword cane in his hand, the blade dark with blood. Iskander fought with his knives, like some sort of dervish, fending ghūls off of Christine. She calmly sighted through the rifle and picked off as many as she could at a distance.

Griffin hauled me to my feet, and we fell back-to-back. Another ghūl rushed at me, but shied away at the sight of the glowing end of the wand. Behind me, I half-felt, half-sensed Griffin's movements as he fended off another. A few more tested our defenses, but together we wove a wall of magic and steel none of them dared try to breach.

There came a long, chilling howl from somewhere across the desert. As if it had been a command, the ghūls broke off their attack. With a few final snarls and barks, they vanished back into the night, leaving behind only their dead. Christine fired after them twice more, before lowering her rifle.

"They'll be back," she predicted. "Maybe not tonight, but soon."

"Agreed." Iskander had removed his coat and vest before lying down to sleep, and his white shirt contrasted sharply with his bronze skin. Well, where it wasn't dyed with drying blood, anyway. Nodding at Griffin and I, he said, "I couldn't help but notice how well you two chaps fought together. I suppose you must practice a great deal, to be so attuned to one another's movements?"

My face grew uncomfortably hot, and I prayed he couldn't make it out in the firelight.

"Yes," Griffin said. "We practice every chance we have."

Christine turned her laugh into a cough, although not very successfully. "Griffin, help Iskander and I drag the bodies out of the camp. Whyborne, check on the camels."

The camels were understandably nervous, and I found the body of a ghūl among them, apparently kicked and bitten to death by the animals. My fez still lay beside my pallet, so Daisy only mournfully mouthed my hair while I checked her over for wounds. Fortunately, neither she nor the other camels appeared injured.

We regrouped by the fire. "Your skills are most impressive," Griffin said to Iskander. "Where did you learn to fight in such a manner?"

Iskander hesitated, as if uncertain whether to answer. "My mum, actually."

"Really?" Christine asked. "You never mentioned it!"

"It isn't something I speak of often. Or ever." He stared east, where the sun would soon rise, like an ancient pharaoh surveying his lands. "She came from a tribe of nomads—not Bedouin, although most wouldn't know the difference. Desert dwellers who roamed from oasis to oasis, nothing more than a whispered rumor to those in the black land along the Nile. Even when she settled down to become as proper an Englishwoman as they would allow someone of her heritage, she still danced with the knives. Just in case, she always said."

How extraordinary. I imagined she didn't have an easy time of it in England. "In case what?" I asked.

He shook his head. "She never said. But she taught me everything she knew."

"My mother taught me how to shoot," Christine said, although I caught the note of sadness in her voice. Thinking no doubt about her mother's drunkenness, and her childhood, and Daphne.

Iskander smiled at her. "Perhaps we have even more in common than we realize."

Christine's face softened, and a tiny smile of her own touched the corner of her mouth. "Perhaps we do."

I glanced away, wishing I might gracefully take my leave. With nothing in a hundred miles, I had no real excuse to do anything save sit there like a lump, however.

Griffin cleared his throat. Christine and Iskander jumped, turning away from each other with identical guilty looks. I refrained from rolling my eyes, although it took some effort.

"Dawn isn't far off," Griffin said. "We might as well get ready to move again."

I picked up my blanket and shook the sand out. "We can't be too far behind if Daphne sent her ghūls back to attack us."

"Let's hope you're right." Griffin began the task of refilling our canteens from the water skins. "If we can come upon them during the day, perhaps we can find some way of capturing her."

"I'll continue to look through the *Arcanorum*," I promised. "There must be some spell in there about forcing an entity from the Outside to return whence it came."

Iskander looked troubled at my words, and I wondered if he doubted either our ability to capture Daphne or mine to exorcise her. But he said nothing, only collected the saddles and went to ready the camels.

Chapter 18

Unfortunately, it seemed fate and the weather had other plans.

The morning's travel continued as it had the past two days: the endless rocking motion of the camels, the tedious stretch of lifeless desert, the cloudless sky broken only by the occasional vulture drifting by. But as the sun reached its zenith and the glare threatened to blind me, Christine reined her camel to a sharp halt. Shading her eyes with her hand, she peered across the landscape. "Do you see that, Kander?"

I squinted at the horizon. It appeared oddly indistinct, more of a smudge than the usual clarity I'd come to expect from the desert air.

Iskander's face took on a grim look. "Sandstorm."

"A what?" I asked.

"Blast it!" Christine stood up in her stirrups and scanned our surroundings. "We need to get to the highest ground we can find. A rock or some sort of shelter would be ideal, but we'll have to make do with what we can get."

Christine kicked her camel into a fast trot, making for a slight rise not far away. Daisy bolted after, and I grabbed my fez to keep it from flying off my head. "What's happening?" I shouted at Iskander.

He glanced back at me. "A sandstorm. The camels are well adapted to survive them. We aren't. We need to get the tents up as soon as possible."

It didn't sound promising. I peered again at the horizon and was shocked to discover the smudge had grown. Within a few minutes, it towered over the landscape, a huge wall of red dust, rolling toward us like a great wave.

As soon as we reached the top of the rise, we dismounted. "Kander, Griffin, help me with the tents!" Christine barked. "Whyborne, get our baggage off the camels, especially the water."

I did as she ordered. The camels seemed to sense what was happening, because Daisy made only a half-hearted attempt to snatch my hat. The tents we'd brought were much smaller than those we'd lived in at the dig site, each barely large enough for two people and their baggage. "Make sure the stakes are anchored," Christine ordered. "Or else the whole thing will come down and you'll risk being buried."

As quickly as we worked, the storm was still almost on us by the time we had the tents up. "If dust gets in the tent, pull your blanket up over your mouth and nose and keep your eyes closed," Christine ordered as she hurled our belongings into the tents. "Damnation!"

The first stinging particles reached us ahead of the main storm, which had grown into a massive wall of red filling the horizon. Griffin grabbed my wrist and pulled me into one of the tents with him.

I shoved bags and water skins aside, clearing space for us as best I could, while he tied the flaps tightly shut. My head brushed the canvas ceiling, and there wasn't enough room to lie down without bending my legs. The ropes sang in the wind, and I desperately hoped nothing gave way. Sand hissed against the canvas, and all light vanished, leaving us in utter darkness.

"Do you think the camels will be all right?" I asked.

"They'll be fine. As Iskander said, they're made for life in this inhospitable clime."

Lightning sounded not far off, followed by a dull roar of thunder. I shivered. "How long do you think it will last?"

"I don't know."

"Do you think—"

Griffin silenced my question by pressing his lips against mine. When the kiss finished, he murmured, "I think you should relax. The storm will last as long as it lasts."

He cupped my face with his hand, urging me closer. Our stubble scratched and caught like two sheets of sandpaper, but his mouth was still soft and warm.

"Hoping for some practice?" I asked when our lips parted.

He chuckled. "Always."

In the darkness, trapped in our little tent, there wasn't anything of a practical nature to be done. I stripped off my coat and vest, down to my shirtsleeves, and he did the same.

There wasn't much room, but we curled up on our sides facing each other, my right leg thrown over his hip. "I'm sorry we quarreled back at camp," he whispered. "Over the wand. If I worry for you, fear for you, take it as a measure of how much I care."

He undid the buttons on my shirt as he spoke. Sliding his hand through the gap in my shirtfront, he teased first one nipple then the other, obliterating any response I might have made save for a gasp of pleasure. At least the wind and blowing sand would muffle anything but a shout.

I traced his side with my fingers, before dipping down to rub my palm against the hard flesh pressing against the front of his trousers. "Right now the only wand I'm interested in is this one."

He snorted. "That's my man of words."

"Oh, hush."

"Make me."

I kissed him, deep and hungry. He returned the favor, sliding his tongue past my lips. I sucked on it, hard, drawing a muffled groan from him. His hands left off touching my chest and moved to undo the buttons on my trousers.

I did the same for him, drawing out the rigid length of his cock. The feel of his fingers on my member sent a shudder of ecstasy through me. The rough pad of his thumb slid across the tip, smearing the liquid there. I wrapped my hand firmly around his length and began to stroke him, silken skin sliding around the glans.

We were filthy with sweat and dust, unshaven and unwashed. But none of it mattered, just his lips on mine, the raggedness of his breathing. The firm stroke of his hand on my length, tugging me to the next height of pleasure and the next. His hip under my thigh, tensing as he pumped into my hand.

He broke apart from our kiss, gasping my name, a shudder going through him. "Yes," I growled, pressing my forehead against his.

"Ival," he groaned, and his hand tightened on me, growing more insistent. I let go of his softening member and gripped his shoulder, pushing against him as he tugged on me, until I could stand it no more, pleasure cresting and breaking like a wave as I spent myself.

We lay in the darkness, listening to the sand on the canvas, the moan of the wind around the ropes, as our breathing evened out. I reached blindly for my coat and fumbled out a handkerchief, using it to wipe away the traces of our passion.

"Relaxed now?" Griffin teased.

I settled my head on his shoulder. "Yes. Thank you."

He chuckled and pressed a kiss to my forehead. "Any time, my love. Any time."

~ * ~

Many hours later, we emerged into a world of dust. The air was crystal clear, but our tents sagged beneath the weight of accumulated sand. The camels, as predicted, were fine, although not happy about being roused. As Iskander checked them over, Griffin walked to the western slope of the rise and stared out. "We have a problem," he said.

I joined him. "The tracks," I realized in dismay. "The sandstorm blotted out all trace of the ghūls' passage."

Griffin let out a long sigh. "Yes. I don't know how we're to find Daphne now."

I stared out across the bleak, unforgiving landscape, hoping for a clue. There had to be something, didn't there? But Griffin was the expert in such matters. If he couldn't find a solution, how could the rest of us? "What do we do?"

"We can't abandon Daphne." Christine joined us, glaring out over the desert as if it had personally arranged the sandstorm to thwart her.

"No one's said any such thing," Griffin replied. "I suggest we continue on in this direction and hope to find either tracks, or some indication we're near the fane."

"It can't be much farther," Christine agreed. "Nephren-ka made this journey many times himself, and he wouldn't have wished to abandon his kingdom for long, lest the priests begin to conspire against him. We're bound to find Daphne soon."

I felt less certain. A thousand miles of sand and rock stretched out before us, and Daphne could be anywhere among it. But what other option did we have? "How many days of water are left?" I asked.

Christine's mouth flattened. "We can continue another day before we have no choice but to turn back," she admitted reluctantly. "Unless we find an oasis."

Gazing out over the lifeless desert, an oasis seemed an unlikely stroke of luck indeed. But I didn't wish to dash whatever shreds of hope she still clung to. "I'll retrieve our things from the tents," I offered.

Christine nodded. I left her and Griffin discussing the situation. Our belongings had become jumbled in the mad rush earlier, some of our things ending up in Christine and Iskander's tent, and vice versa. As I pulled out one of Iskander's packs, the strap came loose with a loud rip.

"Drat," I muttered, going down on one knee to inspect it. As luck would have it, the entire seam had torn, dumping clothes and personal articles everywhere. At least it wasn't Christine's underthings I needed to sort through.

I inspected the seam, trying to determine if it could be fixed quickly, or if I needed to transfer his things to other packs. The corner of what looked like a native robe hung out of tear, covered in embroidery.

What on earth?

I pulled the robe out of the pack. Embroidered sigils and symbols, many of which I recognized from the *Arcanorum*, covered the entire surface. It was the same robe as the one worn by the mysterious men who had threatened us at the hotel and later tried to kill Daphne.

"What are you doing?" Iskander demanded. He hurried toward me, a look of horror on his face and his hands curling into fists. "That's mine!"

"Griffin was right." I rose to my feet, and the wind caught the robe still clutched in my hand, unfurling it for all to see. "You've been in league with our enemies all along."

Profound silence settled over our camp, as if the desert itself held its breath. Iskander froze a few feet from me, staring fixedly at the robe as if he could somehow make it vanish. Griffin drew his revolver and held it loosely at his side. As for Christine, she looked from the robe to Iskander, then back at the robe.

"What the devil is that doing in your pack?" she asked, but the words lacked her usual force.

Iskander tore his gaze from its folds at last and turned to Christine. "I-I can explain. Just give me a chance."

"Can you?" Griffin asked coolly. "Because the robes are identical to those of the men who've been trying to kill us."

Iskander held up his hands, as if to fend away Griffin's accusations. "I know how it must seem."

"What it seems like is you've been in league with these persons all along." Griffin watched Iskander through narrowed eyes. "The night Daphne awoke to find an assassin cutting his way into the tent—you weren't really knocked on the head. You allowed him into the camp, didn't you?"

Iskander closed his eyes, as if at some pain. "I...I did."

"You knew about Nitocris and the ghūls all along."

Christine gasped. Iskander's eyes flew open again, and he aimed a beseeching look at her. "No! That is, I knew about the ghūls, yes. And things about Daphne caused me to me wonder—her uncanny knowledge of the hieroglyphs, her pallor, other signs. But I didn't know for certain until she touched the amulet of Wepwawet and the god burned her."

No wonder the man seemed to adjust to the reality of ghūls and sorcery so easily. He'd only pretended to be surprised the night in the tomb. And to think I'd admired his resilience.

Christine's posture went absolutely rigid, her lips tight against her teeth. "Explain yourself, Mr. Barnett."

"My mother. The reason she knew how to wield the knives, the reason she taught me, was because our family fights ghūls." He laughed without humor. "Believe me, I know how mad it sounds. I thought it was mad myself, when she would tell me the stories as a child. She said we were the Wolves of the West, sworn to guard the dead from the hunger of the ghūls. Worshippers of Wepwawet, driven into the desert when the followers of Allah came. As time went on, our numbers shrank, until only a handful remained. To survive, we became *shardah*. A mirage."

"That doesn't sound like a dialect I know," I said. "Is it some form of Arabic, or—"

"Whyborne, please," Griffin interrupted.

"Oh. Yes. Sorry."

Iskander ignored my questions, focused only on Christine's face. But her eyes fixed on some point on the horizon, away from him. "I believed it nothing but stories," he said, spreading his hands apart helplessly. "Proof Mum was still an ignorant savage, despite all the trappings of civilized life. I did everything I could to distance myself from her. Then the summons came."

"What summons?" I asked.

"To come home. And she went." He took a deep, steadying breath. "She left my father and I, took a ship to Egypt, and never returned. Eventually one of my uncles sent word she died. How…why…he didn't say."

I found myself moved to pity, despite everything. "I'm sorry."

"Don't apologize to him, Whyborne," Christine snapped.

Iskander flinched at her words. "Mother chose Egypt over us. Her old family over her new one. It broke Father; he became a shade, going through the motions of life but utterly withdrawn. After he died, I decided I had to find out what mattered so much to her. So I came to Egypt myself."

He sighed. "The color of my skin meant I never fit in to English society. But as soon as I arrived here, it became obvious I wasn't truly Egyptian, either. I was still trying to find my place, to find my answers, when I met you, Christine."

"Dr. Putnam," she corrected. I winced.

"Dr. Putnam," he agreed quietly. "I couldn't find the *shardah-iin*. They had truly become a mirage. I thought…well. I doesn't matter now. I still believed it all to be silly superstition when we opened Nephren-ka's tomb. Dr. Putnam made her triumphant return to

America, and I remained behind in Cairo. And the *shardah-iin* finally contacted me.

"News of the tomb had reached them, and they grew alarmed. I thought them ignorant, but for the first time I had an opportunity to find out what truly became of my mother. I agreed to travel with them, find out more about the Egyptian side of my heritage." He laughed, but it was a hopeless sound. "And I found out she wasn't just a superstitious savage after all. The stories were true. The ghūls existed, and she died fighting them."

Christine seemed unwilling to ask questions, so it fell to me. "What happened?"

"You must understand, there are not many *shardah-iin* left. Few outsiders wish to marry infidels, let alone wander the wastes as nomads. *Shardah-iin* depart, as my mother did, for better lives. When the ghūls suddenly increased their numbers a few years ago, they had no choice but to call on anyone who might lend aid."

"Do you think this increase connected to the return of Nitocris?"

Iskander looked startled. "I...I hadn't considered it. The fighting was terrible and vicious. Many died. And now our numbers were even smaller than before. They were afraid. They wanted me to join them."

"And you did, without telling anyone you might have confided in," Christine said at last. She didn't look at Iskander as she spoke; her profile might have been carved in sandstone, like some long dead queen's.

"I took an oath to never reveal what I knew!" A spark flashed in Iskander's eyes. "I swore I would never tell anyone! The *shardah-iin* have survived only through secrecy, and I couldn't betray them, not even to you." His lip curled slightly. "And I'm not the only one who kept secrets. You never bothered to mention Dr. Whyborne is a sorcerer, despite the fact you talk about him constantly."

She did? What on earth was there to say about me?

"Keeping your oath is one thing," Christine replied, "but deliberately sabotaging our work, endangering our lives, attempting to kill my sister, and...dear God! You cut through the ropes on the statue."

"No! Sod it, Christine, I wouldn't put you in danger." Iskander took a step toward her. Griffin countered his move, stepping toward Iskander and firming his grip on his gun. Iskander stopped.

"Then what?" Christine asked, giving no sign she'd noticed either of them.

"I never joined the *shardah-iin*," Iskander insisted. "Examine the robes—you'll find no trace of dust, no sign I ever wore them. Yes, I allowed my cousin into camp in the hopes of killing Nitocris. But I had no idea they would go so far as to cut the ropes on the statue. Not until the moment I saw another cousin amongst the scaffolding and realized what he must have done. Certainly, I didn't realize he would put a cobra in Dr. Whyborne's tent, or destroy his notes. You have to believe me!"

"No, Mr. Barnett, I don't." Her expression betrayed no remorse, but a slight tremor infected her voice. "The only thing I must do is order you to leave."

He swayed slightly. "Christine—"

"You do not have permission to use my name, sir!"

He drew in a sharp sip of breath, like a man receiving a mortal blow. "Please, Dr. Putnam. Don't send me away. Let me help you. Let me...let me make things right, if I can."

"You cannot." She turned her back on him. "Take your supplies and your camel and leave. Now."

He glanced helplessly at Griffin, who offered him no more mercy than Christine, then at me.

Pity couldn't help but stir my heart. His position must have seemed untenable, caught between the demands of family and loyalty to Christine. But what could I do? Christine would never allow him to remain.

I gave him a helpless half-shrug. "You had better go, Mr. Barnett."

His shoulders slumped in defeat. In silence, he gathered his things, loaded them on one of the camels, and mounted. "Thank you for the loan of the camel," he said quietly.

No one answered him. His back hunched and his head bowed, he turned his mount's head east and rode away alone.

Chapter 19

The three of us didn't speak much for the rest of the day. There didn't seem anything to say, at least not without upsetting anyone. I suspected Griffin was glad to see the last of Iskander, having distrusted him from the first. As for Christine, I couldn't truly imagine the sense of betrayal she must have felt. First her sister, then the man she'd fallen in love with.

And now we were reduced to three, alone against whatever force of ghūls Nitocris could summon. Not to mention we had no idea if we even followed her trail anymore.

"What's that?" Griffin asked.

I blinked out of my morose thoughts to see him pointing south. The still, clear air of late evening revealed what at first looked like a tumble of rocks, only far too regular to be natural.

"Ruins?" I asked, glancing at Christine.

She shaded her eyes and stared for a long moment. "Perhaps." The lack of enthusiasm in her voice hurt to hear.

Maybe seeing them closer would restore some of her spirits. "I think we should look at them."

"Agreed." Griffin guided his camel in their direction, and the rest of us followed.

As we drew nearer, the thrill of discovery stirred my blood. "They are ruins—and this far into the desert! Can it be Nephren-ka's fane?"

Griffin looked grim at the prospect. "We should be careful."

We saw no signs of ghūls or Nitocris as we approached. The ruins consisted of little other than half-fallen pillars and statues. A double row of huge columns formed a great square, which had probably once been roofed over to form a processional. Within lay a space almost like a courtyard, at its center a smaller square of single columns. Inside this inner sanctum, a shape reminiscent of an obelisk leaned at an angle, propped up by the columns it had fallen on.

"An obelisk?" Christine wondered aloud. "Either this temple was built well after Nephren-ka's time, or this was some sort of prototype of the form."

"This isn't the fane?" Griffin said.

"No. At least, I don't think it is." Christine gazed about. "Why don't we stop and look around? We'll have to turn back first thing tomorrow anyway. At least we won't leave entirely empty-handed. Perhaps I can write a paper on this site before Nitocris kills us all."

We dismounted within the inner ring of columns. Christine and I both went for the obelisk, as it seemed the most likely to give us a clue as the age of the ruin. "Horus," she said, carefully brushing sand off of one of the carvings. "Smiting his great enemy, Set. And look, here is Wepwawet, guiding the dead through the hazards of the underworld..."

Our eyes met. "The priests built this," I said, seized with conviction. "The ones who wrote the inscriptions on the wall back at the necropolis. This must be some kind of—of outpost, meant to watch and hold back the enemies of life, should they burst forth from the fane."

"That is the most absurd bit of poetic nonsense I've ever heard you spout," she replied. "You have absolutely no evidence for any of it. Really, Whyborne, I expected better from you."

I glared at her. "I'm right. I know it."

Griffin joined us, leaning against the obelisk and giving me a skeptical look. "It's a good story, but—"

"I know," I replied doggedly. Because I did. I just wasn't sure *how* I knew.

Which meant I needed to find out.

"Just stay here and let me work," I said. "Don't ask any questions until I'm done."

"Sunstroke," Christine opined to Griffin as I returned to the camels. I ignored them both.

I'd placed the wand in a pack on Daisy, within easy reach should the need arise. Taking it out—and rescuing my fez from her inquisitive lips—I walked a slow circle around the remains of the inner sanctum. I did my best to concentrate only on sensation, and banish all the niggling thoughts urging me to doubt. I focused on the wind against my face, bearing with it the dry, lifeless scent of the great desert. The fading heat of the evening sun, the cosmic fire, on my skin. The sand shifting under my shoes. And far away, so deep I barely sensed it, the smell of wet rock and cold water from a vast underground river, buried beneath the desert.

The elements spun around me, like the model planets of an orrery, all moving on their own courses until suddenly they aligned.

Yes. This was what I'd sensed.

I used my shoe to draw an X in the sand. I made another circuit, farther out, and a third just outside the boundary of the outermost columns. Each time, I marked where the sensation of alignment came over me. I sighted along the Xs, then stared out across the desert along the same line. Did I see a shadow on the horizon, or some distant structure? Impossible to tell, but I had my guess.

"What the devil was that all about?" Christine demanded when I rejoined them. I was actually rather impressed she'd bitten her tongue this long.

"There are stories of lines of power on the earth," I began.

"Good gad, man, you can't be serious. You sound like one of those absurd spiritualists who claim the pyramids are aligned according to some mystic principle."

"Let him finish," Griffin said.

"I know how it sounds," I admitted. "But hear me out. When we were in West Virginia, one of the yayhos told me they could enter our world only in certain places, Threshold being one of them. What if there are certain geographical points which are different in some way?"

"Like Widdershins?" Griffin suggested.

"No, no. Well, maybe." I considered. "I assume Blackbyrne had some reason to found the town where he did. My point is I do sense something, a certain alignment of forces, if you will. I don't think I would have been able to sense it without the wand, but it is there. We might as well follow it for a few hours, just to see."

Christine considered for a few moments, then nodded. "Very well. I've no better ideas. But if we don't find anything, we'll have to turn back or risk running out of water. There's no sense wandering around in the desert until we die."

The bright light of the moon made night travel easy, and within a few hours the shadow on the horizon resolved into a low line of rocky hills. The wind through the cliffs set up a strange piping sound even at a distance, and I shivered every time a gust summoned forth another cacophony.

"Where are we?" Griffin asked.

Christine shook her head. "I've no idea. I've never heard of there being anything in this part of the desert but sand and more sand. I wonder if anyone has even set foot here since Nephren-ka's time, four-thousand years ago."

"Or at least lived to speak of it," I said.

"Let us endeavor to be the first," Griffin replied.

The heights grew gradually closer, revealing broken slopes and sheer cliffs. "Tracks," Griffin said suddenly. "Look."

Even I could tell a great many creatures had passed through here, although I couldn't have said for certain whether they were ghūls or gazelles. The tracks made for a gap in the cliffs, and we followed.

As we drew near the cleft, Daisy suddenly tossed her head. Christine's camel did the same, and Griffin's let out a bellow of protest, as did our pack animals. They came to a jumbled halt, sniffing the air and fighting to turn aside, growing more and more agitated as we strove to set them back on course. Christine's insults to their parentage and hygiene proved an ineffectual goad, and she finally dismounted with a curse.

"We'll have to leave them here," she said. "Grab what you can, which won't weigh you down—canteens foremost. Lanterns. Rope. Ammunition."

Had the shrill piping of the wind upset the camels, or did they sense something waiting for us on the other side of the rocky cleft? Perhaps it was only the scent of the ghūls. But as I stroked Daisy's quivering neck to soothe her, I couldn't quite believe it. Whatever lay in these hills, it harbored no love for any living thing.

As if hearing my thoughts, Christine said, "This...well, I won't pretend it doesn't worry me. Daphne is my sister and my responsibility. If either of you wish to turn back, I wouldn't think any less of you."

"Of course you would!" I gave her an incredulous look. "You'd march in there alone, cursing our names with every step. Your last words would be, 'Too bad Whyborne couldn't be bothered to come, the coward. I could really have used his help.' You'd pray there really is an afterlife so you could return to haunt me. Probably stand in the corner of my office and glare, or make the walls at home bleed, or some such nonsense."

She tried to look vexed, but laughter won out. "Well, yes," she admitted. "But it sounded noble, didn't it?"

"You sounded like a character out of the terrible adventure fiction Griffin loves to read," I replied as I shouldered my pack. "Really, do you think we'd come this far only to cower with the camels while you go to face ghūls and whatever else this accursed place holds? I hope you have a higher opinion of us."

"Honestly, Whyborne, you do take the wind out of one's sails. Had you been present at Patrick Henry's speech, you would have demanded liberty or death before the poor man could even open his mouth."

I ignored this bit of absurdity. Once we'd finished gathering our things, I exchanged a glance with Griffin. If he feared what lay beyond, it didn't show on his face. Stubble darkened his chin, and his clothes exhibited all the creases and dirt of our travels, but his eyes were calm and clear as he checked his revolver. When he tucked it into its holster, I held my hand out to him silently.

He took my hand—then used it to pull me to him, tilting his head back to kiss me softly. Christine stood only a few feet away, and I wanted to protest against such an intimacy in front of her.

But I wanted the kiss more.

"Ready?" he asked, when we parted.

A part of me wished I'd left him safely back in Widdershins after all. The other part of me was desperately, selfishly glad to have him here with me. "Yes."

Christine settled the strap of her canteen more comfortably across her chest. "If you two are quite done, can we get on with it?"

Heat rushed to my face, but Griffin only chuckled. "Lead the way," he said.

I'd expected the narrow gap to open up into a wadi beyond, much like the Valley of Jackals. But as we emerged from amidst the shattered cliffs, the moonlight instead revealed a great bowl, completely cut off save for the cleft through which we entered. Power whispered along my skin, like a mild electrical current. I'd been right; this was a place of arcane energy. Great cliffs towered up on every side, poised like lurking animals. And within their threatening embrace crouched what could only be the Fane of Nyarlathotep.

Directly before us squatted a small temple at the head of a causeway flanked on either side by a line of statues. Row upon row of mastabas, the resting places of the non-royal dead, stretched to either side of the causeway. At the causeway's end rose a low wall, half-destroyed by the centuries. And beyond the wall, butted up against the far cliffs, loomed a pyramid made from some black stone.

"The lightless pyramid," I whispered.

"Yes." Christine sounded as breathless as I felt at the sight. "Look at the stone it's made from—I've never seen anything like it in Egypt. It must be our destination."

"Stay sharp," Griffin murmured, even as he drew his revolver.

"We aren't the only ones to find it."

Below us on the gentle slope leading to temple and causeway, Daphne's pale hair and skin gleamed in the moonlight. She strode across the sand, and a flood of ghūls followed at her heels. Their golden-brown fur blended with the sand and one another, making it impossible to count their numbers, but there couldn't be less than a hundred. Some went on all fours and some on two. In their midst, I glimpsed a few who seemed more human than their fellows.

"Oh dear," I said. "There are a great many of them, aren't there?"

"Too many to fight," Griffin said flatly. "We have to turn back."

Christine shook her head. "We can't leave Daphne."

"Nor can we battle our way through a hundred ghūls to reach her."

Daphne stepped onto the causeway. A few minutes and she'd be at the pyramid, where the Lapidem surely must rest. There must be some way to stop her—but what? How?

The hair along the backs of my arms stood on end, some instinct whispering deep inside. Without warning, the temperature abruptly shifted from the warmth of an Egyptian night to the freezing chill of an icehouse. My breath steamed in the air, and frost spread across the rocks of the cleft.

"What's happening?" Griffin asked in alarm.

I licked my dry lips. "I think the Fane of Nyarlathotep has slept for centuries. And now it's waking up."

The nearest statues on the causeway turned their heads.

For a moment, I thought the low light and my own nerves had conspired to trick my eyes. But no, the nearest statues along the causeway moved, their faces turning toward Daphne and her ghūls with slow malevolence.

Nephren-ka hid this place from Nitocris. She certainly wouldn't be welcome here now.

"What the devil?" Christine breathed. "How...how is it even possible?"

"Magic." The same force which filled the valley like a bowl, tingling against my skin and quickening my breath.

One of the statues stepped ponderously down from its plinth. It clutched in one hand a flail and the other a sword, both carved from stone. With the stiffness of a sleeper waking from a long nap, it lifted the sword—and swung at Daphne.

Whether she'd expected such a defense or not, she was no fool. The sword connected only with empty air as she darted to the side. Her ghūls swarmed forward, although how they might injure a statue,

I didn't know. The flail caught two of the creatures, and even from the distance I heard their mad yelps and the crunch of breaking bone.

Daphne called out, though it sounded more like a bark than human speech. It must have been an order, however, for the ghūls surged around her. She broke into a run, making for the pyramid at the end of the causeway. A handful of ghūls raced before her, and others flanked her to either side. As they passed each statue, it came to life and moved to attack. The ghūls made targets of themselves, while Daphne forged ahead and left them behind, sacrificed to protect their queen.

"Come on!" Christine ordered. "While they're in confusion!"

To my horror, she sprang from cover and ran down the shallow slope. Griffin swore and dashed after her, leaving me no choice but to follow. I'd assumed Christine meant to blindly plunge into the midst of the mass of fighting statues and ghūls, but instead she cut to the side and ducked into the narrow space between the rows of mastabas. Who lay within the low, square tombs? Priests of Nyarlathotep? Nephren-ka's family? The workers who built the fane?

She immediately crouched down and put her back to the stone. When we caught up, she whispered, "If we can sneak amongst the mastabas while the statues and ghūls keep one another busy, we can almost reach the wall around the pyramid. Then it's just a quick dash past the fighting."

"Oh, is that all?" I asked.

"Shh! Follow me!"

She darted across the gap to the next mastaba, and Griffin and I followed. As I crossed the gap, I chanced a quick look in the direction of the causeway. At this range, I could better make out the details of the living statues. From a distance, I'd assumed them to be gods, or perhaps images of Nephren-ka himself. But beneath the double crown of Upper and Lower Egypt, they had no faces.

I froze, transfixed by the revolting sight. The nearest statue struck a ghūl with its flail, sending the humanoid body flying straight at me. I jerked back as it crashed down in a heap of broken bones and pulped flesh, only feet away.

"Whyborne!" Griffin called.

"I'm fine. I—"

The crunch of stone on stone interrupted me. The statue had…not spotted me, because it had no eyes. But its featureless head turned toward us now, and it strove to fit its colossal body between the mastabas.

Oh dear.

Griffin seized the back of my collar and hauled me after him.

"Run, damn it!"

I ran, stumbling after him and Christine. The cold air burned in my lungs. I drew the wand and clutched it in one hand, and the iciness of the metal nearly seared my skin.

One of the sealed doorways to the mastabas fell open, almost directly on top of Christine. She yelped and leaped back, nearly knocking over Griffin and myself. Amidst the cloud of dust rising from around the fallen stone, a thing of bone and resin-soaked rags stumbled out of the open tomb.

CHAPTER 20

GRIFFIN FIRED OFF a shot, and its brittle skull exploded into fragments. The remainder collapsed into a pitiful heap.

Crash after crash sounded, the doors of the mastabas bursting open all around us.

"Son of a bitch!" Christine shouted. "The provenance of the entire site will be ruined!"

"Worry about living long enough to excavate!" A mummy missing the lower half of its face stumbled in my direction on stiff legs. And least the damn things moved slowly. Now if only there weren't quite so many of them.

"Take my sword cane," Griffin said, tossing it to Christine. She drew the blade and hacked at the shuffling corpses blocking the way. I didn't dare ponder whether the mummified remains were merely inanimate things given a ghastly semblance of life by magic, or if they retained any memory or awareness of the people they had once been. They reached for us with withered fingers; one caught my coat, its grip terrifying in its strength. Griffin shot the thing, and I wrenched loose.

"Thank you," I managed to gasp.

Together, we made our way through the houses of the dead. Griffin fired off shot after shot, and Christine bashed anything which got in her way. I whispered the secret name of fire, the end of the wand glowing red as it had before.

A ghūl lunged from between the mastabas, just behind me. I let out a cry of shock. At the same moment, one of the resurrected mummies latched onto the ghūl, its claw-like fingers digging into matted fur.

I struck the mummy with the wand. Its resin-soaked bandages went up like a torch, the flames spreading instantly to the ghūl it clung to. Both of them screamed and clutched at each other as I retreated as quickly as possible.

We emerged from the mastabas at the end of the causeway. A huge, struggling knot of ghūls and colossal statues blocked the entrance to the walled complex beyond. Of Daphne there was no sign—she must have already slipped through.

Christine broke into a run, forcing Griffin and I to run as well. We plunged into the mass of the fight, shooting and striking at any ghūls which came near. One of the statues swung at Christine, but she managed to duck beneath the heavy arm, and it flattened a luckless ghūl instead. For a moment, I thought we actually might get through.

A ghūl tackled Griffin, knocking him onto his back. Their struggle caught the attention of the last statue on the causeway.

"Griffin!" I shouted in warning.

He kicked the ghūl hard in the stomach, shoving it off of him. But the statue had already lifted its stone sword. Even as I watched, it began to fall, intending to crush Griffin into a pulp.

I didn't think. For once in my life, I only acted, hurling myself between Griffin and certain death. The wand in my outthrust hand cracked hard against the descending stone, even as I shouted the words of the spell. The one I'd never yet gotten to work against stone.

The limb shattered into rubble. Pebble-sized shards pelted my face and arms, but most of it flew in other directions, away from us.

Griffin stared up at me with a sort of awe. "Th-thank you," he managed. Then he grabbed me and yanked me down, just as something heavy passed through the space my skull occupied an instant before.

Oh, right. The statue had two arms.

Keeping a grip on me, he rolled us out of the statue's reach, before scrambling to his feet. A ghūl charged us, only to be taken down by the crack of Christine's rifle. She had made it to the shelter of a doorway set in the base of the pyramid. As the statue turned ponderously, Griffin helped me up, and we both ran to join Christine. She sighted and fired past us. "Help me with the door! It moves on a pivot."

We added our strength to hers, shoving the massive door shut. A ghūl tried to crawl through the narrowing gap, but Griffin punched it hard in the muzzle. The door slammed into place, leaving us in utter darkness.

I sank to the floor, my back against the door, and gasped for breath. My heart galloped like an entire herd of horses in my chest, and the muscles of my legs ached. A dozen bruises, cuts, and scrapes I hadn't even been aware of receiving made themselves known. I wished I could simply curl up on the floor and go to sleep.

Cloth rustled nearby. "Here, Whyborne. Light this." Christine pressed a candle into my palm.

The wick flared to life at my command, the light seeming tiny against the heavy darkness enshrouding the pyramid. In contrast to the icy cold outside, the air in here was hot and close. As I lifted the candle, the shadows reluctantly drew back, revealing a small antechamber. Inscriptions and illustrations covered the walls, but even a quick glance showed them to be abnormal. The crocodilian hybrid known as the Eater of Souls, which condemned the unjust to a second, final, death in the afterlife was depicted grown fat and huge, with rivers of blood pouring from its mouth. In another scene, the great serpent Apep devoured the celestial boat containing the sun, ensuring it would never rise again. I shuddered; these pictures would truly have been blasphemous to the ancients.

By the light of the candle, Christine took out her small lantern. "At least the flame is orange," she said. "If it begins to glow blue, the air is stale."

"I take it Daphne is the one who opened the door initially?" Griffin asked. "I didn't see."

"Yes. I glimpsed her briefly, before she disappeared inside with two or three ghūls." Christine examined the door. "Let's try to wedge something beneath it. It might not keep the ghūls out forever, assuming any survive the statues and the risen dead, but at least it will slow them down."

I watched Griffin carefully as we worked. The room wasn't technically underground, but it certainly gave the same feel. "How are you holding up, old fellow?"

He looked utterly exhausted: filthy and unshaven and spattered with ghūl blood. But he smiled when I put my hand to his shoulder. "I'll manage it, never fear," he said. "Don't worry for me, Ival."

"Good man," Christine said gruffly. "Come along, you two, and keep an eye out for traps. Speak up if anything looks in the slightest bit suspicious."

The antechamber let out into a corridor which wended its way back through the monumental pile of stone. After a short distance, it descended via a long set of stairs. The air grew even hotter and closer, and soon the lantern light showed a dusting of sweat on all our skins.

"No bats," Christine observed grimly. "Nor scorpions."

"I take it that isn't a good sign," Griffin said lightly, but with a note of strain in his voice.

"No," she agreed. "Ordinarily tombs and pyramids are filled with the various creatures of the desert which take refuge amidst tumbled rock or cracks in the cliffs. One cannot go anywhere without becoming covered in guano and cobwebs."

"The camels wouldn't draw near," I reminded her. "Perhaps other creatures are equally sensitive."

"And yet here we are," Griffin remarked.

"I've always held humans are the stupidest of animals." Christine cast us a rueful grin. "We've no notion when to turn and run screaming."

The stair ended in a larger chamber, the walls bearing similar depictions as those of the antechamber. In the center of the floor lay a bundle of what I took to be twigs, despite being a hundred miles from even a shrub. Then I realized the nearest twigs formed the shape of an out flung hand.

Christine knelt by the remains. "Whyborne, come here," she said. "Do the bones appear oddly charred to you?"

"Charred?" Griffin voiced trembled slightly on the word.

"Well, not charred, exactly." She prodded at them curiously. "More like melted by acid."

Griffin gasped, and I silently cursed. Whatever did this was surely not the same creature which killed his partner and left a horrible scar on his leg. "Griffin..."

"God." He stared at the bones with an expression of blank horror. "There's his skull. Look at the hole melted in it. He must have sc-screamed. And kept screaming."

"Griffin..."

"Did he scream even after his face was gone, like Glenn—"

"Griffin!" I seized his arms. "Look at me." He continued to stare at the bones, so I took his chin in one hand and forced him to face me. "Look at me," I repeated. "This isn't Chicago. You're not alone. Christine and I are here with you."

He swallowed convulsively. His pupils shrank to mere pinpricks and his muscles stretched tight as piano wires beneath my fingers. "It's the m-monster from Chicago. I know it is. What else could do such a thing?"

"It can't be the creature from Chicago." How could I get through to him? "Griffin, Chicago is thousands of miles away. This daemon, whatever it is, is bound to the Lapidem. It couldn't have been there."

"Not the same entity," Christine mused. "But the same species, perhaps? Assuming such concepts apply to whatever these creatures are."

"You aren't helping, Christine," I snapped over my shoulder.

"Well, I'm only saying! Look here: this poor fellow was probably part of a band of particularly intrepid thieves, or perhaps a priest who wished to destroy the Lapidem. At any rate, he disturbed the stone, and the daemon killed him. Griffin's partner disturbed whatever the other daemon guarded and it...well, acted according to its nature." She spread her hands. "Therefore all we have to do is keep Daphne away from the Lapidem, and we won't have to worry about the daemon coming for us."

I didn't find her words particularly reassuring, but Griffin nodded tightly. "Y-you're right. We have to keep going."

"Perhaps you should return to the antechamber," I suggested.

The hurt look he gave me made me wish I'd kept the thought to myself. "I won't let you down."

"I know." I brushed the hair from his forehead. Then, despite Christine's presence, I pressed my lips to his forehead as well. "I never thought otherwise, darling. Come on, now."

Beyond the ragged remains of the bones, a flight of steps descended even lower into the pyramid. More images covered these walls, as blasphemous as the others. Set stood in triumph over the hewn body of Osiris, and later, Apep strangled Set in turn. The grand galley bearing Ra sank in the river of the underworld, so the sun would never rise again.

God. No wonder Nitocris wished to find this place. If the ghūls were creatures of darkness, of course they would want to ally themselves with the forces of chaos, which sought the destruction of the sun. Eaters of the dead must perforce hate the living.

Was that why Nephren-ka hid this place from his wife? He had yet been mortal, after all. Did he fear she would overthrow him and his kingdom of the living, and replace it with an empire of the dead? A sunless wasteland of hunger and want, every city turned into a necropolis in which the ghūls might feast.

Of course such a thing was impossible. No boat carried the sun through the underworld every night, and no monstrous snake lurked ready to devour it whole. But my studies of the *Arcanorum* had shown me metaphor often cloaked magic, and this one was unpleasant enough I didn't wish to know what the truth might actually prove to be.

We passed more skeletons, some with bits of metal melted to them, which might have been knives or other implements. Griffin didn't look at them, but I knew each one shook him to his core. And yet he persevered despite his fear. My chest swelled with pride at his bravery.

"Be careful," Christine said, holding up her hand. A pit, perhaps ten feet long, opened in the floor ahead of us. As we approached cautiously, a rush of cool air blew against my face from below.

"A dead drop," Christine observed, peering over the edge. "Fortunately, Daphne left us the way across."

How Daphne knew what to expect, I couldn't say, but there was indeed a bridge of sorts laid across the drop. Only instead of wood, the ghūls had lashed together what appeared to be human leg and arm bones.

"I'll cross first." Christine got down on her hands and knees and tested the sturdiness of the ladder. With a shrug, she crawled across its rickety length. As soon as she reached the other end, she scrambled to her feet and wiped off her hands on her trousers. "It seems to be stable enough. But don't linger."

I went next. The sharp ridges dug into my hands, and the horrid, greasy feel of the bones almost made me gag. The stench of rot clinging to them certainly didn't help. "What do you think is below us?" I asked, even as I tried not to look down.

"There's a fresh breeze, which means there must be another cavern or corridor. Something connected to the outside." Christine shrugged.

Once we'd all safely crossed, we encountered another set of stairs. If Christine's hypothetical underground caverns existed, we must be almost on top of them. More inscriptions lined the corridor at the foot of the stairs. But this time, a flicker of light came from the opposite end, and the murmured words of a chant echoed down the stone hallway.

"Daphne," I whispered.

"Yes," Christine agreed, breaking into a run.

I swallowed a curse and bolted after her, followed by Griffin. The sound of Daphne's chanting grew loud even over the pounding of our footsteps.

Her ghūls spotted us from their guard post near the entrance to the innermost room. They charged, snapping and slavering. Griffin shot one. The other grappled with Christine, its claws tearing at her shirtsleeves. I struck it a sharp blow with the wand. Its hold loosened, giving Christine the space to skewer it with the sword cane.

It collapsed, and we ran toward the room at the end of the corridor. It lay at the very heart of the pyramid, an odd, almost hexagonal space. Along the back wall lurked a stomach-turning depiction of the chaos god, Nyarlathotep himself. In front of the great statue crouched a curiously angled stone pillar I took to be an altar.

And on the altar sat a box of irregular proportions, made from some metal I couldn't name.

Daphne stood before the altar, her chanting reaching a crescendo. We were too late. The ritual had already begun.

Griffin flung himself upon Daphne without hesitation, aiming a blow at her head with the butt of his revolver.

Faster than seemed possible, she spun, one of her hands gripping his wrist. Her nails had grown long, and she bared sharp, white teeth at him. He snapped his knee up, but she twisted aside before he could bury it in her gut. With a cry of rage, she hurled him into the altar. He struck the box, and they both went flying to the side.

"Griffin!" I shouted.

Christine swung her rifle like a club, aiming for her sister's head. Daphne ripped it from her grasp and flung it aside, then backhanded Christine. Her strength was shocking, more like a ghūl than a woman.

"Daphne!" I cried, brandishing the wand at her. The serpent's head burned red-hot, distorting the air above it. "Stop this, I implore you."

Travel across the desert had been no kinder to her than to us. Her golden hair had gone dry and tangled, and her familiar clothing hung practically in rags. I searched her face for some trace of the friend I believed I had made.

"And why should I?" she asked, tilting her head to the side. She stalked toward me like a hunting cat, her hands curled into claws. "You've disrupted my ritual. Come to take the Lapidem away from me. Why shouldn't I just kill you now?"

I swallowed against the fear threatening to close my throat. "I can still save you. Use a spell to send Nitocris back to the Outside."

"Save me?" She arched a skeptical brow. "Save me from what, exactly? From becoming powerful? From controlling my own destiny?"

"But you aren't in control. Look at yourself!" I gestured to her claws, her teeth. "Nitocris is changing you. The thing inside you isn't even human, and soon you won't be either."

An incredulous laugh escaped her, like the bark of a jackal. *"You have the audacity to accuse me of not being human? I smell the ocean in your blood."*

What on earth did she mean? Had Nitocris driven her mad, and now she raved, making wild accusations?

"Daphne, please." Christine rose to her feet, clutching at the altar for support. Daphne's blow had split her lip, and blood trickled down her face. "Please, just listen. I'm sorry. Whatever happened in

Wisborg, I swear, if I'd known I would have come for you."

Daphne's lips twisted into a sneer. "Would you?"

"You know I would." Christine dashed the blood from her face with her sleeve. "Don't you remember when we were girls, lying in bed and listening to Mother and Father fight? The only thing I wanted was for us to escape together."

Daphne's sneer faded. "You told me to sing," she whispered.

Christine nodded. "Yes. We'd sing together to blot out the sound of them cursing each other and us."

"I remember." Daphne's eyes lowered and her lips parted. Her body swayed toward Christine, and for a moment, I truly believed she would go to her sister.

Then her face hardened. "I remember," she repeated, but now she spit the words from between clenched teeth. "I remember you caused a scandal. I remember Stephen left me. I remember mother browbeating me into marrying that bastard Adolph, because he had a title and some money, and would overlook your shame." The tendons in her neck bulged, and her hands curled into fists. "And now you come and say you want to *save* me. But you don't. You just want to take away the one thing in my entire life I chose for myself. Well, I won't let you."

She flung back her head and howled. The sound of the jackal, coming from a woman's throat, cut through the hot air and put ice in my bones. But even more chilling were the answering howls from farther up the corridor.

The ghūls had broken through the door.

I scrambled back. Daphne stood in the entrance to the room, grinning crazily. I cast about frantically, looking for some weapon or means of defense against the ghūls, and saw Griffin.

He knelt on the floor before the statue. In front of him lay the box he'd knocked off of the altar. Its lid had come open when it hit the ground, and he stared fixedly at whatever lay inside.

No. Oh no.

I ran to his side. Within the box I glimpsed a dark crystal of some unknown mineral, its purple-black surface shot through with veins of pulsating red. Griffin stared at it, pupils blown wide, like some small creature mesmerized by the gaze of the viper which meant to swallow it whole.

"No!" I slammed the lid of the box shut, hiding away the crystal. He didn't react, so I shook him hard by the shoulder. "Griffin!"

The color had vanished from his face. "The vast plains...fire...the stars burning...and it—oh God! It looked back at me!"

No. My heart stuttered at his words, but I couldn't deny their meaning.

We'd interrupted Daphne's ritual. And Griffin had gazed into what must be the Occultum Lapidem.

The daemon had been summoned. And it was coming for Griffin.

Chapter 21

Bands constricted my chest. I couldn't breathe or move, only stare at Griffin's face. He gazed back, and realization bloomed in his eyes, before shifting to horror.

The howls of the ghūls broke my paralysis. Daphne stepped farther into the room, her teeth bared and her claws ready to rend. Christine retrieved her rifle from the floor, but its bore remained pointed at the floor, her indecision palpable.

There was no way out. Even if we could get past Daphne, the pyramid possessed no side corridors or rooms. We were trapped and at the mercy of the host of ghūls descending on us from above.

The wand twisted in my grip and vibrated against my palm. My head pounded in time with my heartbeat. Dust sifted through the air, coating my sinuses and throat. Could I try to summon the wind? Or would I end up sucking the air out of the room, as it had no other ventilation? Perhaps if we'd been at the dead drop…

The dead drop. Moving air from below. A hollow space beneath the pyramid.

No. It wouldn't work. I'd kill us all.

Daphne gathered herself with a snarl. From the corridor beyond glowed the nitrous reflection of dozens of eyes.

"Christine!" I shouted. "To me!"

I half-expected her to ignore my summons, but she didn't hesitate, stumbling to my side. "Grab the box," I ordered Griffin. "And hold onto me."

Hands gripped my coat. Hoping I wasn't about to make a fatal mistake, I raised the wand high and focused on the stone floor directly beneath us. Bringing the tail of the wand down onto to floor, I commanded the stone to obey me.

For a long moment, nothing happened. Christine spoke my name urgently, claws scrabbled on stone, and Daphne laughed—

There came a great rumble. The entire pyramid convulsed, and the crash of falling masonry sounded all around. The stone beneath us shattered, and we plunged into darkness.

I opened my eyes onto blackness so complete I wasn't entirely certain I *had* opened them after all. Choking dust clogged my nostrils, and every inch of my body ached. I shifted my arms and legs carefully, testing for broken bones. A sharp pain in my left shoulder rewarded my efforts.

The sound of rustling cloth came from the blackness. "Whyborne?" Griffin's voice, thank God. "Ival! Answer me!"

"I'm alive," I said, or tried to. The dryness and dust in my mouth cracked my voice. Moving carefully, I sat up. My shoulder twinged again, but I didn't think it broken. "Christine?"

"I'm here."

My head spun, but a few moments of stillness settled it again. "What happened?"

A hand groped at my back. I reached behind me and found the familiar shape of Griffin's fingers. "You collapsed the floor beneath us, I believe," he said. "And possibly the entire pyramid on top."

"Right. Yes. I meant to do that. Um, the bit with the floor, anyway." I patted my pockets, trying to recall where I'd put my matchbox. "I remembered the air from the dead drop and Christine's theory there might be caverns or some such beneath us. It was desperate, but I didn't know what else to do."

"At least warn us next time," Christine said.

I ignored her. "What happened to the ghūls and Daphne?"

"It sounded as if something collapsed above us," Griffin said. "If the pyramid caved in…it's hard to believe anyone else got out."

"Oh." Should I be glad? Or sad? Or…something?

"Whyborne…I'm sorry." Griffin's hand tightened on mine. "About the Lapidem. I didn't mean to look at it. But it seemed to draw me in. I couldn't turn away. It showed me…things."

"What sort of things?" Blast, where were the damned matches?

He took a deep breath. "I'm not certain I can even describe them. Great black mountains made of glass, huge and terrible, against a sky like no color I've ever seen before. Stone towers. A void of stars. And then...a creature." He shuddered. "And its eye...burning yellow, with a misshapen pupil. And I knew it looked back and saw me, just as I saw it. It's...coming for me. Isn't it? The thing which melted and burned the skeletons. The thing like..."

Like in the Chicago basement. Not the same entity, as Christine had said, but surely of the same kind.

I finally found the matches. Pulling one free, I whispered the name of fire.

"Yes," I said, as the tiny light bloomed. "It probably is."

Griffin's face was haggard: bloody and dusty, his jaw dark with stubble and hollows beneath his eyes. But he seemed composed for the moment. "Here—I still have candles in my pack."

He managed to pull one free before my match burned down to my fingers, and I lit it. The metal of the oddly shaped box gleamed back at me when I lifted the candle to take a look at our surroundings.

The passage we'd tumbled into was clearly not natural. Chisels had worked the stone at some point. Had this passage been carved at the same time as the rest of the fane, or did it predate even the works of the Egyptians? No bas-reliefs or hieroglyphs showed on the walls to give any hint.

Some of the pyramid's innermost chamber had come down with us in a pile of shaped stone and broken statuary. I waited for Christine's inevitable lecture about destroying an important archaeological find, but she said nothing.

Concerned by her silence, I turned to her. She stood apart from us, staring into the blackness of the corridor where it ran off into the unknown depths. Like us, she was covered in dust and ghūl blood. Her arms were folded over her chest and her shoulders hunched.

"Christine?" I asked tentatively. Had she been injured? But she didn't look hurt.

"Daphne's dead." Her voice cracked on the word. "And it's my fault."

"Of course it isn't. Don't be silly."

"I'm not. Daphne's dead, and we're going to die, and...and..."

"Christine?" I asked, when she didn't go on. Dear heavens, was she crying?

She didn't answer. I dripped wax onto a nearby rock and secured the candle's base to it. Despite the various aches in my bones, I made it to my feet.

Christine had embraced me once, when I'd nearly died at the hands of an insane necromancer. Otherwise, we kept our distance as was proper. But when I put my hand to her shoulder and felt her shuddering with suppressing sobs, I turned her around gently and pulled her to me.

"Don't cry," I said. My own throat constricted and my eyes burned.

"I'm not crying," she sobbed into my shoulder. "All this is my fault! I never should have abandoned Daphne as I did. I thought she would be fine, and when I learned she wasn't, I should have done something. Brought her to live with me and attend school, or-or something. Instead, I was stupid and selfish and—"

"You didn't know. You couldn't have known."

"It's n-not an excuse. And when she married the damned graf I thought she'd found her place in life, and was wrong to carry a grudge and not write back to me. Everything which happened since, to her and everyone else, is my doing." She drew in a shaking breath. "And these last weeks, I thought...I thought we'd reconciled. Become friends as well as sisters. I thought everything would be all right between us. And instead she's dead! I'm a terrible, awful person and you should have nothing to do with me."

"Hush," I murmured. "You're not terrible, or awful. It's—it's all right."

"Don't lie to me. It isn't all right."

"I know." I closed my eyes and pressed my face to her hair. "I know."

I don't know how long Christine and I held one another in silence. Eventually her sobs eased, and she pulled away.

"Do you know, I'm actually glad I sent Kander away." She wiped at her eyes with the back of her hand. The dust mingled with her tears and smeared into mud. "A part of me wishes I hadn't...hadn't let pride get the better of me. But at least he'll survive. I'm just sorry I dragged you into this."

"Don't be absurd. We aren't dead yet. The first thing we have to do is find our way out of this catacomb, or whatever it might be."

"Yes." She nodded firmly. "You're quite right. Forgive me for... well."

"Nothing to forgive, old girl." I straightened her collar carefully. "You know I love you, don't you?" I felt stupid, saying the words aloud. But Christine had always been more of a sister to me than the one who shared my blood.

She punched me lightly on the arm. "Yes, yes. I love you, too. Now let's see if we can get out of here."

"At least we've only the one direction to choose from for now."

"True."

Griffin had poked about the rubble and managed to retrieve most of our belongings. The box containing the Lapidem, he insisted on stowing in his pack, on the logic the daemon would be drawn to him either way. Christine's rifle, his revolver and sword cane, the wand... and my fez. After losing so many other hats, I began to suspect the thing carried a curse, and I'd be stuck wearing it until the end of time. Once we sorted our things, we lit our spare lantern, which survived the fall inside Christine's pack, and started to walk.

The rough-hewn corridor ran straight and level through the bedrock. "What era do you suppose this is from?" I asked Christine, in the hopes a bit of conversation might keep our spirits up.

"There's no way of knowing, without any decorations or artifacts." She touched the wall lightly as we passed. "The chisel marks were left rough instead of smoothed down, as if the work was never completed. Perhaps it was an early version of Nephren-ka's tomb, abandoned when he chose a place in the Valley of the Jackals instead? He wouldn't have been the first pharaoh to build more than one resting place."

"To spend your life, preparing to die..." Griffin murmured.

"That might be overstating the case a bit," Christine replied. "But the ancients certainly thought a great deal about eternity. There is something...odd about this corridor, though."

"What?" I asked.

"It's almost as if it's been swept clean. I mean look at it—now that we're away from the rock fall, there's not even any dust."

There was indeed an unnatural lack of any of the ordinary detritus which gathered in even the most deserted of locations. No animals, I might have understood, if they avoided the place as one of dark power. But no dust? Something must pass through here, often enough to keep it clean.

Griffin froze. "Do you smell that?" he asked.

I took a deep breath. Beneath the coolness of stone and our blood- and sweat-stained bodies, lay a curious fetor reminiscent of a chemical laboratory. "What is it? It's getting stronger."

Griffin's face drained of all its color, and his eyes widened. "The thing in the basement, the thing which digested Glenn. It smelled like this." He shook his head wildly, lifting his revolver in a shaking hand. "It's the daemon. Run. For God's sake, run!"

We bolted along the dark corridor, the lantern in Christine's hand flinging insane shadows over the walls. A wind began to blow from behind us, strengthening the corrosive stench. A rushing sound accompanied it, growing closer and closer, as if something vast poured through the empty space at our backs.

I risked a glance over my shoulder. An oncoming wall of slick blackness filled the entire corridor, like paste squeezed through a tube. No wonder the place had been swept clean. From the center of the roiling darkness, a single eye glared at me. It burned from within with some yellow fire, the blazing iris punctured by a hideous tripartite pupil.

The sight stole the strength from my legs, and I stumbled badly. Griffin heard the scuff of my shoe and spun around. The roar of his revolver was deafening in the confined space.

The daemon didn't even flinch at the shots.

I seized Griffin's arm with one hand, pulling him with me, while gripping the wand with the other. The thing was said to be a daemon of the night. If bullets wouldn't harm it, perhaps fire would.

I half-turned even as I ran, pointing the wand back at the thing. This had to work—if it didn't, we'd die screaming.

Flames burst from the wand, fueled by desperation into a streaming lash of fire. Their orange light reflected momentarily in the oily, jelly-like surface of the daemon. The stench of burning combined with its searing fetor, and it loosed…not a sound, but something I felt within my head.

Griffin cried out and clutched at his temples. The thing's eye closed against the fire, and it jerked back. Knowing we dared not waste a second, I locked my fingers on Griffin's arm and hauled him reeling along with me.

"I see light ahead!" Christine called.

"Hurry! The daemon won't stay back for long!" I shouted.

The corridor came to an abrupt end. At some distant time in the past, what had no doubt been a concealed entrance had collapsed into a slope of rubble. Sunlight peeped through a narrow slot at the top of the slope, barely high enough for a man to fit through on his belly.

Christine didn't hesitate, clambering up the slope and flinging herself down to crawl through the tiny entrance. "Go," I ordered Griffin, pushing him at the gap next. "I'll hold it off."

"But—"

"Go!"

I could already hear the rushing sound coming closer again. As Griffin wriggled through, the tripartite eye appeared, glowing balefully as it hurtled toward me.

Christine had set the lantern down by the gap while she crawled through. As Griffin's boots vanished, I picked it up and flung it with all my strength at the oncoming horror.

The lantern shattered, remaining oil going up in a blaze. The daemon slowed, its hideous pupil contracting to a pinpoint. I didn't wait to see if it halted altogether. Flinging myself onto the rocks, one hand gripping the wand, I eeled through the narrow gap, for once thankful for the narrowness of my shoulders.

Halfway through, my pack caught on some projection. I swore frantically and tried to push myself forward, but the tough canvas refused to give. "Help! I'm stuck!"

In response to my cry, Griffin and Christine grabbed me by each wrist and heaved. I wriggled frantically, struggling to find some angle which might help. And all the while, I expected to feel the searing touch of the daemon on my exposed legs. The fire must have gone out by now. It would nearly be on me—

With a loud rip, the pack gave way. I popped out of the gap like a cork from a bottle of champagne. Behind me, the daemon checked its rush, as the burning rays of dawn fell on the rocky slope and through the narrow crack.

We all collapsed onto the stony ground, gasping for breath. The tunnel had let us out somewhere amidst the shattered hills surrounding the fane. Where, I didn't know, and didn't care as long as there wasn't anything trying to kill us for the moment.

Eventually, Christine stumbled to her feet. "Will the sunlight keep it back, do you think?"

I nodded. She helped me up, then Griffin. "Then we'd best find the camels and get as far ahead of it as we can," she said. "I don't want to be anywhere near here come sunset."

Chapter 22

The camels were nowhere in sight.

We stood in the spot where we'd tethered them. Only uprooted stakes and snapped ropes remained. Some panic had infected them, perhaps when the magical defenses of the fane roused, and they'd broken free and fled, taking with them everything we weren't carrying ourselves.

I shook my canteen, which was unfortunately light. We had no food and only enough water to last a few hours beneath the sun. I drew a steadying breath and tried to think rationally, but no solutions came to mind. We were in the middle of the unknown vastness of the desert, without any resources. And even if we had water and food, on foot we'd be far too near the fane when the sun went down and unleashed the guardian daemon.

I looked at my companions, hoping against hope one of them had some suggestion to alleviate the bleakness of our position. Christine stared at the uprooted tethering stakes with an expression very close to despair. As for Griffin, he wandered over to a nearby boulder and sagged against it.

"Take my canteen," he said, gazing out over the desert instead of at us. "It will buy the two of you a little more time."

Christine and I exchanged a confused glance. "What nonsense are you spouting, man?" she asked.

"The daemon is coming for me." He crossed his arms over his chest and hunched his shoulders. "It's...entangled with me, somehow.

It knows exactly where I am. I can feel it. It won't stop until I'm dead."

My mouth went dry, but I forced my voice to remain firm. "We won't let it hurt you." How we'd stop it I didn't know, but there must be some way.

Griffin, however, only shook his head. "And I won't let it hurt you. If the choice is between all three of us dying, and two of us having at least a chance at survival, there's no choice at all."

Something squeezed all the breath from my lungs. He didn't—he couldn't—mean it. "Y-You can't be serious. You're suggesting staying here and just—just letting it kill you?"

"No." Griffin swallowed thickly. "I don't want to die like that. Like Glenn. Like the skeletons in the pyramid. I've one bullet remaining—"

"No!" I grabbed his coat, hauling him to his feet and forcing him to face me. Terror tightened my chest, crushing my lungs. "Don't say such things!"

He wrenched free from my hold, stepping back to put distance between us. "If it saves you and Christine, if it at least gives you a chance, what other choice do I have?"

No. No, no, no. He couldn't do this. He couldn't. "You can choose to fight!" My voice broke. "Griffin, you can't give up!"

"I'm not!" Tears shone in his eyes, and he dashed them away with the back of his hand. "But I can't watch you die the way Glenn did, melted and d-dissolved by some horrible creature. Don't ask it of me."

"I'm asking you to fight back." I grabbed his shoulders again, and this time he didn't pull away. The tears spilled over onto his cheeks, and each one seared my heart. "And maybe I will die, maybe we all will, but I'd rather perish at your side than—than go home without you. You're the world to me." My tears blurred my vision, and I could no longer make out his face. "And I'm so afraid I've cost you too much, when you've given everything to me, but...but...I can't..."

His arms went around me. Somehow we ended up seated on the ground, a tangle of legs and arms. "You haven't cost me anything." He gripped me hard, as if to force me to understand. "I love you, Ival. And I don't want to die, I don't, but I d-don't want to l-lose you."

"Then don't leave me! You said you cast your lot with mine, you *promised*." I wrapped my arms around him as tightly as I could.

Christine flung her arms around us both, sobbing. "D-Damn it, Griffin! Do you think Whyborne and I will allow this?" She thumped him on the back, as though seeking to pound sense into him. "I've already lost my sister. I refuse to lose you as well. Stop t-talking such utter n-nonsense."

His tears scalded my neck, but he nodded. "A-all right. All right."

I closed my eyes and clung to him, and to Christine. Maybe we would all die here in the desert, from the sun or thirst or something terrible summoned up from the outermost void. But at least we'd face it together.

A camel-scented breath blew against my ear. I thought I'd imagined it, until a soft lip began to inspect the back of my neck.

Startled, I pulled away. Daisy stood there, still bearing her saddle and packs, regarding me with soft, curious eyes.

"Daisy!" I leapt to my feet. "Look, everyone, it's Daisy!"

Griffin managed a smile, even as he wiped off his face with a handkerchief as filthy as everything else we possessed. "I see."

I hugged my camel about the neck in relief. "I should have known you wouldn't leave us behind, girl. You're the best camel in all of Egypt."

And so saying, I took off my fez and let her happily chew it to pieces.

Although clearly my Daisy was an extraordinary camel, even she could only delay the inevitable. The water she carried would get us through the day, but no more. The same held true for the food, unless we chose to ration it stringently. But we were better off than we had been, and we set out across the sand with somewhat revived spirits. My feelings remained tender after the fright Griffin gave me, and I took his hand while we walked. We'd decided to switch off riding Daisy to conserve as much of our strength as possible, with Christine going first.

"Whyborne," she said after a while, "what Daphne said in the pyramid. About you having the audacity to accuse her of being inhuman. *'I smell the ocean in your blood.'* What do you think she meant?"

I'd forgotten the incident amidst the confusion and terror which followed. Now I could only shake my head. "I haven't the slightest clue."

"What did she say?" Griffin asked with a frown. "The Lapidem...I wasn't aware of anything outside it."

"I told her Nitocris had made her into something less than human. She seemed to find the statement hypocritical. It's all nonsense. I can't begin to fathom what she might have meant." I shrugged. "Perhaps...well. If she was not entirely, er, stable before her marriage, between her husband and Nitocris, she might have no longer been sane."

"She seemed quite sane in Cairo and at the excavation," Griffin pointed out.

"The woman killed and ate her husband, Griffin!" I winced.

"Forgive me, Christine."

She sighed. "No need to ask forgiveness for speaking the truth."

I gestured at myself. "Look at me. I'm perfectly human. My parents are perfectly human. She must have sensed my use of magic and jumped to some mad conclusion. She probably assumed I'd been possessed as she had, in order to get power."

"You're probably right," Christine said, although she didn't sound entirely convinced. A moment later, she pulled Daisy to a halt. "Damn it. On the horizon. Riders."

I shaded my eyes and peered in the direction she indicated. Riders indeed, mounted on both horses and camels, making their way toward us at a fast clip.

Griffin released my hand and drew his revolver. "Is there any chance they're friendly?" he asked Christine.

"Were we closer to the inhabited lands, perhaps," she said, urging Daisy to kneel so she could dismount. "Out here? The odds seem slim indeed."

There was nothing to do but wait for them to close with us. They spread out as they neared, moving to circle around us. A cloud of dust rose from their horse's hooves, stinging my eyes. The riders wore embroidered robes, and many of them held scimitars or rifles in their hands. Slowly, they came to a halt, save for two who approached more slowly. Neither spoke, but one swung down off his horse. He walked forward a few paces, before seeming to lose his nerve. Pulling off his head cloth, he revealed the familiar features of Iskander Barnett.

"Er, hello," he said sheepishly. "We've come to rescue you from an army of ghūls. Except it doesn't look like you need it."

"On the contrary." I leaned against Daisy's flank, almost boneless with relief. "I don't think I've ever been quite so happy to see anyone in my life."

"I'm glad to be of service," he replied, but he eyed Christine warily as he spoke. "Dr. Putnam, I..."

He trailed off as she marched up to him. For a moment, it seemed as though he might flee. But instead he straightened his back and stood his ground, waiting for her outburst.

Grabbing him by the front of his robes, she ordered, "Don't ever lie to me again, Kander." Then she pulled his head down and kissed him.

"Huh," Griffin said. "I suppose she forgave him after all."

Iskander and Christine broke apart. "Oh," he said, looking as dazed as if she'd struck him. "I...I didn't know...but what about Dr. Whyborne?"

"What about me?" I asked.

He flushed. "The two of you are close, and I thought—"

"Don't be disgusting!" Christine hit him on the arm, although not hard.

The other lead rider observed the scene through dark eyes, which, though not hostile, didn't strike me as particularly friendly either. "So these are the American fools," he said in accented English. "The ones who almost unleashed Nitocris upon the world."

"We didn't know!" I exclaimed hotly. "If you'd only warned us, perhaps we could have done something to save Daphne."

"She's dead?" Iskander asked.

"Yes." Christine turned to the leader and fixed him with a level glare. "And the Fane of Nyarlathotep is destroyed. Besides, how dare you judge us, after almost dropping a statue on my head!"

The leader ignored her complaint. "You are fools, but Iskander assures us you aren't evil. We will give you supplies and camels to return you to Cairo, and here we shall part."

"Um." I shuffled my feet uncertainly. "Actually, there's something we could use your help with."

There came a murmuring from the men. Their leader only frowned. "And what would that be?"

"There's been an accident, of sorts."

"An accident?" Iskander repeated worriedly.

"With the Lapidem." My gaze went automatically to Griffin. "I'm afraid the daemon which guards it awoke."

"Oh dear." Iskander stared at us. "And it's after Griffin? Bloody hell."

"Do you have the stone?" the leader asked.

Griffin nodded. "It's in my pack."

"The solution is simple enough. We will take the Lapidem deep into the desert where it can be safely hidden."

"And us?" I asked, disliking his tone more and more.

"You and the woman may come with us. The daemon has only marked one man, so he will remain here. Once he's dead, it will return to its lair."

"What? No!" exclaimed Iskander, at the same moment Christine shouted: "You damned coward!"

"Why should I endanger any of my people for a stranger?" the man asked coldly. "The *shardah-iin* are too few as it is. With every passing year, our numbers grow smaller. Meanwhile, more and more foreigners overrun this land, looting and despoiling its treasures." He gestured contemptuously at me. "You all think yourselves so wise, so enlightened, and thus refuse to listen to a warning when it is given. I brought the *shardah-iin* to slay Nitocris and her ghūls, as is our ancient pact. If they are gone, I have done my duty. Tell me why I should risk lives to save an arrogant foreigner stupid enough to meddle in ancient magics?"

Cold fury crystallized in my chest. I strode forward until I stood by the man's stirrup, glaring up at him. He watched me impassively in return. "Because once the daemon is done with Griffin, it won't return to the fane," I said. "It's bound to the Lapidem. If you take the stone into the desert, as you propose to do, it will follow. And one day, no matter how carefully you hide it, some other poor soul, maybe even one of your own, will open the damned box. Your choice isn't whether or not to help us save Griffin. It's whether you want to close your eyes and blindly hope everything will work out all right, or put an end to it tonight by helping us kill the accursed thing."

The man snorted scornfully. "And what makes you believe you have any chance of destroying such a creature?"

In the end, the words were far easier to speak than I'd expected. "Because I'm a sorcerer."

The leader, who eventually introduced himself as Asim, determined we should retreat to the nearby ruins and wait there for nightfall. The *shardah-iin* had not come unprepared. Believing they would have to face an army of ghūls, they'd brought a camel train laden with jars of oil as well as other supplies. The riders themselves bore rifles, bows and arrows, knives, and scimitars.

Griffin and Christine rode spare camels, while I took Daisy. As we traveled, I listened to the *shardah-iin* talk amongst themselves. Their tongue was clearly related to Arabic, but had just as obviously developed along its own divergent lines. I wondered if I might convince them to teach it to me. Perhaps I could compile a dictionary, or write an analysis. Then again, if they valued secrecy as much as Iskander said, they might not want me to divulge their existence to even the scholarly circles in which I moved.

Iskander brought his horse alongside Christine's camel, and they both dropped back. Most of what they said was inaudible, blown away by the wind, but I picked out Griffin's name once or twice, and mine several times. "What on earth are they talking about?" I wondered to Griffin, who rode beside me.

He glanced casually back. "At a guess, she's taking the opportunity to lay out a few facts for Mr. Barnett," he said. "Including the nature of our relationship."

"Oh." The tips of my ears burned from more than the hot sun. "Why?"

"Knowing Christine as I do, I suspect she would prefer he know what he's getting into, before things go any farther. Past lovers, damaging secrets which might come out, that sort of thing."

"And us." But as he said, it made sense. If Iskander viewed us as criminals or perverts, Christine would leave him behind without…well, she would probably take a backward glance, being fond of him. But leave him she would. I hoped, for her sake, he would be able to overcome any revulsion he might feel.

"You called yourself a sorcerer," Griffin said abruptly.

I fixed my gaze on Daisy's scruffy mane. "Yes. I suppose I…well. I realized you were right all along. I wanted to be a scholar, because it was safe. Familiar. I could tell myself I was just doing what I'd always done: reading books and applying what I learned to a problem. And even though there's truth to it, the implication there's no real difference between studying philology and casting spells is a lie."

"Whyborne—"

I shook my head. "Let me finish, while I have the courage. If I called myself a sorcerer, it meant becoming something new. Different. So I hid from it, and grew angry with you when you tried to point out the truth." I drew in a deep breath. "I'm sorry."

"You're forgiven." He looked hopeful. "Will you be more cautious, then?"

"I'm always cautious," I replied with a little smile, which seemed to reassure him. Thank goodness, because I didn't want a quarrel, not when we would be facing terrible danger in only a few hours. If something happened to one of us, I didn't want our last words to be bitter.

Because in truth, the lie about being only a scholar, a dabbler, had held me back. It allowed me pretend to be if not helpless, at least without responsibility.

But I wasn't helpless. And given the dark turns our lives had taken, the horrors we'd faced, it was my responsibility to arm myself as well as I might against any future threats. If we survived tonight, I'd stop pretending to be a dilettante and throw myself fully into the study of the arcane arts. I'd become a true sorcerer.

And woe betide anyone who dared to threaten us again.

CHAPTER 23

WE REACHED THE ruins with only a few hours remaining before sunset. By that time, I thought I'd managed to formulate a plan.

Some of the younger *shardah-iin* pitched lean-tos for shade. Iskander led us to one, where a water skin and bag of dates had already been set out. "It isn't much," he apologized. "At home...well, in their tents, they're much more hospitable. You aren't really seeing them at their best, I fear."

"These are hardly ideal conditions," Griffin said. He held out his hand to the other man. "Thank you for your timely rescue."

"If only we'd been a few hours earlier," Iskander answered ruefully, shaking Griffin's hand.

"Late is better than never." I shook Iskander's hand as well. "And vastly better than dying of thirst in the desert."

He departed. Christine went to speak with some of the women *shardah-iin*, leaving Griffin and I momentarily alone.

Griffin offered me the water skin. I took it gratefully and drank, then passed it back to him. I watched his throat work as he swallowed. Dusty, filthy, burned brown by the sun and in dire need of a shave, yet the sight of him still moved me.

"I have an idea," I said, the words sticking in my throat. "But it... well. Involves you. Which is why I wanted to ask you before suggesting it to Asim. If you say no, or don't think it's workable—"

He lowered the flask. "Just tell me, my dear."

"I want to use you as bait," I said in a rush. "It's wretched of me, I know, but hear me out. Light of any kind is anathema to the daemon. Fire didn't stop it altogether, but it did slow the creature down long enough for us to escape. Did you notice the *shardah-iin* have oil with them?"

"Yes."

I picked up a date, then set it back down, my appetite gone. "What if we dig a trench in a circle around the inner sanctum and the obelisk and fill it with oil? Once the daemon is within the circle, we light the oil, trapping it in a ring of fire. Then we can concentrate on killing it."

"And I'm the bait which lures it into the circle," Griffin said.

God, how could I even suggest putting him in such danger? But what other choice did we have? "If you and the box with the Lapidem are in the center, we can be sure of the creature's path." I looked up at him. "Griffin, please, I'll be by your side the entire time. I swear. I'd die before I allow anything to happen to you."

Rather than condemn me, he popped a date into his mouth. "A good plan. It's what I would have suggested myself."

"No, you would have suggested leaving you to die." I didn't mean to sound bitter, but I couldn't help it.

No one lingered nearby, and the lean-to gave us some privacy. He took my hands in his. "Whyborne...when you said you'd cost me too much...what did you mean?"

"You know. Your family."

Griffin sighed. "Tell me you don't believe my search for my brothers somehow means I regret choosing to stay with you."

"No. Well, not entirely." My shoulders slumped, but I owed him honesty. "I suppose I worry what will happen if you find them and they force you to the same choice as your adoptive family. How can I ask you to give that up twice? I was so grateful when my parents sent the Christmas invitation, because I thought perhaps we could make things up to you, and...ugh, well, you see how that turned out. The motorcar would make a better replacement family than Father and Stanford."

To my surprise, Griffin chuckled. "So you did nothing to prompt the invitation? I'd wondered."

"Dear heavens, no!"

"Whyborne. Ival. You don't have to do anything to replace my family. You *are* my family. I hope to find my brothers. I hope they are happy in their lives and will be happy for me in mine. But they'll never take the place of you, or Christine, or Heliabel."

"I know you've been sad about losing your adoptive parents, though," I said.

"Of course I have." He tugged me closer. "I think it only natural, don't you?"

"Yes. But I hate seeing you unhappy."

"I know. As I hate seeing you unhappy whenever you come from visiting your father. I grieved for my relationship with Ma and Pa, and the rest of the family. But grief is part of life. Not something you have to fix for me." He sighed. "You've been my rock through all of this, the one person in the world I knew would never let me down. You've already given me everything I need."

"Oh." I felt a little foolish, but mostly relieved.

Griffin pulled one hand free and reached for the sack of dates. "Come. Eat a bit and get your strength up."

"After I've talked to Asim." I rose to my feet.

"Do you think he'll see reason and agree with your plan?"

"He will," I vowed. "Or else I'll have Christine knock some sense into his head."

Fortunately, Asim agreed with my plan. Several hours later, I woke to find Griffin and Christine seated nearby, talking quietly as they reloaded their guns with ammunition from the *shardah-iin*. My neck ached, and all the bruises I'd gained from the last few days made themselves known. I sat up stiffly, my muscles protesting every movement. My eyes felt gritty, and my mouth tasted like the inside of an old boot. The shadows of the great pillars reached across the sand, the sun lying low on the horizon.

"What time is it?" I asked groggily, reaching for my pocket watch.

"Not long before sunset," Griffin replied.

"You shouldn't have let me sleep so long."

"It did you good, didn't it?" Christine asked practically. "Far better than staying up and worrying would have. Have some goat meat and water."

I took a strip of dried meat from her. The stuff was tough as leather, and I gave up after a few bites. "We should get ready, so everything will be in place before the sun sets," I said.

Griffin shouldered his pack, which contained the Lapidem's sealed box. We crossed the sands to where the obelisk leaned drunkenly to one side. The *shardah-iin* took up position amidst the surrounding pillars, ready with such weapons as we thought might be effective against the daemon. Iskander joined us by the obelisk, as did Asim. A few torches blazed up behind us, but not too many, lest the daemon shy away from our trap.

"Stay behind me," I told Griffin.

"Don't be absurd." The blade of his sword cane flashed orange in the final light of the sun.

Darkness came quickly in Egypt, the transition from day to night in the clear air far more sudden than I'd experienced anywhere else. One moment, long blue-purple shadows lay over the sands. The next, darkness fell across us like a cloak.

"How long do you think it will take the daemon to arrive?" Iskander asked in a low voice.

"An hour? Two?" Christine replied. "It moved fast, but it still has some rough terrain to cross between here and the fane."

In the darkness, all around the ruins of the ancient temple, eyes appeared, reflecting the light with an eerie blue-white glow. Daphne's voice echoed out of the night before us.

"Plenty of time to kill you, then," she said.

"Daph—" Christine began...then fell silent, any joy she felt at her sister's unexpected survival cut off when Nitocris stepped into the light.

And it was Nitocris. If anything of Daphne remained, she had been entirely subsumed. She no longer dressed in modern clothing, but in the linen sheath of an ancient queen. A necklace heavy with gold and gemstones hung about her neck, and a headdress shaped like a serpent rested on her blonde hair. Her eyes had shifted from dark to blood red, and a long pair of jackal ears sprouted from her head. When she grinned at us, she displayed teeth larger and sharper than anything human.

My mouth went dry with horror. The sepulchral smell of the ghūls blew on the wind, turning my stomach. How many were there? A dozen? A score? A hundred? They far outnumbered the *shardah-iin*, at any rate.

"Surprised to see me alive?" Nitocris asked. "It was a near thing."

There came the hum of an arrow loosed from a bow. Nitocris's arm moved in a blur, dashing the arrow from the air a foot from her head. Dear God, had I thought her a ferocious enemy beneath the pyramid? Her final transformation made her seem nigh unstoppable.

"As you see, my reflexes have grown much faster than those of a mere human," she said, her lips drawn back to reveal her teeth. "And what have we here? The Wolves of the West, mange-eaten dogs of Wepwawet. They fancy themselves saviors, but I see nothing but a band of ragged nomads, whose line will end here tonight." Her gaze returned to Christine. "Now give me the Lapidem, sister, and I might let you live."

Christine raised her rifle. "My sister is dead," she said, and fired.

Nitocris jerked, and blood spattered her arm where the bullet grazed her. "As you wish." Spinning to address her ghūls, she shouted,

"Kill them! Kill them all, and we'll feast on their corpses in the light of the moon!"

The ghūls surged forward, a river of brown-furred bodies interspersed with their more human kin. Their eyes glowed with insatiable hunger, and their muzzles gaped into red, tooth-lined maws.

The *shardah-iin* unleashed a volley of gunfire and arrows. Sharp howls echoed; the first rank of ghūls fell, their corpse-candle eyes extinguished. Dark blood stained the sand.

But there were too many of them. They swarmed over the bodies of their dead, jaws snapping and slavering, compelled by the bidding of their mad queen. A *shardah* went down beneath gore-encrusted claws. Knives flashed in the torchlight, guns fired, and screams rang out. My heart pounded in my chest, and my lips went numb. Beside me, Griffin tensed. I knew he wanted to dash out and join the fight.

"Wait," Asim ordered. "We must keep the Lapidem from them. If Nitocris gains command of its magic, there is no knowing what terrors she might unleash."

Some of the ghūls broke through into the courtyard, making for the obelisk. Christine lifted her rifle, sighted, and fired. The nearest went down with a hole through its forehead. She repeated the action twice more. But they came in a wave of darkness, of ears and teeth and misshapen bodies.

The camels went mad, squalling and screaming. Daisy! Surely she hadn't come through all of this to be killed by ghūls.

But it wasn't the ghūls which caused the extremity of terror in the camels. A stiff breeze blew out of the desert, and its fetid, acidic stench overpowered even the reek of the ghūls. The same nauseating smell which filled the catacombs beneath the fane.

No. It couldn't be. The daemon couldn't reach us this quickly, could it?

The stars vanished on the horizon as something black moved across the sky. A flaming orange eye appeared like a baleful comet, punctured by a tripartite pupil.

No longer trapped beneath the ground, it resembled a gigantic stingray, huge and terrible. Rather than traveling over miles of uneven ground, it had flown on vast wings. It was truly a daemon of the night winds.

And it had come for Griffin.

"Dear God in heaven," Griffin whispered.

The creature swooped down from the sky, wings smashing through the outer line of columns. Stone crumbled, the ancient structures tumbling down and crushing everything beneath. I caught a glimpse of an orifice on the daemon's underside, ringed by squirming, gelatinous feelers. It fell upon a cluster of ghūls, the host of feelers around its mouth striking them stinging blows, and they screamed as their flesh melted. One was entirely enveloped; within seconds, the daemon let its half-dissolved bones fall to the ground.

I grabbed Griffin's shoulder in an instinctive attempt to steady him. "Hold on! It's almost inside the trap!"

Some of the ghūls fled its coming, vanishing into the night on all fours. Nitocris shouted orders in a language which seemed more like yips and barks than anything human.

"Fall back!" Asim shouted. "Inside the circle!"

The daemon snatched up a *shardah*, her screams of agony audible even over the sound of falling masonry and howling ghūls. Griffin jerked beneath my hand and drew his revolver.

"Hold!" Asim ordered, grasping Griffin's other arm.

Griffin looked utterly wild, his eyes huge, his body shaking. This must have been his worst possible nightmare, the horror from Chicago writ large. But his nerve didn't break, and he remained at my side, facing the monster down even as it drew closer and closer.

The daemon burst through the second line of pillars, seeming not to even notice the destruction it caused. Its burning eye fixed on Griffin. Christine and I instinctively stepped in front of him.

Then it passed over the oil-filled ditch.

I shouted the name of fire. The ring exploded into flame, bathing the scene in orange light.

The daemon loosed a shriek of pain which grated on my ears and vibrated in my very teeth. It recoiled from the fire, wings and feelers retracting sharply. In the light, its surface shimmered with a thousand colors, like a slick of oil on water. It was semi-translucent, like a jellyfish, the shadows of what might have been organs showing through its obsidian skin.

"Kill it!" Asim shouted.

Christine's rifle spoke, and a dozen flaming arrows embedded themselves in the daemon's gelatinous flesh. It shuddered and shrieked...but it didn't stop coming.

Asim charged, brandishing his scimitar, and the rest of the *shardah-iin* went with him. Griffin drew his sword cane and followed, crying his own wordless challenge.

Its feelers lashed out. Asim's scimitar sliced through the ones reaching for him, and they dropped wriggling to the sand. My heart leapt. The plan would work! We'd whittle the damn thing down if we had to, but we would kill it.

More feelers extruded from its body, replacing those which Asim had severed. As if there'd never been an injury at all.

Asim had only an instant to stare, before the regrown feelers wrapped around his head. His screams were the most horrifying thing I'd ever heard.

Griffin at least avoided the feelers. His sword cane sliced and hacked at one of the vast wings. Others joined him, struggling to bring it down. Rents opened in its homogenous flesh—and sealed immediately.

"Nothing's working!" Christine cried.

I had to do something—but what? The fire spell was too small—I'd need a huge conflagration to kill the damn thing. There was no water in reach, and the creature hovered in the air above the earth. Perhaps the wind? Could I knock it back, or to the ground, or even onto the other side of the flames where it might not be able to pass back through? At least that would buy us some time.

The wind would play havoc with the sand, scouring everyone in its path, but they wouldn't die. I gripped the wand in both hands and began to chant.

A flicker of motion out of the corner of my eye was my only warning, before something struck me with enough force to send me flying.

I rolled across the sand, pain igniting my side. Nitocris stood above me, her sharp teeth bared, her red eyes lit from within by a hellish fury. The orange light of the flames painted her skin and turned the gore spattered on her linen dress to black.

"You should have joined with me when you had the chance," she growled.

I scrambled to my feet. She backhanded me, sending me reeling. My ears rang, and I tasted blood. Whatever Daphne had been, whatever remnants of her I had seen in Cairo and on the excavation, she was gone now. Only the monster remained, called forth by madness to wear her skin.

Screams and cries came from the direction of the battle with the daemon. I glimpsed the fray, turned to chaos by the jumping flames: the *shardah-iin* trying to bring down the thing, Griffin and Christine in their midst, and the daemon barely affected by anything they did.

Griffin must have realized the hopelessness of the situation. "Run!" he shouted. "Fall back and save yourselves! It will follow me!"

The *shardah-iin* scattered at his command. Griffin turned and ran, through the inner ring of pillars, toward the heart of the temple. Christine went with him, ignoring his shout of protest.

And the daemon followed.

"No!" I cried, reaching out toward them.

Nitocris struck me again, hard enough to spin me around. I collapsed heavily against the half-fallen obelisk. Her steps came nearer, soft against the sand. "I'm done toying with you. Time to die."

My thoughts scrambled—I had to fight her—no, I needed to save Griffin and Christine. But I had no way of doing either. We would all die here in this wretched place, and only scraps of melted bone, gnawed by ghūls, would remain to show we'd ever lived.

I pushed myself up off the base of the obelisk, the worn bas-reliefs beneath my hands. The flames revealed their shapes to me: Horus, using his spear of lightning to strike down his enemy Set.

Lightning.

If I could plant the wand at the tip of the obelisk somehow and leap clear at the right moment...

I scrambled up. "Griffin!" I shouted. "Lure it beneath the obelisk! Now!"

I didn't have time to make certain he'd heard. Nitocris was on me, so I ran in the one direction she must not have expected—up the incline of the leaning obelisk.

As I half-dashed, half-climbed up the slender finger of stone, my feet slipped dangerously. It was higher than I'd thought, and my head swam. I had to look down, though, in order to make certain of the daemon's position.

Griffin had heard me, it seemed. He dashed under the incline of the obelisk, the dark shape of the daemon gliding after him.

Then Griffin fell, either from misfortune or because his strength was gone. Christine tugged on his arm, both of them framed by the fire, but they were too slow. The daemon drew closer and closer, and, oh God, it was almost on them now.

Powerful arms grappled with me from behind, and Nitocris's teeth sank deep into my left shoulder. I bit back a scream.

The daemon passed beneath. In mere seconds, it would be on Griffin and Christine. I had no time to fight off Nitocris, let alone find some way of setting the wand.

There was only one thing left to do.

I wrapped my arms around Nitocris, the wand gripped in my right hand jammed tight against her spine, and hurled us both from atop the obelisk.

We plummeted, her shriek of rage and startled terror ringing in my ears. I sensed the line of power beneath me, everything aligning on a single axis, the power surging through the wand. The words to call the lightning ripped my throat in a scream, and the wand came alive in my grip.

The world turned white as the lightning answered.

Agony such as I'd never known exploded through me, even as a titanic crash of thunder swallowed my cry. My body arched helplessly, and I fell...

I lay atop something sticky, half-fluid, sight and hearing seared away. The stink of charred pork clogged my nose. I tasted nothing but blood. I blinked, saw dim shapes moving against a backdrop of flame.

"Ival!" Griffin shouted, the sound muffled and far away. He bent over me, his face coming into focus. I tried to reach for him, but my arm was nothing but a mass of pain and blood. The movement sent me spinning down into darkness.

CHAPTER 24

Several weeks later, I let myself out the door of our room in Shepheard's Hotel. My coat hung awkwardly from my left shoulder, since there was no way to fit it over the sling around my right arm, let alone the bandages beneath.

As I made for the gardens, intent on a bit of a morning stroll, the door to Iskander's room opened. Christine slipped out, smiling rather smugly as she eased the door shut behind her, as if to keep from waking the sleeper within.

"You look pleased," I remarked.

She grinned. "With every reason. What are you doing about at this hour? I can't believe Griffin let you out of his sight."

Griffin hadn't left my side since the destruction of the daemon. The lightning bolt had struck the wand, destroying it. The electricity passed directly into Nitocris's body, and thence into the daemon just as we crashed down on it. According to Griffin, nothing remained of the daemon except for piles of stinking, gelatinous goo. Either the fall or the shock of the lightning across her heart had killed Nitocris as well.

As for me, the lightning had arced up my right arm in a swathe, searing the flesh from the tips of my fingers all the way to my shoulder. Burns, ruptures, and blisters marked nearly every inch of skin on my arm in a pattern oddly reminiscent of snowflakes, or frost on a window. Between those injuries and the bite wound from Nitocris, I'd slipped into fever.

Although Christine swore she'd been absolutely certain of my recovery, I suspected both she and Griffin feared for my life throughout the long trip back to Cairo. As for myself, I was glad enough to remember almost nothing of those days. The *shardah-iin* arranged a sort of travois for me, which my devoted Daisy dragged all the way back to Cairo. Apparently, I'd spent most of the trip either unconscious or raving. The fragments I did recall featured Griffin dripping water between my cracked lips, changing my bandages, or wiping sweat from my brow.

Even after our return to Cairo, the experience left him reluctant to be parted from me for more than a few minutes. I suspect he feared I might suddenly relapse into fever and expire without his constant supervision.

"He's finishing up his shave," I said. "I reminded him I'm almost entirely healed, and he can't spend the rest of our lives hovering. He agreed to let me walk to the garden without him."

"It's a start, I suppose," Christine said. "You gave the poor fellow a rather awful scare, you know. How's the arm, by the way?"

She fell in beside me, and we strolled to the doors leading out to the garden. The sun was only a pink glow on the horizon, and we had the place to ourselves.

"The doctors say the bandages can come off in another week." Thank heavens; my arm rather resembled that of a mummy. The pain had decreased appreciably, though it still woke me at night from time to time. "I have control over all of my fingers, and there doesn't seem to be any damage to the nerves. The arm will be weak, thanks to the inactivity, but I'll have plenty of time to exercise on the steamer home."

"Yes." Christine came to a halt near the far end of the garden, staring out over the hedge. "I shall accompany you."

I winced, but I couldn't say I was entirely surprised. "You're officially shutting down the excavation?"

"I have to take Daphne's remains home to Mother."

I'd been insensible at the time, of course, but apparently the *shardah-iin* cremated Nitocris's body on a pyre, along with the remains of the daemon, before vanishing back into the desert and taking the box containing the Lapidem with them. Some of those ashes now rested in a small urn in Christine's room.

The official story had us all entering the desert in search of the fane. A poisonous snake bit Daphne, and she died despite all our attempts to save her. My injuries were put down to a far-fetched combination of jackal attack and freak lightning strike. I don't know if our story entirely convinced the doctors, but they had no more plausible explanations and thus no choice but to accept it.

"You'll lose the firman," I pointed out. Unfair as it was, the Antiquities Service would turn over the Valley of Jackals to someone else, no doubt citing the early end to excavation as their excuse.

Christine's mouth pressed into a line. Then it relaxed, and she gave me a rueful smile. "Yes. But there are other places than Egypt to excavate. The world is filled with undiscovered wonders."

"And you mean to find them all," Griffin teased as he approached.

He'd lost a good deal of weight during my convalescence, leaving his cheeks thinner than usual. But the dark circles had vanished from under his eyes, and he'd regained his composure and good humor.

"Of course," Christine replied.

"And will Iskander Barnett be accompanying you on these adventures?"

"Perhaps." Christine's look turned thoughtful. "It's too early to say. But…well. He's a good man, and should things work out, he might someday become a part of our little family."

Griffin stopped at my side, resting his hand on the small of my back. We'd made love last night for the first time since my injury. He'd gone cautiously at first, as if my wounded arm made me more vulnerable to other hurts. But my enthusiasm won him over quickly, and convinced him I was not, in fact, any more breakable than before.

I took a deep breath of the morning air. The perfume of the garden mingled with Griffin's sandalwood cologne and Christine's lavender soap. "Would you like us to go with you?" I asked her. "When you return home to Philadelphia, that is. You don't have to face your family with no one at your side."

For a moment, I thought pride would cause her to refuse. Then she nodded. "Yes. Thank you, gentlemen. I'd prefer not to be alone."

"That you have no need to worry about," I assured her. I put my good arm around Griffin's shoulders. On my other side, Christine wrapped her fingers around the strap of my sling. We'd come through death and terror and pain, but we'd faced it together and seen it through. For now, we only stood in companionable silence, and watched the sun rise on a new day.

About The Author

Jordan L. Hawk is a trans author from North Carolina. Childhood tales of mountain ghosts and mysterious creatures gave him a life-long love of things that go bump in the night. When he isn't writing, he brews his own beer and tries to keep the cats from destroying the house. His best-selling Whyborne & Griffin series (beginning with Widdershins) can be found in print, ebook, and audiobook.

If you're interested in receiving Jordan's newsletter and being the first to know when new books are released, please sign up at his website: http://www.jordanlhawk.com. Or join his Facebook reader group, Widdershins Knows Its Own.

Printed in Poland
by Amazon Fulfillment
Poland Sp. z o.o., Wrocław